ALMOST A SCOT

Lords of the Masquerade
Book Six

Jade Lee

ARE YOU SIGNED UP FOR DRAGONBLADE'S BLOG?

You'll get the latest news and information on exclusive giveaways, exclusive excerpts, coming releases, sales, free books, cover reveals and more.

Check out our complete list of authors, too!

No spam, no junk. That's a promise!

Sign Up Here

www.dragonbladepublishing.com

Dearest Reader;

Thank you for your support of a small press. At Dragonblade Publishing, we strive to bring you the highest quality Historical Romance from some of the best authors in the business. Without your support, there is no 'us', so we sincerely hope you adore these stories and find some new favorite authors along the way.

Happy Reading!

CEO, Dragonblade Publishing

Additional Dragonblade books by Author Jade Lee

Lords of the Masquerade Series
Lord Lucifer (Book 1)
Lord Satyr (Book 2)
Lord Ares (Book 3)
Lord Scot (Book 4)
Lady Scot (Book 5)
Almost a Scot (Book 6)

The Lyon's Den Series
Into the Lyon's Den
Lyon Hearted

PROLOGUE

TWO WEEKS BEFORE Iseabail's sixteenth birthday, her mother woke her half an hour before midnight. Iseabail resented the hard shake on her shoulder. She'd fallen asleep a bare hour ago after an entire day spent helping sows birth their young. Delivering piglets wasn't glamorous work, but they were a valuable commodity in Scotland and to her clan in particular. Baron Bain liked his ham.

"Ssst!" her mother hissed at her. "Get your paints. Now."

She was bone tired and stumbled in the dark, but her logical side knew better than to argue with her mother when the woman was in *that* mood. Her illogical side complained that her mother had been especially irritating for the last year or more, so she might as well complain because it vented her spleen.

"Where are we going?" she asked, her voice heavy with her grumbles. "And why bring paint? It's too dark."

"Isssy!" The word was either a diminutive of her name or a curse-like hiss. And it was punctuated with the heavy impact her of boots against her chest. The command was obvious. She was to put them on as fast as possible while her mother shook out a dark cloak made of sackcloth.

Sackcloth? She was supposed to put that on?

Iseabail started to pull off her night rail, but her mother shook her head. And when she reached for her plaid, the woman's expression turned downright murderous. Iseabail frowned. Her only protection was her plaid. That's what she'd been told from the day she was born. It was her identity as a Spalding daughter and the baron's niece. It's what kept her safe as she helped with livestock or when delivering bairns. Otherwise, who knew what would happen to a lass wandering the land?

She knew.

She'd tended to a few who'd run afoul of her uncle's own men. But everyone here knew her identity and no strange men wandered their lands. Not if they wanted to live. So the danger came from the clan's own workers—especially those who oversaw the market like greedy pigs—and it made no sense to hide her identity from them.

But her mother had her moods, and so Iseabail did as she was ordered. Soon she had her paints in a bag slung across her shoulder while the sackcloth rubbed irritatingly against her skin. Then her mother gestured her through the antechamber of their shared bedroom. Two attendant women lay there, both sleeping heavily in their cots.

Iseabail's steps slowed. That was not a natural sleep. Especially Grandmother Bain. That woman would wake when a cat walked by. She turned wide-eyed to her mother who said nothing as she tugged Iseabail along.

The moment they crossed into the castle stairwell, her mother increased speed. Iseabail quieted her steps until even her heavy boots were silent. There were too many men sleeping about the castle for her to want to disturb anyone.

They made it all the way down and out a door to the kitchen garden. Mother grabbed leaves as she went, crushing them between her fingers. As they made it to the stable, she whisked the pulp down Iseabail's forearm.

"What's that for?" Iseabail whispered.

"Just in case."

She wanted to ask, in case what? but there was no time as her mother began saddling her horse. Iseabail did so as well, whispering an apology to the poor thing for taking her out again without a proper sleep.

"Quickly!"

How were they getting past the sentry? Her clan had built up the wall around Spalding Castle until it was a towering thing that blocked out too much of the winter sun. Now it was a dark wall of blackness with only a few ways in or out. Her mother approached the door where one sentry sat bored and yawning.

"Wot's—"

"Don't be bellowing yer yap an' wakin' the dogs. There's a babe come early. Let us by."

"Whose bairn—"

"None o' yer business. Now open up fer us."

"I haven't heard anything—"

"Ach, we just got back a few hours ago. Do ye think we'd be leaving again if it weren't important? Now open the gate or I'll be cursing you with the birth blood." She peered through the darkness. "Otis, is it? Are ye that thick as to deny me?"

The man grumbled, but he was quick about opening the gate. It was the smallest opening of the keep, set for quiet comings and goings. Iseabail and her mother clomped through. Iseabail turned to say thanks—it never hurt to be polite to her uncle's men—but she never got the chance. As soon as they were through, her mother pushed her horse to a fast trot. Iseabail kicked her horse to follow, and they were quickly down the path.

Thankfully, it was a full moon, and they could see well. Truthfully, Iseabail knew this road so well she could—and had—traveled it nearly asleep, but within an hour they were far enough out that the situation changed. An hour's ride put them at the edge of clan territory. She'd only been out here a handful of times in her life and never at dark, but her mother did not slow their pace. Nor did the woman offer any explanations.

But something happened soon afterwards. It was past midnight now and the air was still. Quiet enough, at least, to hear a man's cry, somewhere behind them. Perhaps there was the clatter of hooves behind them, coming fast, but it was hard to tell.

Iseabail was too occupied by the sudden slap of her mother's hand on the back of her horse.

Her mare burst forward, but it was late, the creature was tired, and they had already come a long way. They didn't have enough speed.

Iseabail watched her mother looked behind them, her face shifting through fear, fury, resignation, and then finally a hard-jawed determination. She didn't know what it meant. She didn't understand anything that was happening, but she kept going even as her mother turned both their horses up a steep incline.

It was hard going for them both. They had to backtrack as they climbed, rushing closer and closer to the gurgle of a fast-moving stream. At least that's where she thought they were going. It was hard to tell until her mother abruptly pulled up.

Iseabail dismounted, taking the time to walk her horse to the stream to drink, but her mother shook her head.

"Forget them."

Forget the horses? Had she gone mad? But her mother kept issuing orders.

"Out of your dress. Say in the shift. Where are you paints?"

"What—"

"Do as I say! Our lives depend upon it."

That would have been a startling statement if it had been shouted. Instead, it was spoken with a dark kind of finality. It was the same voice she used at a sickbed when hard truths had to be faced. So Iseabail pulled out her kit, then stripped quickly while her mother began mixing the paints and wetting the brushes.

They could both hear the horses coming closer. The men were even less quiet, shouting back and forth to one another. Iseabail knew the words and the men. Her uncle was here, and he'd brought half the clan out after dark to find them.

A *hunting* party.

"He'll kill us for the insult," Iseabail said, her shivers making her words stutter.

"Aye," her mother agreed, her voice grim. Then she shoved a

brush into her daughter's hand. "Paint on your body. Cover it."

"Paint what?" she asked as she hastily shoved the brush into the dark ochre.

"Symbols. Dots. Anything."

"But it won't mean anything," she protested even as she began stroking orange onto her calves.

"They won't know that," her mother said as she dipped her fingers into the blue paint. It was bright and pretty, Iseabail's favorite color, and her mother was using it all up and down her arms, around the dark smudges of the crushed herbs from before.

Next came the white, as thick and ghostly as possible, thumbed into her cheeks and around her eyes. Hard presses, quick dots, bursts of zigzagged lines that made no sense.

"Mother," she whispered. "What is this for?"

Her mother looked at her, shaking her head. "It won't be enough," she said, the words half-gasped. "I'm sorry. So sorry." Then she gripped her daughter's shift and pulled it straight off. Iseabail's body was naked in the moonlight, except for the paint. "They must see something awful so they remember it."

Something awful? Her naked body?

Her mother meant the paint which she spread everywhere. It covered her nipples and dripped into her mons. Her mother used all the paint. The white went everywhere, but she didn't spare the other colors. Then, when they could both hear the creak of the saddles of the men coming closer, she threw the paints aside and dragged Iseabail into the freezing water.

Iseabail gasped, the cold a shock to her system. She started shivering immediately, but that was nothing compared to what her mother did. The woman joined her in the water, her skirt pulling in the frigid water. She must have been freezing, but that didn't stop her from using her paint covered hands to smear the junk all over her face and neck. And then she began chanting. Nonsense words filled with reverence and power.

It might have been a prayer to the moon. It could have been a child's first babble. Or it was the darkest witchcraft dredged up from the bones of the earth. Such was the power of her mother's voice that Iseabail couldn't tell what was true and what was not. She began swaying with the force of her mother's magic, her body thrumming despite the cold.

One by one, her uncle's men appeared around them. Front and back, all eyes upon her and her mother. What Iseabail couldn't see, she could hear, and it was the muttered curses of superstitious men.

Her knees were weakening, her head fuzzy. She could no longer feel her feet from the cold. The only real thing in her mind was the sound of her mother's voice and the heat from her two hands where they held her shoulders. Then her mother lifted both hands and she heard the men gasp in surprise.

A moment later blood dripped into her hair, across her face, and down her front. She knew it by the smell, not the sight. And by the way her mother used the bloody knife to score a sharp cut down her sternum. It was a shallow cut, but it bled dark enough against the white paint. And then her mother stopped.

"It is done," she said.

Her uncle ambled closer until he stood directly before them. Iseabail finally felt her nakedness as her wits sharpened from the burn of her cut. But she said nothing. She was too busy trying to control the way her teeth chattered.

"What's done?" he asked, menace in his tone.

"My power, my gifts, and my magic. It's all gone into her."

Iseabail jolted. No! If her uncle thought that, then he had no use for her mother. He barely tolerated her as it was because she brought luck to the clan. But they'd had a few bad years. Mismanagement of the stock and too much rain meant many of the men grumbled that her mother had turned against them.

Her mother had, but not in that way. No woman had the power to control the rain. Worse, no woman had the power to force men to plant crops when it was time and in places that wouldn't flood. But none of them wanted to hear that.

"It's powerful magic, it is," her mother continued. "Formed

of blood and soil, air and water." Then she turned to the men surrounding her. "Look well now because if she be forced—if her body be touched against her will—then all the magic in her will lash out. It will kill the soul that wants her in violence."

There was no magic to kill a soul. She had been taught that from her earliest days. Her magic was in the bringing of life in crops, in sheep, and in people. Her mother's magic was medicine and careful management, but she had also said a woman must always speak in ways the listeners comprehend. In this case, violence would be met with violence.

Or so she swore.

Her uncle seemed unimpressed. "And what of you, witch woman? If your magic is in her, why would I keep you?"

"Do you think magic can be controlled so easily? She has power, but no teacher except me. If you wish to use her, then you need me to teach her how to do it."

"And what if I found another?"

Her mother snorted. "There is no other the equal of me. I come from—"

"The betrayer of Scotland. Your mother promised us success at Culloden, and what happened? Death to the highland clans. Destruction of all we hold dear." He leveled his knife point at her, though he still stood on the stream bed. "You and your ma did that."

"You and your kin did that," she returned. "We told you what to do. You ignored us."

It was an old fight between her mother and her uncle. Mary Spalding, Iseabail's grandmother, was the witch who blessed the highlanders headed to Culloden. She prophesized a victory, but the laird didn't believe her. He held his clan back, collaborated with the English, and was rewarded with land and a title while the other clans died.

Then he blamed Mary for his sins.

And her daughter.

And now her granddaughter, Iseabail.

Old fight, old blood, and all of it as ridiculous as it was real. Every man here looked upon her naked body and flinched, fearing dark magic. Every man here thought about burning her and her mother alive as witches. But in Scotland, every clan struggled to survive, and none would so easily dismiss the medicines that Iseabail and her mother understood. Strong crops to feed them, strong babes to carry on.

Iseabail and her mother survived so long as the clan thrived. And now her mother had made it clear that Iseabail was the valuable one. Iseabail held the magic. Her mother was little more than an old crone mumbling rhymes to children.

Her uncle pursed his lips. "Very well then." He held out his hand. "Come out of there. The girl is purple with the cold."

It was true. Her entire body felt frozen solid.

There was no choice. Her mother guided her out, both their steps slow on the slippery rocks. Once out, her mother wrapped her in her shift. A man offered Iseabail a blanket, obviously eager to show his willingness to aid her and not be cursed. She wrapped herself in it and waited for the shivers to ease.

None helped her mother.

They returned to the castle by dawn, a slow procession of misery. Iseabail was numb with cold, her mind blanked from exhaustion. And the paints on her skin itched.

Her mother fared worse. She caught a chill that night. A cough that would not ease, wracking her body night and day. Then one summer night a month later, she went out to tend a new mother and her sickly child.

She never arrived.

CHAPTER ONE

REUBEN BATES PULLED off his gloves as he walked into the pub. The fine leather had cost the earth, and he loved the feel of the fur inside as it slid across his skin. Unfortunately, they were too refined for a highwayman, so he tucked them away in his pockets.

He smiled at Molly, the barmaid. She was a talkative girl and the granddaughter of his quarry. So easy to charm her as she spilled out a life story too common in this remote village in northern England. She and her family survived thanks to a small garden and a talent for making mead. Then one day her older brother started "working" up north. His job paid well, and everyone was happy.

Except, of course, the people her brother stole from. And it was Reuben's job to get one particular locket back.

He could infiltrate the band of thieves. A few years ago, he would have enjoyed some mindless drinking, rutting, and violence. At least it eased the boredom of his life. But that was when his hold on London's underworld had stabilized. When he was a king among his family and friends with money enough to make all his people happy.

They were still happy, but his cousins were older now and pushing for more money, more responsibility. The young needed to prove their worth, but Reuben was thirty-five years old. Hardly old enough to put out to pasture. And yet, everywhere he turned, someone wanted his crown.

So he had come here to recover a necklace for a pretty girl while he figured out how to give his cousins power without getting his own throat cut.

He was rescued from his gloomy thought by the appearance of his quarry. The tavern maid's grandmother waddled in. Her thick ankles and heavy brow endeared her to Reuben. Made him think of his own great aunts, and so he smiled at her.

She peered at him, then called her granddaughter away.

"What you be wanting?" she demanded. She had the thick accent of northern England, but he understood it better than the fake Scottish brogue her grandson adopted when he stopped carriages.

"That lovely necklace you're wearing."

"Wot?" She frowned, not understanding his words and no wonder. The pendant was nearly dwarfed by her skin, the delicate chain too thin to hold the heavy dragon. It was tucked inside the high collar of her dress, but Molly had told him all about it. How her brother had brought it from Scotland, and it was a witch's charm for health and good luck. He'd given his grandmother the thing as a birthday present and the whole family had praised him for his generous gift.

"Your grandson stole that necklace from a lady who wants it back." He raised his hands in a jaunty shrug, as if he were nothing but a clown about to juggle some balls. The woman gaped at him, replaying his words in her mind and roundly rejecting them. In five seconds, she would start pummeling him about the ears.

He never gave her the chance.

He always moved when he spoke. It was the curse of being perpetually on guard. People got used to the animation in his body and never expected the strike when it came. Neither did this woman.

He caught her in the neck, his fingers wrapping around the chain. But he didn't yank it off. Instead, he held there and spoke very quietly.

"If you scream, I will rip this off, punch you in the face, and then be gone before anyone can catch me. And you might or might not survive the blow. Do you want me to do that?"

The lady quivered where she stood, her eyes wide, but her lips pressed tightly together. She was furious, but she was not going to stay that way.

"Your grandson is going to get himself killed. I'm from London and I know it is he who is attacking travelers. Do you think I am the only one who notices? He has not been quiet about his activities. If you love your grandson, then you will give me this necklace and keep him from his foolishness. Otherwise, he will be dead within the year." He let his gaze go flat and hard. "Maybe much sooner."

He saw the fury drain from her eyes. She already knew what the boy was doing. "If I give it to you, you will not hurt Olly?"

"If he attacks a carriage I protect, he will die." He extended a finger to tease along the woman's neck. It wasn't a sexual movement, but it was gentle and that usually made him all the more frightening to people. The combination of deadly intent and softness made the weak shake. It made this woman deflate into misery.

"I will tell him," she whispered. Then she reached to lift the necklace off. He let her do it, though he watched carefully to see if she would try to be clever.

She wasn't...yet.

"He's fallen in with those damned Scots," she murmured. "Made him go wrong."

She held out the necklace, but he didn't take it.

"They aren't Scotsmen, and you know it." He countered, his voice cold. He hated it when people blamed another for their own sins, and so he took a moment to show his disgust of this dirty inn filled with small people. "Clean up your county, grandmother. End the thieving, curb the wild boys." He leaned in tight until he breathed directly in her face. "Leave this world better when you die."

She broke, just as he knew she would. She jerked a dagger from her skirts and stabbed downward at his balls. Not a clean strike for this granny. She wanted him maimed and howling like a child. He caught her in her own shawl, wrapping it around her arm and tightening it across her neck. He could choke her now, and she knew it.

She began to curse, but he cut off her breath with a simple twist of her shawl. Then he used his free hand to take both necklace and dagger. He made it a habit to keep any weapons that had been aimed at him. Which meant he had an impressive collection.

When he had pocketed what he wanted, he looked around the inn. Molly was there, her eyes wide. Her father too, his big hands on a cleaver. So he spoke to the entire room.

"I came to get the necklace back, but I know who leads the thieves." He eased off the shawl to allow the woman to breathe. "You run them all."

Her lips curled in disgust. "They'll kill you."

"Then they'll die." He looked at the two others in the room. "See how little she values your life? I am King Reuben of London. Many better than you have tried and died."

He saw doubt creep into the father's eyes, though Molly looked like she had a pistol in her apron. Damnation, women could be tricky. He shook his head.

"She will be the death of all of you," he said as he tossed the woman backward. Then he stepped away from the door, neatly avoiding the ball that landed in the wall where his chest would have been. "Molly, Molly," he said. "That'll cost you now."

He could have done terrible things to the girl. He saw her eyes widen as the same thought flooded her brain. But he only wanted the pistol. Fortunately, his best friend entered the inn at the sound of the gunshot. He had his pistols at the ready, one trained on the father, the other on the grandmother.

"Are we killing innkeepers now?" Jonathan asked.

"Only if they pretend to be Scottish when they rob carriages."

"What?"

Reuben grabbed the pistol from Molly's hand and headed out the door. He didn't even bother to look at the father or his cleaver. "Granny's blaming it on the Scots."

"Oh. That's rude." He held the door while Reuben stepped out. A moment later they were on their horses headed back to London. "How'd you know it was the granny?"

"Do you know of any young man who would give a necklace to his grandmother and not a pretty barmaid?"

"He could be a doting boy."

"Or he could give the leader of the ring the only prize they'd gotten from the carriage."

Jonathan thought about that. "You're right. That makes more sense."

He knew he was right. He was *always* right. And where had that gotten him? At odds with his entire family who wanted to take over what he managed, to do what he was so good at. Which meant he had to be smarter, better, and rise to a level they couldn't touch.

"Come on," he said. "Let's go home." Where he would marry his way out of his own kingdom and into the aristocracy.

CHAPTER TWO

R EUBEN WAITED A week before returning the necklace. He had questions about such a unique piece and the lady who claimed it. Fortunately, he had friends and relatives alike in London, all willing to impart every morsel of gossip available.

What he discovered was exceedingly boring.

Miss Iseabail Spalding was a Scottish debutante sponsored by the powerful Dowager Countess of Byrn. So far, she'd done nothing exciting except dance with someone who later got himself killed. Yawn. There was a rumor that she had a dowry of five-hundred gold pieces, but that wasn't confirmed. Indeed, nothing about her Scottish ancestry was verified in the usual way of things. And though the necklace was an intriguingly shaped dragon with a dark red stone inside, presumably the dragon's heart, there was little special about it. Any jeweler in London could replicate it, and a new one wouldn't look half so beaten up.

Which meant he would have to go on his usual gut instinct and educated guesses. That began with this necklace. There was something very important about this particular piece. All he need do was discover it and turn it to his advantage. Which was why he waited until the entire household was outside to wave the future Duke of Aberbeag and his new wife Mairi off to Scotland. Easiest thing in the world to slip inside, find Miss Iseabail's room, and wait for her to appear.

The first thing he did was search her room. She had little here beyond what had been purchased in London. Not a single item to remind her of Scotland except a well-made dirk kept hidden in her dresser. And here now was the newest piece of the puzzle, because knives had a history.

This was an old knife of the Murray clan. Add to that a tale he'd learned as a boy of the most famous witch in Scotland, and he had her true identity or at least a good guess. She was obviously not Witch Mary who had predicted Scotland's victory at Culloden. The clans had been destroyed quite literally at that famous battle. Iseabail was probably the witch's granddaughter living in hiding from those who wanted revenge.

He heard footsteps coming up the stairs, so he returned the weapon and settled himself against her bedpost, half hidden by the curtains. He liked surprising people. How they reacted told him a great deal about their character.

She came in and shut the door. Her cheerful expression dropped away, softening her face until he saw high cheekbones worn down with care. It was stark look on her long face and he was struck by the hard elegance of it. She looked to him like a young queen might, one who was raised in hard times and had yet to choose a life of compassion or bitter fury. He rather hoped she went the furious route. What a magnificent creature she would be.

He made a sound by accident. A noisy footfall as he took a step toward her. An extraordinary slip from him and one that forced his hand into brazenness. He might have approached her differently otherwise, but there was no help for it now as she ran to her dresser to grab her dirk.

"I wouldn't do that, lass," he said, "else how can we negotiate?"

Her fingers were on the weapon, but she didn't strike out with it. She was a thinker, this one, not prone to rash actions. But she was also used to fighting, because she held the knife with an experienced hand even as she turned to inspect him from head to toe.

Damn, such a thorough inspection had his cock perking up with interest.

"I know you," she said, her voice polished and nearly clear of her Scottish burr. "Reuben Bates. The man who saved us from the highwaymen."

She remembered him. That had his lust heating up another notch as he swept off his hat and performed an exquisite bow, even if he did say so himself.

"The very same," he said. "And you are the honorable Miss Iseabail Spalding, ward of Baron Bain. You're the granddaughter of the Earl of Spalding, and the only child of his daughter, Lady Alice." His grin widened. "You're also dowered with five hundred gold pieces in a chest brought from the farthest corner of the earth."

Every word was a guess cobbled together from gossip and fairy tales. But he had a good instinct for guessing secrets, and her shocked dismay confirmed everything he'd said even as she denied it. Or part of it.

"The dowry is long gone. The contents merely rumor."

"Oh no," he said with a cheeky grin. "It's real and a great deal more than a meager five hundred pounds." After all, her clan managed a profitable market known throughout Scotland. Whether or not the dowry was there now, it would come eventually. It only needed good management.

Meanwhile she continued to argue. "That's not possible."

"But it is." He fished into his pocket and pulled out her necklace. It flashed in the light, a dragon with a fat belly all done in the vague shape of a shield. "A pretty bauble, this," he said as he turned it over in his hand. "Especially if one knows to do this." With the tip of his thumb, he twisted the hidden latch. The gold popped open and exposed a polished dark red stone, the dragon's heart.

"Oh, you found the catch," she said lightly. "It's not a very pretty stone underneath. I think that's why it was covered."

Well, she was a half-decent liar. Not good enough to fool

him, but maybe some others. And the ruby was exquisite. Polished, not faceted, the light compressed into three bright lines that crossed in the middle to make a star.

"That's not why," he said, humor lacing his tone. "Tell me about your mother, Miss Spalding. Tell me about what this stone meant to her."

Panic edged her expression, ruthlessly suppressed. "I don't know what you think you've heard," she began.

"But none of it's true?" he finished for her. "I think a little bit of it is true. And maybe a great deal more." He did love a mystery, especially ones that involved jewels and pretty ladies.

"It's all exaggeration, rumor, and guesses," she said.

He pushed off the bedpost to saunter forward. He was a big man, but she was tall. He had to step very close to try to intimidate her, and she gave not an inch. Now that was spirit he could admire. He stepped in even closer. Tight enough that she would feel his heat, and he could smell her scent.

She shied backwards as a maiden would, clearly nervous despite her spirit.

"What do you want?" she asked.

He grinned, ridiculously pleased she had asked the very question he'd been tormenting himself with. Fortunately, he had a ready answer. It was glib, but it served his purpose. "What I want is more than you can imagine. What I want from you is something we must discuss."

She held up her hands as if to push him back. "We have nothing to discuss."

He heard steel in her voice which told him he needed to tread carefully. But when it involved a beautiful woman, he rarely listened to the voice of caution.

"Nothing?" he taunted, just to see how far he could push her. "I think we do. Tell me, Miss Spalding, what you would give to have this trinket back?"

It was an honest question. Her answer would set the baseline for the minimum he would ask.

"I have my pin money," she said. "It's not much—"

She cut off her words when he touched her cheek, trailing his finger down along her jaw. Damn him for wearing a glove. He wanted to feel the smoothness of her cheek and the heat from her blush. Instead, he used his smallest finger to tilt her face up so she looked him in the eye. Would she crumble when they locked gazes?

"What would you give to keep your secrets hidden away?" he asked as he stared into the brilliant green of her eyes. "How many people know the full truth about your mother?"

She didn't cower. Instead, she faced him down, her expression finally matching the fiery red of her hair. "You imagine things," she said. "It's nothing but a—"

"A witch's talisman. A sorcerer's amulet. *A cursing stone.*" He hadn't heard that about this amulet at all, but such were the things that people said about witch's talismans. It was a safe taunt.

"It is no such thing!" she exploded, her hand quick as she tried to grab it from his hand.

He was quicker as he lifted it out of her reach.

"Some call it that." He let his voice lower in threat. "And some would call you a great deal worse for having it."

"Keep it then," she snapped.

Did she mean it? He didn't think so.

"I might," he returned. "Indeed, I have a mind to study the thing further. But in the meantime, what could you pay me, Miss Spalding, to stop me from telling everyone in London about your mother's witchcraft?"

He wanted to believe he would never follow through on such a threat. He truly had no desire to hurt the lady. But life took unexpected turns, and he would sacrifice her if it meant someone he loved survived. Such was the business he was in, and she meant nothing to him right now except as someone he could exploit.

"It's not true," she whispered. "She was just a woman."

"The truth doesn't matter," he returned. "It never has." He was surprised she didn't know that by now.

She softened toward him, using the only weapon she had—her beauty and just enough innocence to appeal to his jaded heart.

"You cannot tell anyone about this," she said, her eyes luminous. "The rumors alone could get me killed."

His thumb trailed across her lips. He loved how her eyes darkened at that. She might be an innocent, but she wasn't cold inside. And if the pulse in her throat was any indication, she was responding to him on a very primal level. Then they were a pair, because he was already throbbing with interest.

"Offer me something, Miss Spalding, but choose it well."

"I don't have anything," she cried.

"That's unfortunate because my silence is very, very expensive."

"What do you want?" she whispered. "I'll give you anything."

He chuckled and felt her shiver. "Imagine that," he drawled as he snaked a hand behind her. "*Anything* is exactly what I want."

He thought she'd collapse then in a weeping mess. That's what virgins usually did. They got overwhelmed and broke such that he could take whatever he wanted from the shattered girl. Unless she was a saucy girl who melted against him and offered everything but her virginity. He was prepared for that, too.

She didn't do either. She turned her gaze back up to him, her eyes wet with tears, as she pushed the tip of her dirk into his chin. Or she tried to.

He caught her arm at the last second, holding the blade away from a lethal plunge into his brainpan. It was easy to do. She'd had little force behind the movement, which told him she hadn't intended to kill him. Yet steely anger flashed in her eyes.

"Do you know how many times I have been threatened in my life?"

Plenty, obviously.

"Enough that they aggravate me as so much noise."

He still had one arm around her back, holding her close enough to feel the tension in her body while the other kept her head back. It was a balance of a sort where she stood like a vibrating string on a fiddle.

He really needed to decide how to play her.

"Shall I tell you what I want?" he asked. Rare for him to give up his wants first. Bad choice in a negotiation, but she deserved something for being unusual.

"That would be lovely," she said. Was there a purr in her voice? More likely her Scottish burr, but his cock liked it nonetheless.

"You attend the Finley ball tomorrow night."

She didn't react to his statement, but then again, she didn't need to. He already knew her schedule.

"I should like you to reserve a dance for me. The second waltz, I think."

"The countess will have my head. She insists she must approve—"

"Do not insult my intelligence." Stupid lies set him off. They wasted time and energy. "You have gotten around her all season."

"I haven't," she said with a sniff. "Sadie is the one who takes risks."

Sadie was the third Scotswoman in this house. Well, the second one now that Miss MacAdaidh was off to become a duchess. Apparently, Sadie was the bold one. Of course, she wasn't the one who tried to shove a dirk up his chin. "Then Sadie will happily dance a set with me as well. The one after you, I think."

"I can't force her to dance with you," she said.

"I think you can." And then, so she understood a little more of who she was bantering with, he pressed his fingers hard into her wrist. She needed to drop that weapon now.

She tried to fight him, but her slender wrist was no match for his strength. Eventually her fingers weakened, and the knife dropped heavily to the floor. He covered it with his boot and slid it just beneath his heel. It was a good weapon, and he intended to keep it.

With the dirk gone from her, she tried to jerk back. He didn't want to release her, so he pulled her flush against him. He knew she would fight him, but he wanted to measure her skill. Just how many tricks did this lady have up her Scottish sleeves?

Several, it appeared. She fought like one who had been taught close combat, but there was a panic in her movements that undermined her training. He subdued her easily, but her fear touched him. He did not need to terrify her to get what he wanted. Once he had her pinned against him, her breath coming fast and her cheeks smudged with tears, he whispered in her ear.

"I'm releasing you now, Iseabail." He stretched out her name to taste every letter in it. "Don't attack me again. You won't like the result."

Then he opened his hands and she scrambled back. "I could still scream," she said as she rubbed at her wrists.

"But then we wouldn't be able to waltz tonight."

"You aren't the type to get an invitation," she drawled. "You won't be allowed in."

He grinned. "Leave that to me. Just save the dance. And mind that Sadie gives me one as well."

She shook her head. "Sadie's been in enough trouble. She cannot afford any more scandal."

Ah yes. The murdered dance partner. She might have been cleared of the crime from the constabulary, but society could be a lot less forgiving. "Then you best buy my silence. Accusations of witchcraft against either of you could bring all that ugliness back up."

She stiffened. "It's not true. None of it is true!"

He didn't bother repeating what he'd said before. Truth never mattered, only the strength of the story around a person made the least bit of difference. "I just want a dance," he said. A waltz with a well-sponsored girl at a high society ball. It was the toehold he needed into the *ton*.

"And you'll return my necklace?"

He grinned. "I'll put it on your neck myself." Right in front of the entire *haut ton* if he could manage it. Then he swooped down and pocketed her dirk.

"That's mine!" she exclaimed.

He shook his head. "I make a habit of keeping every weapon that is used against me." He spun it between his fingers as he grinned at her. "And this is a lovely one."

"But it's the only thing I have," she whispered.

He cracked the door to her bedroom. The hallway was quiet now, but he couldn't tell how long it would stay that way. Still, he couldn't resist her outraged expression. She was gathering her fury but was still off balance. That meant he had enough time to steal a kiss.

A quick press of his lips against hers. A tease of his tongue against her soft lips.

She gasped in surprise—the opening he needed—and he was swift to slip inside. Not a bold thrust. He was not a man who stole such things from a lady. But a slight press, a flick of his tongue to give her the idea, and then a retreat.

He grinned. "Now you have something else," he said. Then he slipped out her bedroom and down the stairs. He was light on his feet and fast, gone out the front before any of the servants looked up from their tasks.

The only thing left was to figure out how he was going to break into a ball, dance with not one but *two* debutantes, and not get arrested or thrown out on his very handsome arse.

CHAPTER THREE

I SEABAIL WAS RUNNING, her feet icy cold and cut such that every step was agony. It was the dead, she knew, reaching up from the soil to grab at her. She searched for a place to stand. She needed to catch her breath and think—always she needed to think—but every time she stopped, the fingers of the dead broke through the soil to grab her.

She had to keep moving. She had to find rocks where they couldn't dig through or climb to the top of a tree too far above the ground for them to reach. But no matter how she scrambled, the rocks shifted beneath her feet. And what trees she climbed broke, dropping her down to the soil where the dead finally caught her.

They cut through her ankles first, forcing her to crawl. But once her hands hit the dirt, they caught her wrists and began to pull.

She fought them, but there were too many. Her blood ran in rivulets, and she saw the mouths of the dead drinking it like wine.

One cut through her belly next, and she knew death was near. Best to surrender to it now. Best to let it come quickly. But she couldn't let herself die, not while she still breathed. So she fought and she sobbed until she woke with her blanket binding her tight and her scream trapped in her throat.

Even in nightmares, she never screamed. She hadn't the breath. And she wouldn't give the dead the satisfaction of hearing her terror.

Breathing heavy, she fought to steady her breath. The room was dark without Sadie's comforting snore. That was because her friend had moved into Mairi's empty bedroom. And without her friend here, the nightmares had come back.

It took time to unwind the blankets. It took calm to pull her arms free and push the heavy fabric away. She hated the fabric that twisted around her, couldn't stand to feel anything touch her skin. So she stripped it all away. The blankets, her night rail, even the ribbon that bound her hair. She mentally threw them at the devil while she kicked them off her bed.

Then when the sweat began to dry on her naked body, she sat upright in the middle of her bed and she cursed the dead to hell. No matter how far she ran, the dead chased her. Her mother, her father, the sick ones she'd failed to save, and all the men who'd perished in Culloden.

She wasn't responsible for anything that had happened to them. She hadn't even been alive when the clans perished in battle. And yet they came to her at night when she slept, and nothing she did sent them away.

She closed her eyes, but the dream was too clear for that. With a shudder, she opened them again. She couldn't sit here on the bed like a frightened child. In Scotland, she would rouse a maid to accompany her to the stillroom to mix unguents or check on the food that kept the clan alive. Always something to do in Scotland. But here she had no responsibilities except to be pretty, to dance well, and charm a man into marrying her. Here she had nothing to do but worry that no Englishman could stand strong against her brute of an uncle.

The bottoms of her feet began to itch, the brush of the fabric too much to bear. She would have to step onto the cold wood floor. It wasn't as hard as stone, but it soothed her as she put her weight down. No skeletal remains could grab her here. She was on the second floor standing on wood. She was safe from the dead here.

Or so she told herself.

With nothing else to do, she wandered to the window. The window was shut, the curtains wispy things that did little to ease the draft. Fortunately, it was spring, and the night air would be welcome. Plus, she loved moonlight and she so rarely saw it in London. There were too many clouds here, too much smoke.

She pulled the curtains aside and swung open the window, then lifted her face to the moon. It was half-sized tonight, way up in the sky, and half gone. And yet looking up at it reminded her of her mother. Of reading books by moonlight and memorizing rhymes of healing or worship. Men called it spells and witchcraft, but she knew them to be prayers to the beauty of the land and the grace of being alive.

She recited one now about the black sky above and the green shoots below. Scotland would be coming alive now as spring took hold. She would smell life in the air and not the constant soot of London.

Seven verses tripped off her tongue. Seven blessings to keep away sorrow. And seven wishes to water her soul. And when she was done, she felt better. Not exactly strong, but more herself.

Only then did she look down and see the man in the shadows. She wouldn't have known him except for the dark red burn of his cheroot. A cursed man's eye, she thought, and she jumped back, her heart racing in terror. That one red burn brought back every horror of her nightmare.

She scrambled back onto her bed, her skin prickling with goosebumps. She wanted to hide but the touch of fabric brought back the grip of skeletons on her flesh. What was he doing staring up at her window? Why would anyone stand in the shadows and smoke?

It took several minutes before her terror eased. Several long moments before reason fought back her nightmare. But once logic replaced feeling, new fears surged in her mind. Was someone watching the house? Watching her? Or had she simply surprised someone poor laborer taking a rest in the dark?

It was long, long minutes before she realized she'd been standing there naked, silhouetted in moonlight. Whatever would she do if someone told? The countess would toss her out for sure. No pure woman stood naked in a window.

Where would she go if she couldn't live here? How would she survive?

Was the man still there? Maybe she had imagined him. It could have been a trick of the light. It could have been a stranger taking advantage of an accidental moment and no one would be the wiser. Perhaps he was wondering if he had imagined her standing there.

She had to see if he was there. She had to know if it was someone who might tell.

She grabbed her night rail and pulled it on, though the fabric made her skin crawl. She pulled a wrapper on top of that, though the weight of it whispered of being dragged down into the dirt to die. She wrapped it around her tightly and kept hold of her sanity by force of will.

This was not a dream. This was reality and she would live in this moment. Once she was properly covered, she crept her way to the window and peeked out.

He was still there.

Worse, he had come out of the shadows to stand beneath the streetlight. She couldn't read his expression from this distance. It could have been anything from reverent to mocking. But he held his hat in his hand now, rather than the cheroot. And he looked straight up at her.

Mr. Reuben Bates.

She didn't know what to do. Did she hide and pretend he wasn't there? Did she slam the shutters closed as if that would protect her from him?

Boldness was the only way through now. Hiding would accomplish nothing. She would know what he wanted, even if it was to torment her with the knowledge that he had seen more of her than any decent woman would expose.

She stepped to the window. Her hands were shaking as she appeared now, all but swaddled from head to toe. She heard his response. It was clear as day on this silent street. A whistle of appreciation as he lifted his hat to her. He was just beginning to bow when something else caught her attention.

Another shadow, another man. A big one who dislodged a stone as he moved. Good God, were the nighttime streets of London teeming with people?

Mr. Bates must have heard it, too. Halfway through his bow, he took off running. Not away from the shadow, but toward it as if to catch him. The big one ran fast as well. Down an alleyway and out of sight.

Damn it, who was it? Why was everyone sitting outside her house staring up at her? She pulled the window shut before dropping her head against the cool pane. Would she ever be free of people watching her? Would she ever be safe?

CHAPTER FOUR

Reuben's cock was throbbing, and his mind overflowed with visions of Miss Iseabail Spalding naked in the moonlight. But he still heard the noise and reacted with the ease of long practice.

He ran straight at the interloper.

The man was too large for speed and no match for Reuben on a straightaway. But in the twisting alleyways of London, he could be evasive, especially if he was lucky.

The bastard led Reuben on a merry chase up and around for several streets while Reuben started categorizing what he knew about his prey. He was quick for a man his size, understood the London streets, and likely able to defend himself if it came to blows. But he obviously preferred anonymity over confrontation, which meant he was smart.

Fortunately, Reuben was smarter in that he knew how to stop and listen. A big man had to breathe hard after so much dashing around. Reuben found him with his hat over his mouth behind a pile of rubbish.

"Is that to cover the smell?" he asked as he rounded the corner. "Or quiet yer breathing?" He let his accent roughen up to match the tone of this bastard. That wasn't an insult, but the literal truth by accident of birth. He knew this man and thought him a decent man for a Bow Street Runner.

"Jesus, Reuben, why didn't you say it was you? Would have saved me from running halfway round London."

"It was less than ten blocks, you fat bastard. Millie's cooking's got you slow."

"Aye," he said, patting his belly. "She's a right good cook."

She was also the best childhood friend of Reuben's second cousin. The runner's name was Sammy Watts, and he was a close enough to be considered family. Distant family, perhaps, but in London that meant he lived a mile away.

"What's got you out here this time of night?" Reuben asked.

The man flashed a grin. "Besides the babe squalling at all hours?"

The child was a healthy little boy with lungs that could and had kept the neighbors awake. "Aye."

Sammy moved away from the pile of rubbish and Reuben matched his pace. "Three Scottish gents came to t' office a few days ago. Said they were looking for a girl named Iseabail Spalding. Paid me to find her."

The baron, no doubt, looking for his charge. "Did they say why they wanted her?"

"Said she's a runaway bride." He snorted. "Can't say I blame her. The man's an ugly brute."

"The husband-to-be came here?"

"Not to-be. Says they're married in the Scottish way. No idea what that's to mean, but I can tell he means to whip her for his troubles."

"You mean beat her."

"Nah. Said he's got a riding crop with her name on it." He shook his head. "I wouldn't give a mangy dog to 'im, but that's the law. If they're wed—"

"There's naught to be done fer 'er."

They walked in silence for a bit. Reuben knew where they were going. After all, they lived within a few blocks of each other, and he allowed that they could travel that way together. Reuben kept quiet knowing that Sammy would start speaking eventually. He was one who had to talk his thoughts through before he decided on an action.

"Didn't take me long to find 'er. Only delay was on account of me not thinking she'd be with the nobs. But then I heard about these Scottish ladies causing a stir. One of them was accused of killing a lord."

"That was Sadie Allen, not Iseabail Spalding."

"Aye. But it was enough to find out who they were." He shrugged. "And since the babe was squalling fit to wake the dead, I thought I'd come by the house. Talk to the servants and the like. Didn't think to see her standing bold as brass with her bubbies out." Sammy cast a sidelong look at Reuben. "I wanted to see who her lover was. Didn't think it would be you."

That's why Sammy had stepped out. He'd been trying to see who stood under the streetlight.

"It's not me. I'm not her lover."

"Sure looked like ye were what with bowing before her like some Frenchie courtier."

Reuben shot him an irritated glare. "I'm not her lover. I don't think she has one."

"Sure, she don't." Sarcasm lay thick in his voice. "All them Scots stand naked beneath the moonlight. It's a national pastime."

"Could be," Reuben answered. "There's different and then there's—"

"Scottish different?" Sammy elbowed him in the ribs. "Don't be daft. She was calling to someone an' you know it."

He didn't know it. Her gaze hadn't been out on the street. She'd been looking up at the moon and lifting her face to the breeze. And the moment she looked down to see him, she'd dropped out of sight as if she'd been felled. For all he knew, she'd been doing some spell taught to her by her witch mother or grandmother.

"She's not the type," Reuben said.

"Yer thinking with yer prick. Ye saw her bubbies and now you want to worship at her cunny, not thinking about who else might have seen—"

"Shut it," Reuben grumbled. "You don't know what you saw.

Your eyes ain't never been good."

"Don't take much to—"

Reuben rounded on him, squaring off chin to chest with the big man. "You didn't see it."

Sammy's brows rose but he didn't argue. Instead, he folded his arms across his chest. "Wot's yer interest?" Then he snorted. "Aside from the obvious."

"It ain't that!" Reuben huffed. Except, that was a lie. Any man would be interested given what he'd seen tonight. Clear skin silvered in moonlight. Full breasts on a sturdy frame. She reminded him of a picture he'd once seen of the Goddess Hera. The queen of the gods had held a scepter in one hand and a babe in the other. She'd seemed majestic to him even as his adolescent mind had noted the high, full breasts. Exactly what he'd seen of Iseabail tonight, except she was living flesh and not a marble statue.

"Then wot is it? Exactly."

"I need her to get into a ball tomorrow night. She's going to waltz with me."

Sammy's brows rose. "How'd you manage that?"

"Threatened her."

"Well, I believe yer not her lover. Why would you go to a ball?"

"And how else am I to meet a fine nob to marry if I can't get into a ball?"

"Since when do you want to marry a nob?"

Since the day when he was six that a fine lady told him he wasn't good enough to shine her boots. Since the day he realized every woman knew who he was and wanted a piece of his fortune. Since he'd conquered everything he'd ever wanted in London and was now looking for more. And what else was there for a man like him except a lady wife? A true *ton* lady to bear his name and his children.

"Yer daft, you are," Sammy scoffed. "Always looking fer more. Never satisfied."

He couldn't deny it. Neither could he wipe the image of Iseabail in the moonlight from his mind. "Can you wait with the Scots? Don't tell 'em that you've found her."

"Just long enough so's you can taste those teats?"

Reuben's growl took them both by surprise. He didn't like what she'd done, and he'd liked even less that Sammy had seen it. But he couldn't deny that he knew precious little about Miss Spalding, and he was becoming more curious by the hour. Was she a tart who'd just set out to tempt him? Or was she an innocent witch praying to the moon? Didn't matter. He still needed her to dance with him at the ball.

"Wait to talk to the Scots," he commanded, even though he knew Sammy didn't take orders from him.

"Can't. They want her back, and they've got nothing else in London to distract them from banging on my door."

"Nothing else in London? Are they daft?"

He shrugged. "What do I know if they're regular Scots daft or beyond the usual daft?"

"Can you wait a day? Tell them she'll be in Hyde Park day after tomorrow."

Sammy turned to look at him. "An' how do you know that?"

"Because I'll get her there myself."

"And wot are you going to do when they grab 'er in front o' you and drag her off with that ugly brute?"

He sighed. "I'll let her go. By then, I'll have better things to do."

"An' wot if she offers you a taste of her—"

This time he hit Sammy square in the middle of his chest. He'd warned the man once not to talk about what they'd seen. He wasn't going to allow it again. "She could be the Virgin Mary herself, an' I'd let her go. And as far as you are concerned, that's exactly who she is."

Sammy stood still, his expression hard. "They paid good coin fer me to find her and hand 'er over. That's the law if she's 'is wife."

"And what if he lied?"

"You've got no proof of that, and they've got papers from 'er guardian saying it's true. She's married to the brute, and I got no cause to keep 'im away." He shrugged. "They've paid good coin, an' I got a new babe to feed."

Reuben felt his gut tighten. He'd known Iseabail was not telling the whole truth from the very beginning. He'd thought it was all about her witch of a mother, but what if she was hiding more? What if she'd been lawfully wed? The thought of giving her over to some brute cut deep into his soul, but he had other priorities. And as much as he would enjoy dancing with the Scottish beauty, he was not in a position to stand as her protector. Especially if she were well and truly wed.

"I'm not a man to rescue any woman—virgin or hussy—from her daft Scottish husband."

"Then I have yer word to not interfere?"

"Yes."

"Then I'll wait a day and say she'll be in Hyde Park after yer ball."

"Done."

Sammy grunted his approval, and the two shared a pleasant walk back to their homes. And why wouldn't Sammy be happy? He knew Reuben never, ever went back on his word.

CHAPTER FIVE

"OH NO, SADIE!" Iseabail cried, putting her hand out between Sadie's dance card and Mr. Pierce's pencil. "He can't have that dance, remember?"

Sadie looked at her in confusion. Mr. Keller, however, looked absolutely furious.

"You promised the dance after the second waltz to our friend. The first *honest* Englishman we met on our journey here." She emphasized the word "honest" because, of course, they'd been stopped by English highwaymen first. Reuben Bates was the one who saved them from the blackguards.

Unfortunately, Mr. Keller took offense at the interruption. His back stiffened, his shoulders went up to his ears, and he even sniffed in fury. "I wouldn't think a *Scotswoman* would be so blindly shrewish."

Iseabail frowned. "What?"

"You meant this dance, correct?" Sadie said as she pointed at the dance after the second waltz. "But the next one's available, yes?"

"Yes! You haven't promised it to anyone else, right?"

"I don't know," Sadie said, laughing. "That's what I'm asking you."

It was a comedy of errors and that always entertained Sadie. She loved anything ridiculous and thought it was even funnier when Mr. Keller turned his back on them with another loud sniff.

"Oh dear," Iseabail groaned. "I think we've insulted him."

"Of course you did. I thought that was the point."

"Why would I want to insult a suitor?"

"He's the one with Indian money."

"What's wrong with money from India? Isn't that what the East India company does?"

"It's because his uncle married it."

Iseabail watched the man stomp through the crowd toward the refreshments. "His uncle? But it's not even his money, then. It would go to his cousins."

Sadie shrugged. "All part of the clan, I suppose."

"But it's *money*. Who cares where it's from?"

Her friend had no answer. What was important to the *ton* made little sense to them, but that was why they were guided by the dowager countess. Or so she told them repeatedly.

"So who is this gentleman I'm promised to after the second waltz?"

"Mr. Reuben Bates. He said… Well, he's supposed to… I mean, he asked me to have you save him a dance."

Her friend rocked back on her slippered heels and laughed. The sound was merry and full of mischief, but it never failed to lighten Iseabail's heart.

"I don't remember a Mr. Bates, but clearly he has some sort of power over you."

"Not a whit," she lied. "And you do remember him. He's the one who rescued us from the highwaymen."

Sadie's eyes widened. "Truly? I had no idea he was elevated enough to attend a ball." She looked around at the titled assemblage. This event was as exclusive as Almack's. "Whatever would a peer be doing rescuing us from highwaymen up north?"

Lying about his antecedents, no doubt. "Why is it more believable that a peer would playact being a rugged gunman than a man of lowly ancestry could attend this ball?"

Sadie laughed. "Because no one gets in here without a full pedigree. Even we wouldn't be here without the countess."

Which made her all the more curious about Mr. Bates. "Will you save the dance for him? Please?"

"What are you saving for him?"

Iseabail held up her card and pointed to where she'd written the man's name.

"The waltz?" Sadie gasped in surprise. Her gaze swung back to where the countess was talking with her friends. "Does she know?"

Iseabail didn't need to answer. Sadie already guessed the truth, and it didn't seem to bother her a whit. With the boldness of one who never said no to a lark, she scrawled Mr. Bates's name on the appropriate line.

"Thank—" Iseabail began, but she was interrupted by a pair of gentlemen eager to add their names to Sadie's dance card. Iseabail knew the men. Both were more interested in a bit of fun in the garden than anything approaching matrimony. But at least one of them was an excellent dancer, so Sadie seemed happy to offer up her card. Which meant Iseabail had to do so as well, despite her disinterest in either man.

And so the evening went. Neither of them was popular enough to have her dance card filled, but they made a good enough showing. Sadie was the flirt who made everyone laugh. Iseabail stood beside her hoping for some reflected glory. Normally she could engage well enough to feel like she gave the gentlemen a chance to impress her. She needed a very specific kind of husband—one who could stand up to her uncle—and so far, every pale, mincing Sassenach had disappointed her. Not a one seemed like he could survive a harsh winter, much less her uncle's brutish fury.

Which is why her attention kept wandering to the door where Mr. Reuben would soon step through.

Any minute now.

Any second now the man who had seen her naked last night would ask her to dance.

Good God, what was she going to say to him?

He didn't arrive in the normal receiving line. That wasn't surprising. Many a gentleman arrived after the dancing began. Iseabail watched the main door as best she could, much to the annoyance of her dance partners. It was rude of her, she knew, but she couldn't stop herself. She had to know if he was coming.

By the end of the first set, she accepted the truth. Mr. Reuben wasn't here. Either he hadn't managed an invitation—the most likely possibility—or something else had happened. That meant she didn't need to risk the countess's wrath by dancing with an unapproved gentleman. She didn't need to face someone with whom she'd been so accidentally inappropriate. Her face still burned with humiliation at the memory. And yet, he was also the most interesting man she'd ever met.

The conflict of emotions made her incredibly distracted, and even Sadie noticed.

"I knew it was a lie," Sadie whispered to her before the second set began. "He's not a peer pretending to be a gunman. He's a gunman—"

"Yes, yes. I know."

"You can do better, Iseabail. You have blue blood and a dowry—"

"A rumor of one—"

"Is better than what I have, which is absolutely nothing." She squeezed Iseabail's arm. "You know, the only reason I've gotten as much attention as I have is because I'm the fun one. If you'd smile more, crack that ice queen polish a bit, they'd flock to you—"

"Like flies on honey?"

"Yes."

"I don't want a fly."

"You don't want to be ignored, unwed honey either."

No, she didn't. If her uncle ever caught her without a ring on her finger, she would be unceremoniously hauled back to Scotland and forced on any one of his toadies. That was why she had run in the first place.

"So smile. Come on. The second set is beginning."

Iseabail took the advice to heart. She put on her brightest smile and gave her dance partner her exclusive attention. She tried not to count dances. She didn't want to think, *Three more dances until he didn't show up.* Two more dances until he wasn't here. One more dance to go. And yet it was in her mind despite her best efforts.

So it was with some surprise that when she finished that last dance, she turned to find Sadie grinning at her from the edge of the dance floor. Two gentlemen towered above her. On one side stood one of Sadie's regular waltz partners—a second son with a long nose, a booming laugh, and exquisite dancing skills. That man was glaring fiercely at Mr. Reuban Bates on the opposite side.

"Mr. Bates," Iseabail said as she approached the three. "You've arrived."

Lord Arlo sniffed audibly. "Do you know this man?" He might as well have asked, *Did she know this rancid bit of meat?*

"I do, my lord," she returned sweetly. "He saved my life once."

Mr. Bates grinned. "So I did. And all I asked was for a waltz in return."

"Not so, sir," she returned. "You asked for nothing as you were already paid for that task. This dance is for something else entirely."

She was being testy with him, and she wasn't sure why. Maybe because she was risking things by dancing with him. Or because her cheeks burned at the memory of him bowing to her last night. Or maybe he set her out of sorts because she never knew exactly how she was supposed to act around him and that made her feel unsafe.

Either way, he didn't seem to mind her mood. His grin widened at her curt words, and he held out his hand to hers.

"This dance is the culmination of years of planning," he said. "And I couldn't ask for a more beautiful partner."

Years of planning? How ridiculous. But there was nothing silly in the way he looked at her. His gaze was frank as he took in her gown, her form, and most likely the hot pink spots of color in her cheeks. Damn her red coloring for showing everything. And damn him for being where no man ought to have been last night. He looked at her now as he likely had last night, seeing her at her most vulnerable, and she didn't know how to fight that. Especially when she found her hand in his without her even willing it.

If she weren't the daughter of a witch, she would have claimed he'd bespelled her. But of course, she knew that such things didn't actually happen.

Meanwhile, Lord Arlo still tried to interfere. "Miss Spalding, you know you shouldn't dance with just anyone."

"She's not," Sadie interrupted. "She's dancing with the rogue who saved her life. Mine, too, if we're honest. Now are you going to waltz with me or not? Because—ooh!"

Out of the corner of her eye, Iseabail saw Sadie get jerked onto the dancefloor. Whatever Lord Arlo's thoughts on Mr. Reuben, it was clear he wanted his dance and Sadie's giggle told everyone she was happy to oblige.

And that was the last moment she thought about Sadie.

Mr. Bates absorbed all of her attention without even saying a word. He raised their joined hands and led her onto the floor. Amazing how secure her fingers felt in his. They were both wearing gloves and she was not a small woman, but his hand engulfed hers and his grip was strong enough that it would be hard for her to escape should she want to.

That was as thrilling as it was frightening.

"You are looking very well dressed this evening," she said. Unlike herself last night. "I can hardly believe you are the same man." He certainly didn't seem the same as the one who had watched her from the street. That man had been brash and rough. This one seemed refined and courteous, though both men sported roguish mischief in their eyes.

"I hope my efforts are pleasing?"

"And here I thought only braggart Scotsmen fished for compliments."

He chuckled. "Braggart Scotsmen declare their beauty and pray you disagree so they can fight you."

"You speak true there," she said.

"I merely wish to not offend you with my coarse manners."

He didn't. His manners were perfect. And as for his attire, every stitch, every thread exuded elegance. Every inch conformed to his very muscular frame. His cravat was an exquisite cascade of brilliant white folds, his points stretched rakishly high, and his hair waved a la Brutus in a dashing spectacle. And that was nothing compared to the way his trousers hugged his lower half, thick muscles encased in black. Most women claimed to admire shiny Hessian boots. Not her. She couldn't care less about the footwear. She swooned after the corded breadth of his thighs and the power in his every step.

What she wouldn't give to see this man in a kilt.

He caught her around the waist but didn't pull her indecently close. Too bad. She wanted to feel more of his strength when they danced about the room, but she knew better than to allow it. Already she could hear whispers and see fans pointed in their direction.

"Do they know who you are?" she asked, her voice needlessly breathless. The music hadn't even started yet.

"Some."

"How did you get in? I was watching the entrance. You were never announced."

He grinned at her. "You were waiting for me?"

"Do you always turn words around such that they give you a compliment?"

"Of course. It helps to point out when people admire me. They too often forget."

She rolled her eyes, unsure whether his cheekiness was bravado or true confidence. It didn't truly matter. He was charming and handsome. That was a potent combination, especially when he mixed it with bold dancing.

"Sir, last night I had a nightmare and—"

"I had a vision of such beauty," he said right as the music began and he swept her into motion.

He wasn't elegance on the dance floor. He was power barely leashed as he gripped her about the waist and spun her around. Good lord, he made her head spin quite literally. But if she had no control over the whirling dervish of a partner, then she might as well enjoy it.

She wasn't one to relax into anyone's hold, but she did match her speed and skill to his. He kept her feet moving as fast as his, and she kept her arms strong without being stiff. He seemed to like that as his grin abruptly widened.

"Do you trust me?" he asked.

What a ridiculous question. "No."

"Even better."

Obviously, he liked a challenge because he set himself to force her body to trust his. He spun her quickly while holding her completely safe. He wove them left and right around other couples. A lesser man would have them crashing into someone—everyone—but they always slid through unscathed. And though she couldn't deny the thrill of it all, she also guessed that he was leaving disarray in his wake. He was an excellent dancer, but the other couples were probably jerking to an abrupt halt as they danced past.

He must have realized it, too. She saw his gaze dart about them as a frown darkened his features. Immediately after that, their steps slowed. He matched his pace to the room, and they were now waltzing as everyone else did. Smooth, not so thrilling, but easy enough for Iseabail to take a full breath.

"How many couples crashed?" she asked.

His expression turned annoyed. "Just one stumbled. That idiot viscount who has no rhythm."

That could refer to several gentlemen, but she believed there was only one viscount here tonight. "I'm glad you slowed down."

"Are you truly? No love of speed and frenzy with a partner who can keep you safe throughout it all?"

"I love it as much as any person. But I am a woman on the hunt for a husband. Making a spectacle of myself on the dance floor will not help me in that pursuit." She arched a brow at him. "Not all of us can sneak into bedrooms or ballrooms without consequence."

His brows rose. "You think I bear no consequences?"

"Not like I do."

He snorted. "That is certainly true, Miss Spalding. You might lose invitations to the most exclusive balls. I, however, am risking my life and limb by being here uninvited."

"One wonders why you do it, then."

"Because sometimes one can only go up."

She wanted to ask what he meant by that, but she didn't have time. The music ended; the dancers stopped. As was appropriate, she dropped into a curtsy before him, and he a bow. And when she straightened, he held out her necklace before him.

"As promised, Miss Spalding. Your pendant."

She reached for it, but he was quicker than her. He draped it around her neck, then spun around her to fix the clasp. She had little choice but to stand still while everyone watched what he was doing. Damn it, everyone would think he was fixing his interest upon her, and that she allowed it! Jewelry was not something that was casually offered between unattached people. And yet here she stood, publicly allowing him to give her something that was already hers.

The minute she felt the chain drop against her neck, she stepped away. "Thank you, sir, for returning my pendant to me, but you need not have done it in such a public manner."

"It's only that it fell away when we walked in the park. I knew you didn't realize the catch had broken."

She dipped her head to him again, appreciating that he'd created a lie about it, but she was still annoyed. He was creating a spectacle. Unfortunately, the moment she turned to leave the dance floor, she realized that he had done a great deal more than that. There with the countess stood no less than three footmen plus their host and hostess for the evening.

Were they about to be thrown out of the ball? Her reputation would never recover!

"Oh no," she moaned.

"Oh yes," he returned. Then he held out his hand to her and flashed that cheeky grin. "The only way forward is up."

"A nice sentiment if I were a bird, but I'm not."

He chuckled. "But maybe I am large enough to carry us both."

CHAPTER SIX

UNLIKE HIS USUAL marks, Miss Spalding clearly knew she was being used. Unfortunately, she'd been his only option tonight. No young lady of consequence would dare dance with a common scoundrel like him, and so he had found one he could force. Unfortunately, they were both about the pay a heavy price for his audacity. Unless, of course, he maneuvered them out of it.

Good thing he'd planned for this.

The first person he made nice with was the Dowager Countess of Byrn. After all, if she started complaining that he had insulted Miss Spalding with that waltz, then he was done for sure. He began by talking loudly as he escorted Miss Spalding to the edge of the dance floor.

"You are quite lucky to be sponsored by the dowager countess. Her son and I are good friends, and I have always been impressed by the entire family."

Miss Spalding answered in the way all debutantes must. She smiled and agreed wholeheartedly. "I am extraordinarily lucky and grateful. She has found excellent husbands for all her daughters and now Mairi has wed a future duke!"

Perfect. Miss Spalding obviously knew they were avoiding disaster together.

"A duke? I hadn't heard," he lied. He looked at the dowager countess. "Congratulations on such a wonderful match."

How could the countess respond to that except with a bumbling thanks? At least that was his hope. Sadly, the lady proved much too smart for so easy a ploy.

"Don't try to butter me, sirrah. What cause have you to make a spectacle of my charge?" Her eyes flashed to Iseabail. "I thought you were the sensible one. Take off that necklace at once."

"But it's my necklace," Miss Spalding objected. "The catch broke, and he recovered it for me."

And while the countess was shocked by her charge, Reuben took the moment to turn his charm on his hostess. "It's not the only piece I've discovered. I knew this was yours the moment I saw it at the jewelers. Lady Finley, I believe this exquisite piece belongs to you."

He pulled an old necklace out of his pocket, one that had originally been set with three dull rubies. Those gems had been replaced years ago. What sparkled in his hand now was paste, but it was beautifully done paste and so he presented it with all the panache of a man carrying the crown jewels.

The lady gasped as she saw it, her gaze hopping to her husband and no wonder. The man had pawned it a month ago to pay his gambling debts and apparently, she hadn't realized it was missing.

"I know I travel in circles not as elevated as you, Lady Finley, but it allowed me to have the catch on Miss Spalding's necklace fixed and also to see that this lost item was returned to you."

"Lost item," the woman repeated, her expression tightening. "Thank you, sir, but you need not have interrupted to my ball in order to—"

"But of course, I did," he interrupted. "Tonight is the ball of the Season. I had to come to it. You understand the allure, don't you? The beauty that surrounds me, the exquisite decorations, the perfection you display as hostess."

"Spanish coin will not help you—" she began, but her husband interrupted her.

"Mabel, dear, can't you see he was just having a bit of fun? He went about it the wrong way, but look. Your necklace is returned, all right and tight."

The necklace, yes. Not the bracelet or the earbobs, which he still possessed. And that, of course, was why Lord Finley was being so accommodating. He knew that Reuben was his only hope of ever recovering his wife's jewelry.

"All right and tight," his wife echoed, fury in every syllable. She knew her husband's gambling had gotten out of control. And she no doubt guessed where the other pieces of the set were. "How dare you bring your disgusting—"

"Perhaps I might be of assistance," he said, cutting into her diatribe before she could say something she couldn't take back.

"You—"

"I have friends throughout London. I'm an amiable fellow, after all. We could assist you in limiting your husband's entertainments to appropriate levels."

Not surprisingly, Lord Finley objected. "Now wait a damned moment—"

"We have no desire to beggar anyone, you see." He winked at Lady Finley. "And compromises are possible."

It was a risky strategy to appeal to the lady. That would set every gambling man in the *ton* against him. But the women ruled society, and that's where he wanted to be. So he took the risk of throwing in with the ladies who always wanted more power over their men.

"Interesting," murmured Lady Finley, but she was interrupted by the exquisite timing of the countess.

"What are you doing here?" snapped the dowager. He was confused for a moment, but then he realized she was speaking to Miss Allen. The girl had sidled up to see what was going on, as had everyone else at the ball. Indeed, the orchestra had stopped playing in order to watch him being tossed out on his head. "Don't you have a dance partner right now?" the countess demanded.

"I do," responded Miss Allen with a twinkle in her eyes. "I am promised to Mr. Bates."

"So you are," he said. "Pray forgive me." Then he turned to his host and hostess, bowing quickly before them. Lastly, he turned to Miss Spalding. He expected her to be annoyed with him, but instead of anger, he saw rampant speculation in her gaze. As if she were thinking very hard about him, and he was very curious as to what was her conclusion. "I should very much like another dance," he said as he kissed her hand.

She snorted. "I am sure you would, but alas, my card is full now."

It wasn't, but he didn't argue. "Another time, perhaps." He paused a moment wondering if he should warn her about her kinsmen come to look for her. But he hadn't the time as she cut into his thoughts.

"I still want my dagger back," she said under her breath.

And she might very well need it, but he had no time to delve into it. Meanwhile, he had to entertain the lively Miss Sadie Allen. He took her hand and escorted her to her place on the floor only to be surprised again by Miss Spalding.

She and her partner took positions beside them. This particular dance divided the group into sets of four and so now he had an excuse to watch her. Except her partner quickly made it clear as to why he was there.

"I say, did you return a necklace just to be allowed in a ball? My sister's come out—"

"Dickey," he said, using the idiot's shortened name. "Pay attention to your partner."

"Of course, of course," the man intoned as he bowed to Miss Spalding. "But you see, I know the, um, jeweler who repaired Miss Spalding's necklace."

Yes. Every bad gambler in town knew where to pawn his goods. Meanwhile, he smiled at his own partner. "Are you having a good evening, Miss Allen?"

"It's not boring," the woman responded. "You almost kept up with me and Lord Arlo during the waltz."

He cast her a rueful look. "I'm afraid I got carried away

with—"

"Do you know my sister?" Dickey interrupted. The man jerked Miss Spalding across from him with unnecessary force just so he could keep talking to Reuben. "Lovely girl. Adores me. I could convince her to add you—"

"Are you all right, Miss Spalding? Your partner seems ham-handed."

She answered with a roll of her eyes. Miss Allen was less polite. "Mr. Wells is well known to us," she said dryly.

"Wells—well known," Dickey chuckled. "Good one."

As if that joke hadn't been made a thousand times.

He would have said something scathing, but the dance picked up tempo and they were busy moving in and out of the pattern. He was an accomplished dancer, so he moved with ease despite the way his attention was fractured. He needed to keep an eye on Lord and Lady Finley. Though the footmen had receded to the walls, Reuben was still one bad move away from being thrown out in disgrace.

"Have you always danced this well, Mr. Bates?" Miss Allen asked.

"I learned recently the same way everyone does."

"By being hit with a fan during dance instruction?"

"The instructor wouldn't dare."

He grabbed Miss Spalding's hand this time, feeling the length of her fingers as they spun around. He'd always admired strong hands, especially in women. And long fingers seemed the epitome of class, especially when compared to his thick, blunt digits. He'd been in too many fights to have beautiful hands.

"My sister is quite handsome, you know," Dickey pressed. "She's likely to be quite popular this Season, as soon as she's out."

They separated into lines as a pair of dancers spun down the center. Off the dancefloor, Lord and Lady Finley had separated, each speaking in low voices to their closest friends, no doubt seeking advice. He knew the parties in question. He'd taken time to learn everything he could about them and their friends. But he couldn't figure out what was being said while he was hopping around in this dance.

"I say, after this dance, let's share a pint, eh?" continued Dickey.

"You are annoying me," he growled. It was the only warning the man would get.

Both ladies reacted. Their eyes widened, and Miss Allen's lips curved in delight. There was no repressing her spirit, but he admired the reserved lady more. Miss Spalding looked at Dickey who remained oblivious to his peril and then returned her gaze to Reuben. If he was guessed correctly—and he usually did—she was silently asking him to not make a scene.

Unfortunately, he could not comply. He'd already warned Dickey, and he never did such a thing twice. Though, with luck, the boor would leave him alone throughout the rest of this dance.

A new group of four formed, as was part of the dance, and he was treated to the frankly curious stares of a very young debutante and her haughty partner. Neither tried to speak with him. He was used to such things. But the gentleman was even colder to Miss Allen, and that was beyond rude. So when it was his turn to spin the young girl around, he smiled his most charming smile at her. She blushed prettily, and he whispered to her.

"Your partner isn't nearly as rich as he pretends." It was the truth, but it was also a lie. Nearly everyone here pretended to possess exaggerated wealth. Her particular partner had thick nest egg of blunt—probably the source of his attitude—but it wasn't limitless. And it wasn't going to last if he continued to alienate every man, woman, and underling in his circle.

The girl's eyes widened, and she dipped her chin. Message received, and he'd possibly saved her from a very unhappy future with an obnoxious man. He winked at her and turned his attention back to Miss Spalding.

Er, Miss Allen. Miss Sadie Allen was his partner, not Miss Spalding who was suffering through the missteps of another boorish gentleman. Meanwhile, Miss Allen was sizing him up with a perceptive gaze.

"Why are you doing this?"

"Dancing?"

"Trying to make them like you." She sighed as they walked around each other. "I have to. You don't."

But he did, more's the pity. "Why are you here? There are plenty of Scotsmen who would snatch you up."

She shrugged as they stepped back. The central couple was swinging their way down the two lines. It would appear she didn't intend to answer. Or if she did, he missed it as Miss Spalding caught his eye again. She was looking beyond him to the people along the wall. Her expression was serene as a lady's ought to be, but he knew to look at more than just the face. Her movements were stiff and slightly distracted.

Which meant something was happening behind him.

"I am sure you would find my sister's ball delightful," Dickey said, much too loudly.

Idiot. Reuben was going to carve that on the man's headstone. But rather than give any kind of clue as to his thoughts, he smiled benignly at the man. The couple was coming down the center, the woman linking arms with every gentleman in the line and spinning around before passing on to the next. Even better, the woman was Lady Rebecca, one of his targets for this evening.

His timing would need to be perfect...

He grabbed Lady Rebecca and spun her around with an appropriate amount of force. Then she did a quick spin around the ladies' line before coming back to catch Dickey's arm. She did it just as she ought. Dickey, however, tripped over a well-placed boot.

The idiot went sprawling. Reuben, on the other hand, caught the spinning, off-balanced woman. Lady Rebecca landed neatly in his arms. She was light and compliant as he lifted her up and out of Dickey's way. She gasped in surprise and looked up at him with startled gratitude on her young face. He set her on her feet then bowed deeply before her.

"How dare you!" Dickey screeched from the floor. "You tripped me!"

A female voice interrupted his tirade with a hard scold. "It's a poor dancer who blames his thick feet on someone else."

The words were tart and exactly something that Miss Allen would say. But when he looked up, he realized it was Miss Spalding, her hands on her hips and her expression annoyed. "My feet are bruised from you, as are nearly every lady's here." She looked up to the miss still clinging to Reuben's arm. "Are you all right, Lady Rebecca?"

The girl smiled. "I am, thanks to Mr. Bates."

"He is quick on his feet," Miss Spalding agreed. Then she threw up her hands. "Well, that's done then. An entire dance ruined." She looked to Miss Allen. "Do you wish some lemonade?"

"Pray, allow me to get it for you and Lady Rebecca as well," Reuben said, neatly stepping over Dickey as he escorted the ladies away. They rewarded him by smiling sweetly. Miss Allen took his arm, but it was Miss Spalding who gently steered them around.

What he saw on the other side of the room had his heart sinking to his feet. Host, hostess, and a veritable army of footmen stood there, all ready to throw him out. Damnation. His gamble had failed and now he was taking these ladies down with him.

Unless he could bring Lady Rebecca into his clutches. She was young enough to be enticed. So he caught the young girl's elbow just as she was heading back to her mother.

"Lady Rebecca, if I may, would you please honor me by walking in Hyde Park with me?" Then to make her understand that he wasn't making a play for her specifically—which would surely be rebuffed—he gestured to Miss Spalding and Miss Allen as well. "Perhaps we could all go? As an afternoon lark." He winked at Miss Allen, knowing that she was the one most likely to be amused by his antics.

"Oh, I don't know," Lady Rebecca demurred, glancing nervously toward her mother.

"We won't go during the fashionable hour," he quickly offered. "Just three beautiful ladies and myself, out for a stroll before the others spoil everything. Shall we say three o'clock?"

Miss Spalding held out her hand to the girl. "I should very much like to get to know you better, Lady Rebecca. The Season can be so hard without another woman to talk with."

"But Mama will say even at three o'clock—"

"Then make it two, hm?" she pressed.

The girl wavered, then suddenly brightened. "Yes. Yes!" she said, as if she was thrilled to make a decision of her own. "I shall meet you there at two. We shall meet as if by chance. Mama can't say anything against that."

"I'm so pleased," Miss Spalding said as Lady Rebecca giggled, then dashed back to her mother.

Reuben was thrilled. No matter what was about to happen now, a walk in the park with a titled lady would do wonders for his consequence. Though guilt threatened his composure as his gaze returned to Miss Spalding.

Her clansmen would be there. They would catch her unawares and he would not stop them. After all, if she were well and truly married, then she deserved… No, she probably didn't deserve what was coming to her, but then who did?

Besides, he had other things to worry about as Lady Finley and her lord approached with dark expressions. Time for him to make his escape.

"And now I must offer my apologies," he blustered as he kissed the hand of Miss Allen. "I'm afraid I am due to another event. Nothing so grand as this, but I must dash away."

Miss Spalding looked over his shoulder and spoke in a dry tone. "I'm sure it's very pressing."

She knew he was about to be tossed on his ear. "I look forward to tomorrow," he said as he bowed over her hand. He took his time with his kiss. Her hands were so elegant, he couldn't resist stroking her for a few seconds longer while the memory of how she'd looked in the moonlight teased at his composure.

But then he spun on his heel to bluster and apologize to Lord and Lady Finley that he had had a delightful time, but simply must depart. No one with any brain would be fooled. He was about to be tossed out on his ear. But a great many in the *ton* had feeble minds that could be swayed in his favor.

Or so he hoped.

Indeed, he had wagered nearly his entire life on that one wish.

CHAPTER SEVEN

"WHAT DO YOU mean, you don't know?" The dowager countess set down her tea hard enough that it clicked in its saucer. She was glaring at her son who had arrived ten minutes ago, well after the summons sent that morning.

Iseabail and Sadie were in the room as well, supposedly to practice their penmanship. Neither had put pen to paper since the earl had arrived. Meanwhile, the man leaned back in his chair with a heavy sigh. His gaze encompassed all three women as he spoke, his voice showing his irritation. Or perhaps a lack of sleep, given that he was a new father of a baby boy. One who, apparently, barely slept.

"Reuben Bates has a great deal to recommend him as a husband. He's wealthy, knows secrets about half the *ton*, and he is more honest than gentlemen of excellent parentage. But he also comes from common stock, has rough edges, and his assistance can be bought."

"How common? And how wealthy?" the countess pressed.

That was not what Iseabail focused upon. She was more interested in exactly how much assistance could be bought.

The earl shrugged. "There are thieves and bootblacks in his lineage."

Sadie spoke up. "The same could be said for all the *ton*." She'd been reading about the history of most of the peerage. Iseabail had been shocked to discover how many came from pirates and rebels.

"Half the *ton*," the earl said dryly. "The thing is, he doesn't have a title to overcome it."

The countess nodded. "But he wants one. Yes, yes, we all understand why he is making up to Lady Rebecca. He wants an entrée into society and my two charges gave him that." She cast a glare at Iseabail. "Why didn't you discuss this with me first?"

"I promised him a dance, my lady," Iseabail answered. "I thought if he were allowed into the Finley ball, then he would be an acceptable partner."

The lady sniffed. "But he wasn't invited. He snuck in like a common thief!" She waited a moment after that dramatic pronouncement, then turned back to the question at hand. "How much money?"

"Enough that it's causing him a problem."

Sadie snorted. "How can anyone have *too much* money?"

"The man's brilliant. Everything he's managed has turned to gold. But now he's got people who want to take over, take away, or just take. He needs to delegate his interests to the ones he trusts. There's too much for one man to handle, but then what is he to do?"

"Get a wife, obviously," his mother said.

"And then what?"

"Do what every aristocrat does. Get his wife pregnant and go hunting."

The earl shrugged. "Reuben isn't one to rest."

Sadie shifted in her seat. "Is he a violent man?"

"Undoubtedly. But never to someone he has sworn to protect."

"And he can be bought?" Iseabail asked.

"Yes."

"For how much?" That was the main question. What would it take to buy his help?

The countess leaned forward. "But you said he has more money than he knows what to do with. Whyever would he sell himself for more?"

Sadie huffed. "He must be one of those men who is never satisfied. Always needs more and more money to no purpose except to have it."

"That's not Reuben. He doesn't need money; he needs new challenges. He's so damned good at everything. He tries something, wins, then gets bored." The earl pushed up to his feet. "Well, I'm off to find a special treat for Amber. She's been up night and day with the new baby and could do with something to cheer her up."

"You're trying to find her a gift?" Sadie asked.

"Yes. Something to help. I feel so damned useless with a new baby. I'm thinking flowers or a new face cream, maybe."

Sadie shook her head. "She'd much rather you hold the baby while she sleeps. Rock the baby, bathe the child, even change the nappy if needed."

The earl frowned at her. "But we have servants for that."

"My lord, she doesn't need flowers." Sadie's tone was too tart, but she didn't hold back. She never held back. "She needs to feel as if you are in this with her. That you are sharing the burden with her."

"But I can't—"

"Spare me from husbands who say they can't. Ask your wife what she wants. She'll tell you. And if she doesn't know, then sit there with her until she can. And for God's sake, don't tell her what you can and can't do. You have to be quiet until she can tell you what she needs."

The earl stared at her, his expression thunderous. Clearly, he wasn't a man used to being told what to do. But a moment later, his gaze hopped to his mother. "Is she right?"

"Of course she is."

"Then why has no one said that to me before?"

All three women stared at him with not a one daring to answer so basic a question. In the end, he planted his hands on his hips and glared at the room.

"I'm not an intimidating man. Someone should have said something to me before!"

He was, in fact, a very intimidating man, but his desire to please his wife was to his credit. And so Iseabail said in a soothing voice, "I am sure your wife feels your respect and understands that you want to help any way you can."

"Well, I do," he grumbled.

"And do you think Mr. Bates will respect and honor a bargain made with a woman?"

"What?"

The man's mind was clearly back on his wife, but the countess understood immediately. "You are thinking of him seriously? As a marriage prospect?"

As a *something* prospect. Especially if his morals were more flexible than the standard soul's. "I will not entertain a man who would go back on his word."

"Well, you can rest easy then with Reuben. He'll honor his word. Says it's good business to do what one promises. But if he doesn't promise, then he'll happily turn his attention elsewhere."

Reassuring words. "Thank you, my lord. That was most helpful."

"You're welcome." His gaze turned back to Sadie. "How do you know so much about what new mothers want?"

She chuckled. "My lord, most women know these things. I just put it into words."

The countess sniffed. "And no one taught you to keep your opinions inside. I promise you, Miss Sadie Allen, no man wants a woman with a sharp tongue."

Sadie's tongue wasn't sharp so much as blunt. She had no difficulty saying what was on her mind, whenever it came to mind. Iseabail found that admirable. She had spent so much of her life silently subservient to her mother, then terrified into silence by her uncle, that she had no strength to speak up at all.

Iseabail set aside her quill. "I think I shall change into something else for our walk with Mr. Bates. This dress binds too much." It was a gift from Mairi and a bit too tight in the bodice and loose in the arms. She wanted to wear something that showed her height and cleavage to advantage.

"I don't think so," the countess stated. "I don't want you making up to the man. He's too common for either of you."

The earl was halfway out the door when he heard that. "Mother, he's a good man. He would honor his wife."

"I don't care if he'd put her on a pedestal and shower her with gold."

Sadie snorted. "Whyever not?"

"Because he's not good *ton*. And as my charges, you can both do better." She turned a hard glare on both women. "I will find you good husbands with better pedigrees."

"And less money," Sadie said.

The countess sniffed. "Money isn't everything."

Said the woman who'd always had it.

The countess's gaze softened. "I would prefer you to have feelings for the gentleman you marry. Life is hard enough without marrying a man you cannot respect." She shook her head. "No, the more I think upon it, I believe I shall bar the door to him."

Bar the door! But then Iseabail would never be able to hire him. Thankfully, the earl objected before she could say anything.

"That's too harsh, Mother. I respect the man."

"Then you may meet with him whenever you will, but my girls will not. They are here to find husbands and he does not qualify."

The earl pursed his lips, but decided not to argue. "You will do as you please," he said as he made his bows. "As will Reuben, I expect." Then with a distractive way, he collected his hat and coat and departed.

Which left Iseabail to plead Mr. Bates's case. "You shouldn't bar the door to the man. We've promised to walk with him—"

"Then he will be disappointed."

"—And Lady Rebecca," Iseabail continued. "We cannot afford to insult her."

The countess pursed her lips. "Her mother won't allow it either."

"But she might. Or Lady Rebecca will sneak out. Either way, we must go walk with her. If for no other reason than to protect her from Mr. Bates."

"She is rather young and silly. Just the kind of girl who might be tempted by a rogue."

"Exactly," Iseabail declared as she headed upstairs to change.

"Not so fast, my girl." The countess stood up. "I am not so blind. What is your interest in Mr. Bates? I'll not allow you to marry him."

"But what if I hired him?" she asked.

"For what purpose?"

To kill her uncle.

The thought should have shocked her. Indeed, she had been taught to revere all life, even in one so harsh as her guardian. But if her uncle was gone, then she could stop living in fear of him coming for her. She could marry whomever she chose and not look for a man who would defend her. She could finally beg forgiveness from her parents' ghosts. Indeed, she would have avenged them by killing their murderer. Assuming, of course, it had been her uncle.

She bit her lip. She couldn't say any of that to the countess. She could barely think her own terrible thoughts. Fortunately, she had another answer.

"I want my dowry," she said firmly. "No one believes that I bring anything to my marriage. But if Mr. Bates got my five hundred gold coins from my uncle…"

"Then you could definitely marry well." Her eyes narrowed. "And you think he would do such a thing?"

Iseabail had no idea. "I can ask."

The countess pursed her lips. "Very well. You may walk with him today. But after that, you will have no more interactions with him except in an employment capacity. Do I make myself clear?"

"Yes, my lady."

The countess snorted as she looked out the window. "He had better arrive exactly on time today," she said. "He must in every way appear absolutely proper or I shall bar the door to him myself."

"But why? Almost no gentleman ever arrives on time."

"Because he is not a gentleman. Never fear, I'm sure there will be another way to contact him if necessary. You must understand that appearances are everything. And if I am to allow an encroaching cit into my house, then he must seem to be perfect in every way."

"That is an impossible standard."

"Nevertheless, it is what I require." And so saying, the lady swept out of the room.

CHAPTER EIGHT

"**D**AMNATION, I'M GOING to be late."

Reuben hopped out of the boxing ring and wiped off his face. He'd been teaching one of his young cousins to defend himself. The boy was eleven and ought to know how to hit by now, but of course he didn't. There was no power in his punch and apparently no interest in learning. The boy was an artist, always shaping mud and dirt into sculptures that defied imagination. Fantastical shapes of rock and stick that became dragons or knights of old.

He had no quarrel with the pastime, but in order to survive, the child needed to defend himself. His younger sister Lindy, on the other hand, would give hell to any soul who tried to trespass upon her good nature, himself included. She stood beside the boxing square with tight fists and a furious scowl.

"You need to teach me!" she grumbled. "I can hit ten times harder than him."

"That's why I don't need to teach you," he said. He glanced back at the boy now sitting on his arse in the middle of the ring. He was doing something with his gloves. Stacking them, twisting them, or some other such nonsense that had nothing to do with hitting. "Can you help your brother get home?"

The girl rolled her eyes. "You need to teach me. Then I'll protect him."

He would if he had the time. Instead, he'd spent most of his day sorting the accounts of this small gym. He'd given the task to his brother a year ago and the disaster had taken months to clean up. So now he kept control of this, and a dozen other businesses owned by various members of his family. The boxing club was the most neglected and was, thankfully, not in as bad shape as he feared. But it showed the signs of his neglect in things that needed to be fixed, people who were not working as they ought, and all those stupid details he despised but couldn't seem to allow anyone else to manage.

"Can we talk now about what needs to change here?" his youngest brother Harry pressed.

"Talk fast while I clean up."

"I want to block off that wall and leave a place for the customers to clean up."

"Have you lost your mind? There's barely room to spit in here and you want to close it off more?"

"It's for the nobs. They don't like washing out in the open. That's why they don't come 'ere."

"They don't come here because it's a place for rough fighting. What idiocy are you thinking?" He glanced over to where his niece was leading her daydreaming brother out of the room. With her gone, he stripped down to his falls and washed the stink off himself.

Meanwhile his brother shook his head. "They'd come. I could bring them in."

"No, you can't. I'm the one who knows every toff. You're the one who knows every bruiser."

"But—"

"Damn it, Harry, I don't have time for this nonsense. Ye've got to sack Willie and Roy. They're just big talkers who are too old—"

"They keep the customers happy. Half come in just to hear the tales." He handed his brother a towel. "And if I served better drinks, then the nobs would come too."

"This isn't the place for drinks. Send them up the street."

"Then it's not me who gets the money, now is it?"

Reuben pulled on his shirt, using the time to think. This boxing parlor had been his brother's dream, and so Reuben had helped him with the money to start it. Then he'd had to teach the man how to defend it from thieves and gangs of crooks. Harry had learned quickly enough, thank God, but now he wanted to expand in ways that made no sense.

"Doesn't this place make enough for you? Can't you be happy—"

"With things how they are? No more than you could."

Reuben pursed his lips. Harry was right on that account, he supposed. But the truth was, he didn't have time to supervise any kind of expansion and he didn't want his brother to lose it all on something as foolish as trying to tempt the nobs.

"It's not going to work," he said. "The nobs won't come here. You're too far away from them."

"It'll work."

"No—"

"It's not for the nobs," his brother ground out. "It's for the women."

Reuben paused in the middle of tying his cravat. "What women?"

"I got the idea from Lindy."

"Your daughter?"

"Aye. She wants to learn how to fight."

Reuben nodded slowly. "I can see that you've taught her a fair bit."

"I have. And I've taught some other girls, too. Older ones. Ones that need to know where to hurt a man."

"They're the ones who want a closed off area to wash."

"Yes." His brother faced him square on. "And they're the ones who like fighting Willie and Roy. They're old enough that they don't care if a girl hits 'em. And they know why the girls need to learn."

"You got that all from Lindy?"

"And her mother. Anna's been talking it up. More girls'd come if we had a place for them to clean up and maybe a nice drink or two—"

"Would they pay?"

"Yes."

He sounded certain, but Reuben wasn't convinced. It all depended upon the neighborhood. If the women supported something like this, it could work. But all it took was some righteous soul screaming about what girls ought and ought not do. Then suddenly something simple like teaching a girl how to punch became the focus of every argument, yea or nay. It was too risky without him right here keeping an eye on things.

"It isn't going to work, Harry."

"You don't know that. I do. Damn it, Reuben—"

His brother went on and on. He argued for his choices, explained his reasons, spoke of people who would help and the women who needed to learn. Reuben didn't disagree. He just didn't have the time to supervise it now. There was too much to do, so he finished dressing, brushed out his hair, and then interrupted his brother.

"Get me a hackney. I'm late and I can't miss this chance."

"To hobnob with the dandies?" His brother's voice was filled with scorn. "You've forgotten where you've come from."

Reuben shook his head. "I've got my eye on where I'm going, you idiot. And if it works—"

"Then you'll be gone, and I can do what I want here."

"Maybe." He made his voice thick and heavy. A threat if ever there was one, and his brother knew it. "And maybe I come take this all back from you."

His brother winced. "You wouldn't."

He wouldn't. But he couldn't allow his family to think he'd gone soft. "You do something stupid, and you know I will." After all, he'd done that a dozen times in as many years. He was the rescuer of his family, the one who knew what would work and what would fail. And the one who taught them the value of sticking together to help each other out.

But the circle was growing, and he was damned tired of being the one in charge. It was too much work for one soul, and yet his brother was right about the other thing. Even when there was too much to do, he couldn't help but push for more.

Which was why he needed to get to the Countess Byrn's now.

"Get me a clean hackney. I can't arrive smelling of horse or worse."

Harry headed for the door, his every step thunking down in anger. "We're not done talking about this."

"We are for today."

Then he did his best with his hair and his cravat. He'd spent hours trying to master the more complicated styles that were fashionable these days. He couldn't do it without the help of an elite gentleman's valet, and the man he used wasn't skilled in that way. Besides, he'd have to go home to get done up, and he hadn't the time nor the patience for it.

So he went for casual. It worked with his boyish charm. And he headed out as soon as he was done. His brother did not say anything more, but the rebellion was clear upon his face. Reuben would need to give the man his head soon.

But he couldn't manage it. Every time he'd tried before, whenever he looked away, someone messed up and he had to pick up the pieces. But he also couldn't forget it, and so he was sour and pre-occupied when he finally arrived at the dowager countess's home.

He had his apology ready, complete with flowers for all the women. The butler made him use the knocker, though the man had no doubt been watching for him. It was a subtle measure of how unwanted he was that he stood cooling his heels for more than a minute. But at least the door opened to him, and he was able to step inside with every appearance of jaunty enthusiasm.

What he didn't expect was that instead of being greeted by the butler, the door swung open to reveal the countess on the middle of the stairs, her gaze cold as she spoke two words to him.

"You're late."

Had she set herself there just to appear to advantage above him? Was that truly why he'd been made to wait outside? Just to startle him with her pronouncement?

He believed so. And indeed, it set him in a jolly good frame of mind. Who wouldn't appreciate such theatrical staging? Especially when it was for his sole benefit.

He recovered quickly, well used to the game one had to play with aristocrats. He bowed deeply before her.

"My most sincere apologies," he said. "I'm afraid my nephew required my help with a quick lesson. It set me behind schedule, especially since I was very particular with the bouquets I selected." He should have sent his niece to buy them for him, but he could never trust that someone would select just the right blooms.

He extended the largest bouquet to her. She didn't take it, of course, but she didn't throw them away either. Instead, she nodded to the butler who relieved him of one group of posies, but not the other two. Those he intended to present directly.

Meanwhile, the lady continued down the steps. "Come into the parlor, Mr. Bates," she commanded.

He set his hat and gloves on the table himself given that the butler was preoccupied with the flowers. Or at least the man pretended to be preoccupied. Such was the casual type of insult that the common man suffered at the hands of the aristocracy. Then he hurried after the countess and into the parlor.

She had seated herself in a throne-like chair opposite the door, and the pompousness of that display had his smile broadening. Life was so often like a theater production. If one wanted to play, one had to enter into the ridiculousness of it with a full heart.

He bowed to her again, spreading his arms wide—a posey in each hand—as he entered the room. "I am honored to be so received," he said. Then he looked both left and right. The younger ladies were on opposite sides of the room, and he took the time to offer his gifts first to one, then the other.

"Miss Allen," he said to the one who seemed to share his awareness of the ridiculous. True to her bold nature, her expression was not schooled into bland acceptance, but she openly watched the proceedings with a doubtful air. As if she could not believe the English acted in such a manner. "You are lovely as always." And she was, her bright yellow dress a compliment to her golden-brown hair.

"A pleasure to see you again," she said as she accepted the small bouquet of yellow flowers.

Then he turned to Miss Spalding and felt his breath robbed from his chest. She sat in shadow in the corner next to a writing table, though her bright red hair betrayed her. Her head was down, her hands clasped demurely in front of her. It was the appropriate pose for an unmarried young lady, and yet there was an energy about her, especially when she raised her head.

She had clear purpose in her mind and in her life. It wasn't in any one part of her body. Her eyes were clear, but not unusually piercing. Her hair was in shadow, so the red didn't burn like fire in the sunlight. Indeed, there was nothing in her attitude but sweet acceptance of the bouquet he extended to her.

And yet like recognized like. She had a plan, and he was suddenly very curious as to what she wanted.

He might have stayed that way for hours, studying her features as he searched for what had changed in her from a few days ago to today. Something had brought her to life.

"Mr. Bates," the countess intoned.

"My lady?" He spun immediately to address her.

"My son has a fondness for you and so as a favor to him, I shall be blunt."

"Most wise," he agreed, as if the countess was ever anything but blunt. "I am grateful."

"You should be because I am about to save you a great deal of time."

"Always a benefit."

She waited a moment and he wondered if she wanted him to be more obsequious. Thankfully, she did not. She huffed out a breath and shook her head.

"My son says you are smart, wealthy, and looking to elevate yourself in status. Such is the way of things."

All correct. He dipped his chin in acknowledgement.

"It won't work."

Was that all she had to say? And here he'd thought she had something novel to impart.

"You're too cheeky. The money and the secrets you supposedly know are enough to worm your way in. So many others have managed such a thing, but this constant cheerfulness is an afront that will not serve you."

"My cheerfulness, my lady?"

"You act as if you know things, that you think things, that you can do things that we cannot."

He grinned. "It's true."

"That may be, but one does not allow such a thing in our ranks unless—"

"Unless one is born to it?"

She nodded. "Exactly." She leaned forward. "You do not have the manner to ingratiate yourself. It is too rough, too immodest, too…"

"Cheeky?"

"Exactly. We ladies do not like it." She rocked back in her chair. "That is my message to you. Do not waste your time in the *ton*. We will not allow it."

"But you will allow me to walk in Hyde Park with your charges?"

She pursed her lips. "Only because they promised Lady Rebecca. I shall not condone it again. Nor will they accept any such invitations from you." She arched a brow at Miss Allen. "If they do, then I will consider them no longer my charges."

Well, that was pretty heavy punishment for merely walking

with him. But at least he'd have this one afternoon. He had best make the most of it.

He bowed deeply to the arrogant woman. She probably did think she was helping him or telling him something he didn't already know. It was more than some women would do. She didn't realize that he had been bumping up against aristocratic arrogance all his life. And that he already knew how to break into their ranks. After all, she was right. He had the money and the secrets to force his way into the lower echelons at least.

But he hadn't yet forced himself to hide his God-given charm. And that, he realized with a sigh, was something that would have to happen soon because the lady was right. The *ton* did not appreciate a cheeky cit. So he would hide his irreverence—or at least moderate it—because the aristocracy was the only competition left to him. He'd won everything else.

He straightened to his full height. He schooled his expression to sober. And he spoke in a cultured tone that so far had been markedly absent in his speech. It wasn't easy. He had far better things to practice than his diction, but this was something she would respect.

"My lady, pray let me honor you with an equally blunt response."

Her raised eyebrows showed that she understood his change in demeanor.

"I am joining your ranks," he said coolly. "I have set my mind to it, and it shall be done. I might not marry Lady Rebecca, although she is primed for it. Her family needs my money, and she is a sweet, impressionable girl. There are other ladies whose families are in an equally desperate situation, and they would be wise to allow me to manage their family fortunes." He smiled and let his teeth show in all their wolfish glory. "But rest assured, your Scottish charges are not on my list." He glanced over at Miss Spalding. "Except in that I enjoy their company."

Far from being shocked, the lady frowned at him. Then a moment later, she summed up her thoughts with an abrupt grunt-like word.

"Huh."

"And that we are late to meet up with Lady Rebecca."

CHAPTER NINE

FORTUNATELY, THEY WERE within walking distance of Hyde Park and so had no need of a carriage. Mr. Bates had come by hackney, and Iseabail doubted the countess would grace him with hers. So she and Sadie set off at a brisk walk toward Hyde Park while Mr. Bates kept pace with ease.

Sadie was naturally irrepressible, so she spoke first, laughing at the thing that was on all their minds. "I hope you've no more need of the countess's support," she said. "You've set her back on her heels now and will have to work to get in her good graces."

"Will I?" he challenged, his tone light and his expression filled with mischief.

"Well, of course you will," Sadie countered. "You just said you had no interest in either one of her charges. That's a supreme insult."

He waggled his brows in challenge. "Perhaps you will change my mind."

Sadie laughed loudly at that. Perhaps too loudly as others took notice, but she didn't seem to care. She lifted her head to the sun and sighed happily. "I will not work to change anyone's mind. I find it to be a complete waste of time."

Which is to say that Sadie gave few opinions about anything, leaving her to appear empty-headed and focused exclusively on her own amusement. And that was the greatest lie of all. Meanwhile, Mr. Bates turned to her.

"And what of you, Miss Spalding? Are you insulted that I have not set my matrimonial cap at you?"

"No, sir," she answered honestly. "I worry as to your mental ability."

He laughed heartily at that. Clearly, he had no self-doubt whatsoever. "I am deficient because I do not want you?"

"No, sir. You are a fool to believe that all your machinations will net you a place among the peerage." She slowed her steps long enough to look him in the eye. "That is what you are doing, is it not? Forcing your way into the ball, pressing for a walk in Hyde Park. You want to marry one of them and in so doing increase your status. Or at least that of your children."

"And you think I cannot do it."

"I think it is a waste of time and effort." She glanced back at the countess's home. "They will never accept you or your children. And I think you know that. Which leads me to question your sanity. Why work so hard at something that will never come to pass and that you don't seem to want anyway."

He twisted at that, his brows coming together. "Why wouldn't I want a better standing for myself and my children?"

"If you wanted to be one of them, you would dress like them, act like them, become as polished in manners as royalty."

"Do you find my manners rough?"

"I find you cheeky, and that is not something they like." She lied when she said that. She found him to be bold and original. Rough in some ways and exciting in others. All of that was so much more intriguing than "cheeky."

"The peerage likes cheeky, if it is bold enough."

To prove his point, he tipped his hat to a very stern-looking matron who was approaching from the opposite direction. She was doing her best to appear outraged by his very presence, and while she was busy gasping her shock, he winked at her and spoke in an undertone that did not carry beyond their small circle.

"Your bosom is magnificent, my lady. Your lord is very lucky indeed."

The lady sputtered in consternation, but as they turned the corner, Iseabail could see her lips curve and a girlish blush appear in the woman's cheeks. She was flattered, and Iseabail was impressed.

"Do you know who that was?" she whispered. "That was Lady Graham. She's an intimate of Lady Castlereagh who is a patroness of Almack's."

"Is that so?" he drawled. "And here I thought her just a beautifully endowed woman."

She cast him a sidelong glance. He knew who Lady Graham was. He knew all the players in the *ton*, probably much better than her. "With all your talents, this is what you spend your efforts upon? Teasing prickly ladies in the hopes that their sons will someday accept your sons?"

He prickled slightly as they entered the park. "I shall elevate my entire bloodline. Can you think of a more worthwhile endeavor?"

"Scores of them. Teach your people how to read, discover a new medicine or new technique for making something, spend your money on obtaining healthy foods. Something that will have more immediate impact than pleasing people who will refuse you no matter how big their bosoms."

"Spoken like a lady who is already accepted as one of them."

She snorted. "I am a Scot with a missing dowry. I am no more accepted than you."

"If that is what you believe, then I ask you where are your wits? Why are you here searching for a husband among them if they fill you with such disdain?"

She swallowed and forced herself to speak plainly. "Because, Mr. Bates, as a woman, my options are disgustingly limited." She lifted her chin. "I should like to speak with you about that, if I may. It is my hope that you will assist me in an unusual endeavor."

His brows rose. "I am intrigued."

"Good—" she began.

"But I am currently otherwise occupied." And then he grinned as he tipped his hat to someone just beyond her left shoulder.

Iseabail turned to see Lady Rebecca approaching at a rapid pace. She was grinning as she headed their way, and it was clear that the girl would be skipping if her maid hadn't said something sharp to her. Iseabail shook her head and wondered if she had ever appeared so joyously carefree.

"Hullo, hullo!" Lady Rebecca said as she caught them. "I feared I'd miss you."

"Nonsense," Mr. Bates replied as he extended his arm. "I would wait hours upon hours to greet you."

The girl giggled and blushed prettily, but then her expression sobered. "You must not say things like that, you know. Mama was very cross that I accepted your invitation to walk. She said I must not do it again."

"Because I am scandalous?"

"Because Papa owes you a great deal of money, and she does not want to suggest that I could marry you to end his debt." Her gaze dropped to the ground. "She wants me to marry for love, you see, because she married for money and look where it got her."

Mr. Bates nodded and patted her hand. "I understand. But you see the problem is not that she married for money, it was that she married someone who is very bad at managing money. Whereas I, on the other hand…" His voice trailed off suggestively.

"You're very good at it?"

"Extraordinarily excellent with it." He smiled down at her. "I bought up all your father's debt just so that we could get to know one another."

The girl nodded, her expression sober, and Iseabail saw his entire plan laid out in excruciating clarity. He had needed an entrée into the ball so as to meet Lady Rebecca, and Iseabail had provided that. And now he had a debutante on his arm, one who was young enough to be impressed by his charm. The two would marry, Mr. Bates would never be fully accepted into society, but his children would be because her parentage was excellent.

And he would have no need whatsoever to help Iseabail.

"You know," Iseabail said as she caught up with Lady Rebecca. "You are not responsible for your father's debts. You cannot be a slave to your father's misdeeds."

"Hear, hear," agreed Sadie as she came alongside Lady Rebecca.

Naturally, Mr. Bates disagreed. "Have you no family feeling, then? Do you owe nothing to your clan?"

"Allegiance is something that men invented for each other. Men protect one another, they fight together, and do great or evil things together. Each man is therefore responsible for what the others do as he has a voice in what the clan does." She waved her hand at Sadie and Lady Rebecca. "What voice do we have in what our families choose? Lady Rebecca, can you stop your father from gambling?"

The girl shook her head. "I have tried."

"And he paid you no mind. Neither do I have any say as to how my clan gains or spends their money. And even Sadie who has the most generous cousin as the leader of her clan, what have you to say about how the Aberbeag act in the world? Were you ever consulted?"

Sadie's laugh carried gayly through the air. "You know I was not, but such is the way of the world."

She could say that because Connall was generous with her and the women of his clan. But he was the exception, not the rule. "If I have no say in what my clan does, then why should I be bound by their choices?"

Mr. Bates shook his head. "That is radical thinking that will get you nowhere."

"Is it? You are doing the exact same thing, are you not? You're making up to Lady Rebecca to gain entry to the peerage for your children, if not yourself. You want a voice in the country and the world." She shrugged. "So do I."

"And you refuse to obey the law until someone listens to you?"

She threw her arms wide. "I am not breaking any laws. I simply will not sacrifice my life or my happiness to benefit family who care less for me and my future than a night of revelry."

She was referring to Lady Rebecca's father, but Mr. Bates understood it differently. "There is no love lost between you and your uncle then. What of the rest of your clan?"

She shook her head. "I grieve for the women I left behind, not the men." It was the truth. She had once tried to bring the women together to fight her uncle. But her uncle was not the only brutal man in the Spalding clan. Though several were decent men, there were not enough to fight her uncle's hold. Which meant the women in the clan ended up silent and beaten. Even her mother's disappearance had not roused them. Iseabail was the only soul to search, the only one to demand an answer.

She got a month locked in her room for her trouble.

Meanwhile, Mr. Bates looked at her sadly. "Your clan has not done well by you." He glanced down at Lady Rebecca. "Which is why it is important to choose a man who is willing to fight for you, to give your sons everything they need to succeed, and—"

"Who cares what happens to the daughters?" Iseabail asked.

His head shot up. "I did not say that."

"You didn't need to."

Iseabail lost the war against dismay. She had thought that of all the men she knew, he was the one who could help her. He was the one who might see her worth, but he was not that man. Though he had strength and his own kind of honor, women were a tool to be used for his ambition. He was the same as her uncle in that regard, and she was once again without recourse in an increasingly bleak world.

Sadie, ever observant, dropped back to walk with her. She took Iseabail's arm and patted her hand. "Don't give up yet. There is a man somewhere who will face down your uncle."

"I no longer care about facing him down. I just want to live free of him."

"For that, you need a husband."

"Do I? Do I really?" she asked, a new idea forming as soon as she said it. She had skills. She was a midwife, if nothing else. There were ways to survive without a husband.

"If you aren't married, he can always grab you and force you back home. You have no legal rights as a spinster."

She knew that. But honestly, how would her uncle know she was in London? She'd been here for nearly a month now with no one the wiser. And even if he knew, London was a big city. How would he find her here?

She was mulling over those very thoughts. Could she truly find a life of her own, on her own? Then it all fell to pieces around her.

"There she is!"

She heard the voice, but didn't exactly understand the words. The Scottish accent was thick, and though she'd understood it all her life, her ear had become used to the English tones. But she knew the growl and the menace it carried. And she knew the man whose voice sounded like boulders clashing with broken swords.

Hamish had been cut in the throat once and still managed to survive, albeit with a harsh voice. He was her uncle's right-hand man and the villain who'd been promised her hand in marriage. And he was the sole reason she'd gotten the courage to run as fast and as far as she could.

Yet he was here. She saw him now, right here in Hyde Park, pointing his fecking dagger at her heart.

CHAPTER TEN

FOR ALL THAT he was bent on charming Lady Rebecca, Reuben studied Miss Spalding's face. She was frustrated, and well she should be. It was clear that her life was filled with people who wished to control her for their own ends. That was unfortunate, but Reuben hadn't become one of the wealthiest men in London by turning his attention to every hard-luck story he came across. There were too many of them, and he had other things to do.

Such as charm the beautiful Lady Rebecca into becoming his bride. He'd had other ladies in his sights, but as often happened in his life, one particular option landed easily in his lap. And here she was, whispering to him that she had escaped her home to meet him in the park today completely against her mother's dictates.

He'd already guessed as much, but it was nice to hear the confirmation as well as the tone of defiance in the girl's tone. That was excellent progress. He would play on her sense of duty next since marrying him would erase her father's debts and save her idiot parent from disaster…at least for the moment.

Her tender feelings toward her family would coerce her into marriage. In return, he would curb her father's disastrous habits, set her up in a life of luxury, and then see what new opportunities would arise from having children well settled in the ruling class.

It was the way the world worked, if one was good at the game, and he did not appreciate Miss Spalding's righteous anger at how women were pawns in men's powerful games. He had a tender heart at times, strictly curbed for just this reason. Feeling for the weak interfered in the just application of power.

And so he should have been grateful to see that Miss Spalding was now in trouble. He hadn't seen the men coming, thanks to his irritating conversation with the Scotswoman. His focus was on reeling the naïve Lady Rebecca into his arms. So when he heard her gasp in shock, his head snapped up and he instantly became aware of many uncomfortable things.

The first was that Miss Spalding's clansmen were rough, violent men who were advancing on their party with great speed. That was unfortunate. He'd hoped to avoid them by setting their walk to an early hour. He'd thought that the Scotsmen would be too lazy to watch the area during the less important times.

Obviously, the men had discipline and were now headed toward their quarry. That was enough for him to grab Lady Rebecca and quickly move her out of the way. He set her next to a tree and stood in front of her as her protector.

Second, he saw Sammy Watts settled against an opposite tree smoking a pipe as if he hadn't a care in the world. And he didn't, so long as Reuben stuck to his promise and didn't interfere in whatever the Scots intended for Miss Spalding. But that was a hard thing to do when he saw both Scotswomen settle into fighting stances. Neither had run. They must have seen it would be useless in their gowns and fashionable hats. The men would be on them in seconds.

So the women had decided to fight, and didn't he look like a coward abandoning them to their fate?

He twitched with the need to interfere, but he had promised to do no such thing. And he never went back on his promises. Indeed, most of his fortune was predicated on general faith that his word was his bond.

"Miss Spalding!" he called out and then he tossed her dirk to land at her feet. He'd brought with him thinking to return it to her. It was a sop to his guilt at not warning her what was coming.

And now she scooped it up with the speed of long familiarity.

Meanwhile, Miss Allen spoke up with the haughtiness of one who had never truly faced rough men. "What are ye doing?" she called out. "Frightening good people in the middle o' the day?"

The center man, one with dark teeth and a grizzled jaw, held up his hands as if to show he meant no ill. But his right hand still carried a wickedly sharp knife and his smile looked gruesome with those rotted teeth.

"No harm," he said in a thick Scottish brogue. Fortunately, Reuben had a knack for languages and figured out the meaning easily enough. "I came to bring my wife home. She's sorely missed."

"You've no wife here, Hamish," said Miss Spalding in a clear British accent. "Go back home."

The woman didn't waste time or energy on bravado. She spoke clearly even as she was backing away from the three Scotsmen. She brought Miss Allen with her, tugging lightly on the lady's sleeve. And the two slowly moved to a more defensible position.

At least that was likely her plan, but there was no place more defensible here. It was all open ground and few trees. Not to mention the frightened face of nannies who were grabbing their charges to get away from the fight.

"That's where yer wrong," Hamish returned. "Yer me blushing bride, Iseabail. We were married three weeks ago, we were."

"Three weeks?" the lady snapped. "I've been in London for more than four."

"Ach, but yer token was with yer guardian, and he used it as yer proxy." He fished a grimy piece of parchment out of his placket. "It's signed, Iseabail. Yer mine."

"What token?" she countered. "I am wearing it." For emphasis, she pulled her pendant from beneath her dress.

"Cease yer blathering, woman. Come now or I'll take ye back shackled to me horse."

It was a cruel statement, and one that Reuben knew would

come to pass. This Hamish was one to enjoy mindless cruelty.

"Run, you fool," he rasped out. He didn't know what would come of that. Where was she to go to? But at least in the countess's home, she would have some recourse. A barrister, if nothing else, to investigate the claims and tie the matter up in the courts.

It would give Miss Spalding breathing room to think of something else. But she didn't get the chance. She turned her head to look behind her, and two more Scotsmen stepped out behind them. Five bearded, kilted Scotsmen. And halleluiah, he now had an excuse to interfere. After all, he'd been told three of her kinsmen came for her. Five was clearly more than three, and if Sammy had lied to him, then he felt no responsibility to keep his word.

So he sauntered out to join the ladies even as the five Scotsmen began to close in on the women. He whistled as he moved, pretended to an insouciance that he didn't feel. And it was enough to throw the Scotsmen off their game.

"What ho," he drawled in as posh a tone as he could manage. "Have you no escort, ladies? That's not safe, you know. Plenty of shady sorts in London, hmmm? I should be pleased to walk with you while we find your conveyance."

To the side, he saw Sammy straighten up with a frown, but his attention was centered more on the confused Scots. Clearly, they had no idea what to do when an Englishman acted completely ignorant of the threat they posed.

Hamish growled out a warning, his disgust plain. "Are ye blind, ye bluidy Sassenach? Get gone."

"Blood? Where?" He looked down at himself as if in horror using the pretense of inspecting his clothing to unhook the holsters that sheathed two of his blades. The last thing he wanted was to start throwing knives in the middle of Hyde Park, but he wanted to be prepared just in case. Especially since the Scotsmen didn't seem to be taking the hint. Nevertheless, he tried to reason with them one more time. "I don't know what your business here is, Mr. Scot, but civilized people do not go accosting women in the middle of the most fashionable park in London. The watch is headed this way, and no one here has any interest in your marriage one way or another."

He moved between the ladies and the grumbly Hamish. A protective stance though he looked like a dandy standing like a lost idiot on a battlefield. He was sure the other men were approaching from behind, but he trusted the women to let him know if they came too close.

"I'll beat ye senseless, ye bluidy idiot." Not a clever retort, but then Reuben hadn't expected one. What was more important was that Hamish jerked his head to his two men, indicating that they should attack.

One was big and slow, therefore the easiest of the two targets. Best to dispatch him quickly.

Reuben closed the distance, clipped the thug's outstretched arm while kicking him hard in the knee. The big man went down with a howl and Reuban managed to wrest a very large dirk from his hand. A nice one to add to his collection.

He didn't have the time to admire it, though, as the other one closed in. He was younger than the others, small, wiry, and he held his knife well. His attention, however, was split between Reuben and trying to grab hold of Miss Spalding. Damn it, the man was close enough to get her. One lurch and he would have her, especially since she was distracted as the other two Scotsmen came at her.

Thinking fast, Reuben did a silly feint. It was a useless move except to pull the man's attention away from Miss Spalding. Enough, at least, for her to duck away. Or so he hoped.

It worked.

It also infuriated the young Scotsman enough that he came hard at Reuben, slashing down with his knife in a very odd movement. It was not meant for street fighting as it left the idiot overbalanced and exposed. More likely it was what he used when closing on a wild boar. It would be very effective when hunting.

Useless against a man like Reuben.

A quick punch to the man's throat, and the young one went down like a stone, gasping for breath. Reuben's kick connected with the boy's exposed wrist, and the knife went flying off at Sammy.

Oops. He did not want the Bow Street Runner involved. But Sammy could not resist the lure of a well-made dirk. He put away his pipe and picked up the blade as he sauntered forward.

Hell. Reuben did not want to fight his friend.

Meanwhile, he glanced back at Miss Spalding. She was the target of this attack, and he'd left her and Miss Allen alone to fend off two burly Scotsmen charging from the rear.

He needn't have worried. As he watched, he saw Miss Spalding sink her dirk into the meat of one man's thigh. The other would have caught her then, except Miss Allen got him with a well-placed kick between the thighs. The bastard went down with a howl, then she followed it up with a swift punch to his temple.

He would not move again for a bit.

Reuben grinned. He appreciated a woman who could fight dirty, though he was more impressed by a woman who could kill a man with her knife and step away with nary a drop of blood on her. Miss Spalding hadn't killed her attacker, but he wouldn't survive without someone to stitch up the wound. And rather than waste her time on his pain, she straightened up to face the man who was leading this merry bunch of incompetents.

Hamish wasn't waiting. His face contorted in fury, and he'd pulled out his sword. A damned big Scots sword in the middle of Hyde Park. An intimidating sight to be sure, if one didn't know anything about fighting.

With one hand, Reuben shoved Miss Spalding backwards. She wasn't expecting it, so she stumbled. Meanwhile, he used the motion to quickly duck down and come up on Hamish's opposite side. The man was too slow to recover. Frankly, the sword was too heavy to shift so easily, but the bastard had muscles to wield the thing, so Reuben made use of his quick reflexes. He knew better than to ever stand still in a fight like this.

He moved to the side, then punched Hamish in the ribs, close to his armpit. He continued his attack with rabbit punches, all meant to disarm, not to destroy. He didn't put much power into his attack. That wasn't its purpose. He meant to confuse and distract until—

Now.

Hamish turned to face him. He'd barely gotten his sword back up, but the thing was lifting quickly. If Reuben missed, the sword might very well cleave him in two.

So he didn't miss. Reuben punched him on the temple with a heavy fist backed by the full weight of his torso.

The ugly man went down.

He spared a moment for remorse. A blow like that could permanently damage a man's brain. He didn't regret the action. He did, however, know that a man who was generally prone to violence could get worse after a hit like that. More brutal, more irrational, and more of a danger to any woman who was married to him.

Killing him might become necessary. But not yet.

He turned to speak to Miss Spalding. There was a great deal he wanted to understand from her, but he never got the chance.

Sammy had her. He'd twisted her one arm hard up behind her back. Her dirk lay at her feet, and she flinched every time she moved. Not because she was hurt, but because Sammy was jerking her arm high every time she tried to move or speak or even stand.

Before long, he had her on her knees between them.

Reuben's stomach turned sour. "What are you up to, brutalizing a woman like that?"

"Did you see what she did to them Scots?" He jerked his head to the one howling as he bled on the ground. "She's a wildcat, and I'll not have her in my London."

"That's a bold lie, that is," he countered. "You like a wildcat. You married one."

"I married English, I did. And my lady wouldn't do that to a man."

Reuben snorted, his mind racing as he tried to find a way out of this mess. "Maybe. Maybe not. It depends on if someone was trying to marry her to that man." He gestured to the bastard who was still unconscious behind them.

Sammy didn't argue. "You said you wouldn't interfere."

"You said there were only three."

He snorted. "What do I know how many Scots—"

Reuben lost his patience. "What do you know if he's a fecking liar? What are you doing turning over a woman to the likes of them?"

Sammy stiffened. "Their papers were good. I read 'em."

"Their money was good. You don't know what Scots' papers are like. Reading isn't enough to tell." He stomped over and grabbed the parchment out of the bastard's placard. It looked official enough, but what did he know? He wasn't a barrister.

Meanwhile, Miss Allen was squatting next to the man still howling as he held his leg.

"Shut up!" she snapped as she batted his hands away.

He made a fist in reaction, his face screwed up in fury as he swung out. Reuben tried to stop it, but he was too far away. Didn't matter. Miss Allen had been prepared.

"Very well," she said as she straightened up. "I won't help."

He didn't blame her. The one he did blame was Sammy, who was glaring at the disaster all around him.

"Let her go, Sammy. This isn't your affair."

"They paid me to keep the watch off 'em."

"Then I suggest you get them out of here before the watch shows up."

"But they want her."

Reuben broke. It wasn't a conscious decision. Normally, he felt the fury coming on. Normally, he allowed himself to *appear* as if he'd snapped. It added to his reputation throughout London. This time he really did. He went from calm to red-visioned fury in the blink of an eye.

He punched Sammy hard enough that the man's head snapped back. His grip on Miss Spalding loosened and she was quick to crawl out of the way, but Reuben barely noticed. He was too busy punching his friend bloody.

How dare he send a bastard after Iseabail?

How dare he consider giving her over to these arses?

How dare he put his hands on her?

How dare he? How dare he? How dare he!

If Sammy fought back, Reuben didn't notice it. He also didn't hear anything but the roar of blood in his ears. But he did feel small hands on his arm pulling him back.

He rounded on the annoyance only to see Iseabail holding up her hands to stop him. She was saying something he couldn't hear. And while his breath heaved in and out, eventually her words became clear.

"This doesn't help!"

It bloody well did! His blood was pounding, his fists aching, but the need to pummel the bastards who threatened her beat through his brain and body. He wanted to fight! He wanted to—

"Please," Iseabail was saying. "We need to leave. The watch is coming, and I don't know what they'll do to me."

"Not a bloody thing," he returned. Except he knew that wasn't true. She was Scottish. She'd stabbed a man who was whimpering on the ground. There was a crowd of onlookers and gawkers. The watch would want to blame someone for this mess, and it would likely be her.

"We need to get you back to the countess's home."

"Yes." She looked to the side. "Lady Rebecca, can you make it home by yourself?"

Who?

A young girl stepped out from behind a tree. Oh yes, that girl. Her eyes were wide, her cheeks rosy, and her expression shifted between shock and admiration. "Yes," she said. "Yes, my maid and I should go."

"Yes, you should," said Iseabail. "Right away."

The girl bobbed her head but didn't seem like she would move. It was the maid who had more sense. She grabbed the girl's arm and hauled her back. A moment later, they were all but running in their haste to leave.

"It's our turn now," said Iseabail. "Come on." But she didn't leave. Instead, she squatted down and grabbed the papers from where Reuben had dropped them. Then she looked at Miss Allen, who was still looking down at the blood that soaked the dirt from the howling man's wound. "Leave him, Sadie."

"It needs to be cleaned and stitched."

"So did his wife after he beat her, but he left her to die instead."

Sadie's brows rose. "He's like that, is he?"

"They are all are," Iseabail returned grimly.

Reuben would have agreed with her. He would have stomped away in righteous fury along with her. Except her look included him. And why wouldn't it when he stood there with his friend's blood all over his fist?

Good God, what had he done?

CHAPTER ELEVEN

*T*HEY'D FOUND HER.

That knowledge shuddered through Iseabail's body. It made her hands shake and her mind numb. She'd known it might happen. Indeed, a part of her had always known that her uncle wouldn't give her up so easily. But the more time she'd spent at parties in London, the less she'd felt the threat of him.

Until today.

All the terror and the fear she'd buried down had come roaring back. She'd stood there in her pretty gown in the middle of Hyde Park while five of her own clansmen tried to grab her.

They'd found her.

"Climb into the cab."

Iseabail blinked. She'd been walking quickly somewhere. Away. She'd been walking away. The only reason she hadn't been running was because her legs were unsteady, her hands shaking, and her chest tight with fear.

They'd found her.

"We're going for a ride. There's no reason to walk right now."

She blinked as she looked at the carriage. Sadie was in front of her, already inside the conveyance with her hand outstretched. She looked furious with her mouth set tight and her brows drawn down.

Iseabail knew better than that. She hid her emotions; she kept her expression placid. Her mother had taught her that. Hide, hide, hide. Until you're ready to strike.

"Climb inside," a man said. "You can think of what to do there."

The voice of reason, so rarely coming from a man. She turned to look at him, knowing what she would see. Mr. Bates. Rugged jaw, now clenched. Bright eyes, now narrowed and steady. He held out his hand to her to help her climb into the carriage. Normally she'd shy away from any man right now, but he had helped her. He had fought for her.

She gripped his hand as if it were the only safe point in the world. And she used him to climb inside the carriage.

She wasn't thinking as she sat down. Any other time when she had witnessed something horrible, she would go to a corner of her bedroom and sit alone. She had things that comforted her there. A plant in a pot—a different one every year. A book of whimsical pictures her mother had gifted her. And hard stone on two sides. She would press her back to it, look at the plant and the pictures, and wait until she felt better.

She sat across from Sadie and pressed her back into the corner. She watched as Mr. Bates climbed into the hackney and closed the door. He sat next to her, his body too large for the small space. But rather than shrink from him, she pressed her knee against him and felt the hard strength of him.

He was like a stone wall beside her, and she appreciated his presence.

Meanwhile, Sadie pulled off her gloves where were caked with dried blood. "I would have helped him," she said. "I tried, but he—"

"He swung at you," Mr. Bates said.

"He's not the first frightened man who strikes out with his fists." She took a shuddering breath. "He may die. Even if it gets bandaged right, an infection will—"

"His wife died on the floor of their cottage, both her legs shattered from his fists. He left her there and went to bed." Their daughter had snuck out to find Iseabail. By the time they'd returned to the cottage, it was too late. The woman was dead and all Iseabail could do was find the girl work in the castle and teach her how to sleep with a dirk.

"Was he drunk?" Mr. Bates asked.

"Does it matter?"

He had no answer to that, and she had no desire to explain. And yet, sitting there pressed into the corner of the carriage, she found words tumbling out.

"Ours is a wealthy clan. The market brings in a great deal of money and most of it goes into whisky. Every night. I stop the women as much as I can, but everyone has some."

Sadie leaned forward. "There's nothing wrong with drink. It's the excess that makes it ugly."

Iseabail looked up. How did she make her understand that the Spalding clan was not like the Aberbeag? Sadie's home was led by Connall, and a better laird she'd never met. But her uncle was different.

"I teach the girls that when they drink, they're not fast enough to escape." She swallowed. "Some aren't fast enough anyway."

Mr. Bates shook his head. "I'll never understand the Scots."

She didn't have the strength to argue the many things wrong with that attitude, but Sadie rounded on him with a vengeance. "Don't tell me the Sassenachs never beat their wives. Do you say you've never seen a man mean with drink? This is not a Scottish vice." She sat back with a huff. "Or not *only* a Scottish one."

He didn't argue. Instead, his eyes were troubled as he looked at her. Enough that Iseabail looked away rather than face the questions in his gaze. But to look away brought her back to her fears.

They'd found her.

She gripped her fingers so tight they throbbed.

Sadie twisted in her seat. "Will the watch come for us?"

"Yes," Mr. Bates answered.

"They attacked us first. Everyone saw that."

"Yes."

"But it won't make a difference, will it?" Sadie continued. "Not if he's her husband."

Iseabail jerked. "He's not!"

"Well, of course he's not. But he has a paper saying you are. How do we prove that you're not?"

"I don't know," she whispered. "I don't know." For all she knew, her uncle could have married her by proxy. She'd only heard of that happening in the old tales when women were forced to marry men out fighting battles. The priest married them to an axe or a scabbard. But she'd never heard of it done the opposite way.

"I have the paper," said Mr. Bates as he held it out. "It took it off—"

Iseabail snatched it from his hands and tore it into a thousand tiny pieces. It was a lie. Every word of it was a lie and she'd be damned if another soul saw it.

Mr. Bates snorted. "I would have burned it myself. But I suppose if the pieces are small enough."

Sadie grabbed pieces off her skirt and tore it into tinier bits. Iseabail took those pieces and teased out the thread. By the time they were done, there was nothing but broken threads that would be useless to anyone but a mouse. And probably not even them.

It was very satisfying.

It also took several minutes. Long minutes when they should have arrived at the countess's home ages ago. Iseabail looked out the window.

"Where are we?" she asked.

"Cheapside." Mr. Bates's voice was calm. That reassured her. "I'm taking you to a place to change. You can't appear before the watch in those clothes." He gestured toward Sadie and her blood covered gloves. "Plus, it will give you time to decide on your plan."

Plan? Her plan had been to find a Sassenach husband who

could protect her from her uncle. That hadn't happened, and now she was out of time.

They'd found her.

But she still had a little time. Her clansmen would come back, but they weren't here right now. She needed to think fast. She needed to *act* fast.

She lifted her chin and turned to Mr. Bates. If she were a beauty, she would put all her coy whiles into her position. She wasn't, so she faced him with honesty and simple need.

"Mr. Bates, sir, will you marry me?"

CHAPTER TWELVE

"WHAT ARE YOU doing?" Miss Allen gasped.

Reuben was startled as well. Certainly, he'd been propositioned before. A man in his position had plenty of women who asked to join his bed. But never had one been so bold or so elegant in her question. No feminine wiles, no coy glances, but a simple, forthright question.

He rather admired her for that. He still had to answer in the negative.

"Miss Spalding, you are overwrought."

"Of course, you are," Miss Allen soothed. "But you know, a man will not solve this problem."

"Won't it?" Miss Spalding returned. "It'll keep my uncle from marrying me to Hamish." She looked back to him. "And I've five hundred gold pieces as a dowry."

"But I'd have to go to Scotland and get it from an angry uncle."

She nodded. "But you can handle him. You made mincemeat out of Hamish, and he's the ugliest fighter in the clan."

"It is kind of you to say so, but any fool can get lucky in a fight." He smiled at her. "And you handled your attacker very well. You didn't even get a drop of blood on you."

She looked away. "I knew he favored his right side. He fell off his horse once and the bone never set right. Easy enough to duck inside and cut him."

Easy for her, apparently.

"All I had to do was think of his wife," she said.

"You have a brutal family, that's no lie. I see why you came to London, why you want a strong husband." He shook his head. "But I have no need to tie myself to a crazy Scottish clan."

"We're a rich one, too."

He snorted. "I have more money than I know what to do with," he lied. The truth was he knew exactly what to do with his money, and it was all invested in friends and family who knew their business. For the most part. His days were filled with checking on what they were doing and fixing it when they failed.

"Imagine what you could do with more."

He chuckled, truly impressed by her resilience. She had not descended into the vapors but was putting logic to her untenable situation. "I have no need for Scottish gold. My life is here."

"No, sir, it is not."

He jolted at her audacity, but didn't get the chance to respond as she calmly described every way he had just destroyed his own plans.

"You have bet everything on finding someone to marry among the *ton*. If you fail to force your way in, what happens to you? Will they let you go back to your place in London on the fringe of their world? Or will they punish you? Will you become a pariah?"

The *ton* were not known to be forgiving of their own, much less any encroaching mushroom who thought he could force his way inside. Since his two dances with these ladies two nights ago, his brother's gaming hell had already lost his most elevated customers, several ladies had cancelled orders at his aunt's dressmaking establishment, and worst of all, three of his nieces had lost their positions as maids in elevated households. His family was already being punished for his audacity. He had reassured himself that their business and employment would return when he married someone like Lady Rebecca. If nothing else, he would be able to influence things from an elevated position. Hopefully, their fortunes would rise with him.

If he failed, however, he would have damaged all of them to no purpose. Their prospects would dim accordingly. His would be erased.

"I am not a pariah yet. I still have many possible wives—"

"You beat a man bloody with your bare hands."

He winced and curled his hands into the fabric of his clothes. The blood had dried on his knuckles, and this did not wipe them clean. All it did was ruin his jacket, and yet he could not stop himself from trying to rub the dark stains away.

"Lady Rebecca watched it all. Do you think she has seen such violence before?" She gestured at Miss Allen. "Sadie and I have seen it all. Drunken revels turned violent, bloody gashes from a hunt gone bad."

Sadie blew out a slow breath. "Lady Rebecca has never seen a cut stitched closed. She told me a week ago that a footman hurt himself moving furniture. He bled badly and she had to leave the room, sickened to her stomach. She won't even go in that parlor anymore."

"She's very young," he said grimly.

"And she will not react well to what she saw," Iseabail continued. "Neither will her mother nor any of her mother's friends. You have demonstrated that you are too rough for their tender daughters."

He had no response to that because she was right. He'd made such an effort to show polish in every aspect of his person. He'd refined his speech, learned the complexities of a cravat, and practiced being delightfully bold instead of boorishly scary. He'd taken lessons in dancing and refined his palate.

And he'd just thrown it all away.

Rather than speak, he slammed his hand on the carriage roof. "Take us to the alley beside Palace du Joie," he bellowed.

Miss Allen gasped. "We cannot go in there like this!"

"It is one of the few places we can," he muttered. "She's my aunt." He looked out the window. "We'll go in from the back."

The carriage stopped in the middle of the street, not quite close enough to the alleyway, but the best that could be managed. He already had his coin ready when he pushed open the door. Then as fast as possible, he paid the driver, helped the ladies out, and pushed them toward the dark.

He didn't have to push hard. They were already moving, though a few people on the street gasped at Miss Allen's blood-covered gown. Iseabail moved to shield her on one side while Reuben took the other. They rushed to the back door to his aunt's dress shop.

He rapped three times, very fast, and a fourth a beat later. He was rewarded in a moment as his aunt hauled open the door. She took in his measure with a sweeping glance, then stepped back so they could enter.

"I knew you couldn't contain yerself," she muttered as he pulled the ladies inside. "An' now look what you've done to two more. Ladies they are, brought down by you."

She always was a sourpuss. "This was not my doing," he shot back.

"An' when does that matter?" She folded her arms as she looked at the ladies. "You've got dirt and a tear," she said to Iseabail, "but it's not so bad."

Miss Allen sighed as she dropped her bloody gloves into the nearest rubbish bin. "But I'm a complete mess," she said.

"Aye, but I've got something for you."

"For them both," Reuben said. "Make them fully presentable as quick as you can." Meanwhile he shrugged out his jacket. Damnation, there was blood on his shirtsleeves too. "I'll need it all, too," he groaned.

His aunt jerked her head to the side room. "You know where to go."

He did. His aunt's shop had been his first investment. He'd even spent time stitching crude seams when he was a younger, though that time had been mercifully short. It had been his idea to whisper to the men in the gaming hell that their wives and sisters would receive a discount if they frequented her shop. That had been enough to entice her first titled customers. And with him keeping an eye on the expenses, her dress shop had flourished. In thanks, she allowed him to keep a change of clothing upstairs in her private rooms.

He needed to go there now, but he was loath to leave Iseabail. "This is my aunt," he said. "Aunt—"

"Madame Joie," his aunt said, though her real name was Judy Bates. "My nephew has brought you to ruin, hasn't he? Tut, tut. I'll set everything to rights."

"I've hardly brought them to ruin," he began, but Iseabail interrupted her.

"Actually, he was helping me, and for that I am grateful. Indeed, I'm hoping we can—"

Reuben stepped forward. "That's not up for discussion right now. Change your clothes—I'll pay for it all—and then come upstairs for some tea. We can make a plan then."

Iseabail faced him. Where her friend was still obviously shaken, Iseabail's face was calm, her expression and her attitude set. "Do you think I haven't gone over and over this in my mind? I have feared this moment for weeks—"

"But I am not your solution," he said.

"Are you certain? I can offer you—"

"Everything?" he inserted. It was what she'd said in her bedroom.

She nodded. "And you said that was exactly what you wanted."

It was true. He just didn't want her kind of everything. "I have a plan." He softened his voice. "It does not include you." How those words stuck in his throat, but he forced them out.

"You want Lady Rebecca or her ilk." she shook her head. "That is no longer possible. You must readjust."

How many times had he said that exact thing to one of his relations? One business scheme after another failed because someone was too stubborn to see disaster coming and change his method. Was he that blind? That arrogant?

Of course, he was. But he would not admit that yet. Not with his aunt watching them with a too-smart eye. She would see that he wanted nothing more than to touch Miss Spalding. That part of him longed to be her protector against all ills. And she had some very big ills arranged against her. He knew of no other man beside himself who might save her. But to do so would upend all his careful plans.

"It is not easy to say no to a beautiful woman," he murmured. "And yet I have done it countless times."

She huffed. "I am not coming to you as a beautiful woman. I have things to offer. Five hundred—"

He caught her arm hard enough to silence her. It was never wise to talk money in front of others. "We will discuss this upstairs. Over tea."

She snorted. "Whisky would be better."

His lips curved. "I will send for some."

Then he forced himself to step back. He consciously opened his fingers so that he no longer felt the hard bone in her arm, the strong muscles, or her soft skin. He released her and stepped away though it nearly tore him apart to do it.

Damnation, what was happening to him? He was accounted a decisive man. He'd never lingered over a woman like this. And he'd never struck a friend over one.

He turned for the stairs rather than face his aunt's intrigued smirk. She was guessing at things he'd rather kept secret. So he jerked his head at the ladies.

"See to them," he said. "Then bring them upstairs."

"You take care of yourself," his aunt said. "Then I've got words we need to exchange first."

Bloody hell. Could this day get any worse?

CHAPTER THIRTEEN

REUBEN STOMPED UPSTAIRS and performed his ablutions as fast as possible. He wanted to use this time to think dispassionately about his plans. His world was a complicated chessboard of people and possibilities, and every time he tried to sort through them, his thoughts veered back to Iseabail surrounded by blood and yet remaining untouched.

It was a metaphor, he was sure. Any soul who remained in her circle would be steeped in disaster while she remained intact. She might sport torn clothing, perhaps, or a bit of dirt on her gloriously pale skin. But the only red would be in her hair and her lips.

God, what a firebrand she was. She'd wielded that dirk with purpose. Even now he had no idea where it was. Somewhere on her person, no doubt, secreted away between her breasts or strapped to her thigh.

The image was arousing. How stupid he'd been to think of her as a naïve debutante whom he could exploit. The only distinctive thing about her then had been her height. But she'd surprised him at every turn, and now she proved she had clearer sight than he.

What you want is no longer possible. You must readjust.

Was it true? Were all his plans of marrying into the aristocracy over?

"Are you finished yet?" His aunt's voice cut through his

thoughts.

"Near enough," he said as he ruined yet another cravat. Damn it, his hands were sweating and had softened the starch. What the hell was wrong with him?

"Turn around. I'll do it," his aunt huffed.

He did as he was ordered. He'd been conditioned since childhood not to argue when she took that tone. He didn't always obey her, but never argued. This time he allowed her to set his cravat in a complicated style.

"Well done—" he began, but she clucked her tongue to make him silent.

"There," she said as she stepped back. "I'm going to hire two more girls."

"What? You told me that business was off."

"It is. Which means it's the perfect time to train two new ones. I've the time to teach them now."

"But not the money to pay for them or the room to keep them." Young apprentices cost only what it took to feed and house them, but sometimes that was the difference between money for coal and not. He'd be damned if he let his aunt freeze in winter.

"You leave that to me," she said. "I know what I'm about."

He shook his head. "Let me see the records. Girls can be expensive."

"An' when will you do that?" she pressed, her hands on her hips. "I've been asking you to come by for months now."

He winced. It was true. But there had been so many other things to do. His brother's gaming hell alone took up half his time. The money that flowed through there needed to be tightly controlled. "Bring them to me now—"

"And then when do you talk to the ladies? You said something about a new plan?"

"Don't listen in to my conversations."

"Then don't have them in the middle of my workshop."

She was right. He knew she was, but damn it, everything was

coming to a head right now. He needed to stay focused on marrying into the *ton*. Once he did that, he would be in a better position to steer titled women to her shop, rich men to his brother's gaming hell, and a better class of people to the boxing club.

Meanwhile, his aunt dropped her hands on her hips as she stared at him. "Who is she to you?"

"Who?"

She clucked her tongue. If he were younger, she would have flicked his lips with her hard fingernails. "You haven't the time to play stupid. The redhead. Who is she to you?"

He kept his eyes averted. "No one. A girl I used to gain entry into the *ton*."

"And I'm the Queen of England."

"Stop pestering me!" Aunt Judy was one of a few people in the world who dared challenge him, but even that privilege had its limits. Apparently, she didn't realize how close she was to being cut from his life as an interfering old biddy.

"I'll stop when you stay out of my shop," she said with a snort.

"I'm the reason you have a shop."

"And you've been amply repaid for that."

"Have I? I watch your books so you don't overdraft, my name keeps out the thieves, and I send you customers."

"Since when? You've not been to see my books in years, the thieves stay out because I have good locks and I live right here. As for customers, I've had three cancel their orders this week. Because of you. So tell me another tale about how you're the reason I'm in business."

He wanted to argue, but she was right. He'd watched her closely when she'd started the business, but over the years, he'd wanted to make sure she could survive when he was busy. It had been a long time—more than a decade—since she'd made any mistakes. And yet he still treated her as if she'd just opened her doors.

He grunted. "Fine. Hire your new apprentices."

"I already have, thank ye kindly. Now tell me about the girls downstairs. Tell me why they have you beating Sammy Watts in the middle of Hyde Park?"

News traveled fast. And if Aunt Judy knew, then the *ton* would already be talking about it. Damnation. He should be out there mitigating the problem, not here arguing with her. "Sammy lied to me. I had to make an answer."

"That doesn't sound like Sammy. Nor you, for that matter. You're a great deal quieter about your punishments than a bloodbath in the middle of Hyde Park."

"It wasn't a bloodbath."

"Tell that to the man with his leg cut in half."

Reuben rocked back on his heel. "Did he die?"

"They took him somewhere to get stitched up. Missy heard it from her sister who was there. Said all them Scots were screaming for the magistrate."

Great. Just bloody great.

"How are the ladies faring?"

"The bloody one's still shaking. Not been in many fights, that one, but she's getting 'erself together. The other one is thinking. She's the one in trouble, isn't she?"

He nodded.

"And you had to defend her. Against Sammy. Why?"

He didn't know. But the sight of Iseabail trapped against Sammy still set his blood to boiling. His hands were clenched into fists at the memory. She'd have bruises from his grip. There'd been terror in her eyes. Terror when she was the coolest cucumber he'd ever met.

"Ach, look at you," she growled. "Yer the smartest of my kin, and you're still as dumb as a block o' wood. You fancy her, you idiot."

He snorted. "I respect her. She's smart, and she can fight."

"So can Missy, but you never got bloody because of her. Think hard, boy. The redhead surprised you, didn't she? Smarter and more capable than you thought."

That was certainly true.

"She's the first in a long while that has done that to ye. And she's got yer pisser all perky, don't she?"

He glowered at her coarse language. "That may be, but I'm well past the time when my cock rules my head."

"That you are. So she's smart, you respect her skills, and you like her looks. That wouldn't be enough to sway you, boy, but then you've got the one thing you inherited from your mother."

He frowned. His mother had passed when he was seven. He barely remembered her except in the tales that his relatives told. "What's that?" he asked.

She tapped his chest. "You've got her soft heart. And that Scottish miss has a problem. A big one, most likely, and you're thinking you're the only one who can save her."

He turned away. He hadn't been thinking that. In truth, he'd been thinking that there must be a Scotsman who was better suited to taking on her uncle. Though from the looks of things, her clan was filled with brutish men all aligned against her. Connall Aberbeag had sponsored her to London, but then he'd gone off with his new bride. If the man were going to help more, he probably would have done it already.

And, come to think of it, if there were a Scotsman to help her, Iseabail would have found him already. The woman was resourceful enough to look close. Instead, she traveled over four hundred miles to London. A waste of time, he thought, because who among the prissy *ton* would be able to handle a man with a claymore, much less a band of them? Not a one. They might do well in a boxing ring, but against real weapons in a real fight? Most of these dandies would piss themselves as they ran away.

He sighed. Iseabail was in trouble, and he was likely the only person she knew who had a chance to help.

"There it is," said his aunt, as she pointed to his nose. "You're thinking what you can do for her."

"And why not?" he shot back. "She's got five hundred gold

coins to pay if I do." Not to mention a profitable market that would bring in a great deal more if properly managed.

"Ye don't need the coin."

He didn't. But he certainly knew how to use it.

His aunt busied herself by setting the kettle to boil. He noted that she was scrimping on the coal in the bin. She was too old to be pinching her pennies that way, but then he reminded himself that she had just hired two new apprentices without consulting him. If she wanted to put her coin into new employees, then he couldn't say a word about the nearly empty coal bin.

But it was hard to hold his tongue. He wanted her to live in comfort, but he had to respect her choices. And so she would tell him if she caught him looking—

"I know what I'm about," she said. "I don't need you nosing into my books, and I don't want anyone telling me how to live."

"And if you run into trouble?"

"Then you can say, 'I told you so.'"

He folded his arms across his chest. "I don't want to say that. I want you to be warm at night."

Instead of answering, she turned her head at some noise downstairs. "They'll be coming up here soon. What are you going to tell her?"

He didn't know. The last thing he wanted to do was rush off to Scotland to teach an evil uncle a lesson. But if Iseabail was right, Reuben had just destroyed his chances of marrying into the *ton*. Not many young ladies wanted a man with blood on his hands.

"It's a simple equation, Reuben. You've got feelings for her, so you want to help her. Ask yourself: is this twitching in your loins something for today or will it last?" She cocked her head. "Meaning, will you get bored of her when her trouble's done?"

He glared at her. He did not want to discuss his loins with his aunt or anyone else for that matter, but the question was a good one. If he admitted he felt an attraction to Iseabail—indeed, how could he deny it?—then he had to know if it was a passing thing or not.

He sighed. "It's not love, if that's what you're getting at." He'd fallen in love a time or two in the past. Hot, lusty affairs that fogged his mind and consumed his coin. The first two ended the moment his purse was empty. Thank heaven he hadn't made his fortune yet. The third had been longer. It might have lasted, though they'd been so young, it was hard to know. She died in his arms of a fever, and he'd stopped thinking of love from that day on.

"Because yer too sensible for love."

She was mocking him, but he answered it honestly. "Because I am not in love with her. I am too calm for that. I have not spent days and nights dreaming of her. I have no wish to marry her or see my babes in her arms."

He said that with confidence though his words brought those very thoughts to mind. She would be a good mother, and they would have smart, beautiful children. She would teach her children poise, and he would teach them prudence. His fortune was built upon knowing when to leap and when to stay still.

He was so consumed with the images in his head that he didn't realize the woman herself had topped the stairs. He had no idea how long she stood there listening, but she spoke up now, her voice filled with the same kind of clear-sighted intelligence that he valued.

"I have no need for love," she said firmly. "I need someone to help me kill my uncle."

His aunt's head snapped up, her eyes wide. "Murder, is it?"

"He murdered my father and my mother."

"You have proof?"

"Of course not."

"A child's memories, no doubt, with no certainty behind it."

She didn't answer. Her gaze was on his, and he was lost in the beauty of her standing there. His aunt had dressed her in a rich green, too bold for a debutante, but perfect for her. Such presence she had. Like a queen commanding her knights. *Kill him for me.*

And he fought the urge to do just that.

He ran to logic rather than give in to what she wanted. "I've no need to go to war with a Scottish clan," he said.

She swallowed and nodded, though he knew she was thinking of a way to persuade him otherwise. A moment later, she surprised him. Again.

"Do you know of anyone? Do you have men who would be willing? For five hundred gold coins?"

"You'd have to marry to get it."

She lifted her chin. "But it should be enough to induce someone, shouldn't it?"

Several someones, but she'd have to be careful whom she selected. So few men could be trusted. Even fewer would have the skills required. Hell, he had no idea if *he* could do it. There were too many unknowns.

"You have no idea what you're asking," he said slowly.

She didn't argue with him. She simply folded her arms and stared at him as a queen might look at a recalcitrant boy. And there between the two of them stood his aunt with a canny look on her face.

"You've got Jonathan," Aunt Judy said. "He's been looking for more work. And he's built up a good group of men."

"She's talking murder. Jonathan and I have never done that. We protect. We escort. We—"

"Took on the highway men for us," Iseabail said. "You recovered my necklace for me." The pendant sat clear as day between the sweet mounds of her breasts. "Have you never killed before?"

Of course, he had. He was a man built for the London kind of warfare. He'd been trained in it since his youngest days and had learned to respect the cost of taking a life. In London, he was an undisputed king among his set.

Scotland was an entirely different environment. A very new kind of challenge.

Even as he told himself that he was not equipped to handle a war in Scotland, his mind started categorizing the things he could use. Iseabail was the most obvious asset. She knew the terrain, the people, and was smart enough to be accurate in her descriptions. Then he could add in all that very interesting Scottish superstition about witchcraft. He might see Iseabail as a queen, but he knew others saw her as a powerful witch. He could use that mysticism to great advantage. It was probably why her uncle was so keen to keep her around.

The possibilities intrigued him. He felt a familiar churn of excitement that had been absent from his life for so long. But to embrace that would be to give up on his ambitions here in London. The one where his children would be among the peerage. He might want to harry off to Scotland on a new adventure, but what would that do to his future children?

He would not give up on them. He'd invested too much time and money in his current scheme. And so his decision was clear.

"I'll send a message to Jonathan. He's your best option." Then he added a bit more, though the words choked him. "He'll make a decent husband as well."

CHAPTER FOURTEEN

ISEABAIL DIDN'T WANT this "Jonathan" to marry her, but beggars couldn't be choosers. Still, she made one last attempt to persuade Mr. Bates.

"You still think you can find an aristocrat to marry you. You're deluding yourself after today's fight."

"I'm sure I can," Mr. Bates said with a smile. "Never underestimate the *ton's* love of money. I didn't want to buy my way in, but I could. Even after today's fight."

Iseabail heard the certainty in Mr. Bates's voice and felt despair settle deep into her bones. Even though he had suggested a different man to help her, she couldn't shake the feeling that without him, she was doomed.

Didn't he understand that she had spent the last decade looking for a man who would stand up to her uncle? She'd found no one in Scotland or England. She hadn't even been sure about him until she'd seen him fight. She'd never seen someone move like him. Fluid and quick. He didn't have a weapon, and yet he'd dispatched Hamish's men like so many children.

And now he was denying her.

She didn't blame him. His entire life was in London. Family and friends were the least of it. His ambitions were here. What did she have to lure him away from that?

Nothing.

Still, it cut deep. She felt utterly alone.

She felt Sadie touch her arm. "You'll be all right," she said. "We'll find an answer."

She smiled. Sadie meant well, but eternal optimism blinded the woman. Sadie was confident because she'd been raised with enough protection to stretch her wings in safety. But that hadn't been Iseabail's experience. And she knew better than anyone that things rarely worked out for the best. Still, Sadie had bolstered her for a moment. Enough that she could turn to address Mr. Bates. "When can I speak with Jonathan?"

He frowned. "I'll arrange for him to see you tomorrow first thing. Do you know what you want to say to the watch?"

She lifted her hands in a shrug. "That I'm not married. That I won't go back to Scotland. That they attacked me." Unfortunately, that wasn't going to work. Everyone knew a guardian had the right to drag his charge back home and force her to marry anyone he willed.

She was a fine one to accuse Mr. Bates of self-delusion. She had yet to face the reality of her own situation. If she went back to the countess's home, she'd be taken by the watch and given over to Hamish no matter what she claimed.

"I can't go back there, can I?" she said, fear chilling her bones. "I need to run."

She'd spoken more to herself than anyone else, but Mr. Bates reacted as if she'd shouted. He jumped forward and barely stopped himself from grabbing her arm. His hand touched her, though, then froze as if knowing he was going too far.

"No need to run away," he said. "There's nowhere to go that is safer for you. Without protection or help, you'd be like a lamb to slaughter in London."

"I know," she said miserably. "That's why I asked for your help." She pressed a hand to her forehead. What was she going to do? Hamish wasn't going to stop. Neither was her uncle. "I have to get married to someone who will stop him."

"Don't be rash," he snapped. Then he modulated his voice. "Let's get you back to the countess's home. She has a great deal of influence."

"But won't the watch be there?"

He shrugged. "She can handle the watch. They won't take you in tonight."

One night's reprieve? That wasn't long enough, but what else could she do?

She let him guide her back down the stairs and into a hackney. She dropped onto the squabs and stared at her hands while Sadie climbed in across from her. He sat beside her, and she had to keep herself from sinking into his body. Despair was winning as she found fewer and fewer places to turn. She'd thought her most desperate time was when she ran across half of Scotland to find Sadie. Now it seemed everything was for naught.

Her uncle had won.

"You're not done yet," he said. His voice was low as he squeezed her arm, but the comfort she found in his voice was short-lived.

"Will your friend fight for me?"

He sighed. "For the right price."

She didn't have any money except for the dubious promise of her dowry. "I'll marry anyone who will kill my uncle."

"Don't be rash—"

She turned to him, anger strengthening her body. "I'm not rash. I'm never rash. I will never be free as long as he is my guardian."

"You won't be free with a murderer as your husband either."

Sadie held up her hand. "Let's talk about other options."

Sweet Sadie. She had no idea how many times Iseabail had gone through them. "What do you have in mind?"

For the rest of the ride, Sadie discussed people or clans who might come to her rescue. None of them would work. Her uncle and the marketplace he controlled were too powerful. The Spalding market was the only place for many clans to sell their goods. Without it, they'd quickly starve. As for the other clans, each one had troubles. After Culloden, none wanted to go to war with anyone, much less a fellow clan. Worse, every whisper of witchcraft worked against her. It took a brave Scot indeed to marry the granddaughter of the most infamous witch in Scotland.

Which meant they arrived at the countess's home without finding a solution. She would have hidden in her bed then, if she could slink into her bedroom. But she didn't because of what they *did* find upon arrival.

Half the *ton* was walking their street. Apparently, everyone wanted to see the murderous Scotswomen, and she was very grateful Mr. Bates had had the foresight to take them somewhere to change. But it also emphasized just how much trouble she was in. She had no doubt the watch was inside waiting for her, and whatever happened could not be hidden.

Her reputation was lost.

So she made one last attempt to grab Mr. Bates. She touched his arm before he swung open the door, then waited until he gave her his full attention.

"Can you not see? Look at all the greedy gossipmongers on the street. The *ton* will never accept you after this."

Rather than becoming dismayed, his expression lifted into a grin. "That makes the challenge all the sweeter when I win."

Good God, was everything a game to him? "You don't strike me as someone who ignores reality." She gestured to the walkers who were not walking by. Every single one had stopped to gawk at them. "They will never accept you or your children."

He appeared to think about that. His expression sobered, and he looked at her closely. She had no idea what he saw, but his inspection was thorough, and her skin tingled the longer he looked at her. And then, as if to further imprint himself upon her, he touched her face.

He wore gloves, as was appropriate, but the calfskin had warmed to his body. He stroked across her cheeks and then down to her lips. She didn't want to surrender to his caress. Indeed, with what she was about to face in the countess's parlor, seduction was the furthest thing from her mind.

But his touch was gentle, and no man had ever touched her so sweetly.

"You may be right," he conceded.

Then he pressed his lips to hers.

Hope surged within her, and though she knew she should not allow it, all her defenses dropped away. She had picked this man. If a kiss would help to sway him, then she would do everything in her power to seduce him.

He swept into her mouth, fire burning into her with the power of his thrust. He stroked her in ways that surprised her—the top of her mouth, the edge of her teeth—and that startled her out of desperation and into need. She no longer thought about how to seduce him. Instead, she felt the solidness of him as he supported her face, the passion in him as he pushed deeper and harder into her. One of his hands stroked her neck and she angled her face to feel that tingling caress.

And as her head tilted, he had more freedom to move within her mouth. She dueled with him. How could she not when he stroked her with such ferocity? A twisting push of tongues while her skin burst with fire. She felt her nipples tighten as she made a mew of surrender.

He was everything she wanted, and—

He broke off the kiss.

He tore himself backwards as if dragged. Then he looked at her while she searched for something—anything—to say. He found words before she did.

"Maybe," he whispered. "You would be worth it."

She wanted to grab him. She wanted to make him stay in the carriage until he promised to help her. But after that kiss, she was too dazzled to react quickly. Then he shoved open the door and hopped down before she gathered her wits.

Meanwhile, Sadie whistled under her breath. "*He* would be worth it," she murmured. "If you can catch him."

Iseabail swallowed, her gaze still pinned to Reuben as he tipped his hat and lifted his chin in the same moment. Damn, he was handsome, especially when his lips curved in that dare-you smile. He challenged everyone who looked upon him to disparage him, dismiss him, to do anything but worship his prowess. And with the last of her pride gone, she tumbled faster than she thought possible.

She wanted him. She might even love him. She certainly adored him whenever he smiled in that cheeky way.

You would be worth it.

His words echoed in her head, and she grabbed onto them as her lifeline. She had one night, didn't she? There had to be some way to convince him.

But there wasn't time to make a plan. She had to get out of the carriage. So she squared her shoulders and grasped his outstretched hand. She descended into the sunshine with a serene expression and firm jaw. Then she waited as Sadie took his other hand and joined them on the street.

"And now," he said with a happy chuckle, "we enter the lion's den."

CHAPTER FIFTEEN

REUBEN HAD EXPECTED that the countess's home would be the center of the *ton's* attention, but he didn't anticipate that the lady's house would be bursting to the gills with all manner of visitors.

The butler threw open the front door the moment the three of them descended from the carriage. Reuben could hear the whispered speculation about them on the street and see the ugly expression of the butler as the three of them approached. The man clearly did not approve of the situation.

Damn it, why had he kissed her? Now his body was burning from the memory, and he had to focus all his wits on the situation at hand.

Once inside the door, they busied themselves with setting aside gloves and hats. All the business of a peer arriving home while Reuben covertly surveyed the situation. The most immediate problem was the watch. Two men stood in the foyer looking both angry and uncomfortable in escalating degrees. Fortunately, he knew the name of one. That might help. Next was the countess who was busy chastising the watch for making outrageous accusations. He'd have to adjust her fury. A little bit of anger at her charges would help soften the attitude of any authority. Too much and she'd help send them all to prison. And lastly, a profusion of ladies all peering through the parlor door at them.

Finally, the countess turned her attention to her charges.

"Thank God you're safe. Girls, I have been worried sick!" She grabbed Iseabail first, scanned her from head to toe, then embraced her. Reuben was close enough to hear her whisper into the girl's ear. "Don't say anything. Let me handle this."

Then she repeated the gesture with Miss Allen.

Next, it was his turn. He smiled and bowed to her, but her expression hardened into anger. "I am very cross with you Mr. Bates. Very cross indeed," she stated loudly. "What nonsense have you involved us all in? The watch at my door. My girls frazzled. I insist you leave immediately and take these odious men with you."

It was clearly a ploy to lay everything at his door while the women were cast as victims. Unfortunately, everyone here—including the men of the watch—knew that Iseabail was the center of this problem, not him.

Mr. Otto Gibson stepped forward. He was the oldest of the two watchmen, and he was distantly acquainted with Reuben. "Begging your pardon, my lady, but it's not Mr. Bates we're looking for. By all accounts, he stepped in to save the miss—"

"That ain't true!" cried another man of the watch, this one unknown to Reuben. "He's in the midst of it all. Jes' ask Sammy Watts. It were a lawful getting of an errant wife." He pointed hard at Iseabail. "And he interfered where it were none of his business."

"Put that finger down," Reuben growled, "or I'll see that you never use it again."

Growling at the watch was not the way to act. Indeed, it was the opposite of his usual charm. And yet, he did not like anyone pointing a dirty finger at Iseabail, and he found himself standing between her and the offending man without even a conscious decision to move. Damn it! He needed to get control of himself.

"Now, now, no need to insult a lady," Otto said. His words were for everyone, but his focus was on Reuben as his bushy eyebrows drew together into a frown. "Reuben, you and me have seen a thing or two. We've got witness statements—"

"And what have they said?" Reuben interrupted. "These witnesses?"

Lady Rebecca abruptly pushed through the growing crowd in the foyer. "I did. I saw it all, and you were magnificent, Mr. Bates!"

He looked at the girl, seeing her rosy cheeks and wide brown eyes. Her mother stood protectively behind her, but there was a thoughtful look in the matron's eyes. One that said she could turn this situation to her advantage. But it was Lady Rebecca who caught his attention the most as she kept talking.

"Those horrible men came for Miss Spalding. They were truly frightening, and I couldn't understand a word they said. Savages, really. Mad savages." She pressed her hand to her bodice as if terrified, but he saw the delight of a woman who loved a good gothic tale, the more outlandish the better. "I was terrified, you understand, but Mr. Bates saw me to safety. He made sure no harm would come to me, and then he..." She gasped in true dramatic delight. "Oh, he saved us all!"

Even though she and her mother stood at the entrance to the parlor, Reuben could clearly hear the gasps from the other ladies within. There might even have been a lower voice from a few gentlemen, it was hard to tell. Either way, it was clear that thanks to Lady Rebecca, the tide of opinion was flowing in his favor.

"I only did what any gentleman would do," he said as he winked at Lady Rebecca. She blushed bright pink, and he knew he had gained an admirer. Several if he played his cards right. So he turned to his acquaintance on the watch and tried to make him a friend. "Otto, I know this is a difficult business. Blood in Hyde Park, upset ladies, and two innocent debutantes caught in the middle, but I assure you, I can explain it all."

"Can ye explain wot ye did to Sammy?" cried the younger watchman. "He said yer friends. If that's wot you do to yer friends—"

"Stop it, Charlie. Let's hear what Mr. Bates has to say."

"It's a terrible tale, Otto. Miss Spalding has come here to find a husband as so many young ladies do. She was fortunate enough to gain the respect and sponsorship of the Countess of Byrn, but her unscrupulous uncle wants to keep her dowry for himself." He leaned in. "Five hundred gold coins."

He made sure to say that last point in a stage whisper. Everyone in the parlor gasped, even though this was common knowledge. Indeed, the countess had made a point of it. Yet still, they all gasped as if they were at a Cheltenham tragedy. And so he gave them exactly what they wanted.

"What was the poor girl to do when those ruffians came for her, claiming all sorts of nonsense? Surrender? Of course not. She fought as any good woman of virtue would. And I—"

Lady Rebecca spoke up. "You could not leave her to fight alone!"

"I could not," he confirmed.

"You're so brave," she said.

He smiled at the girl. "I am most pleased that you are unscathed, my lady."

She giggled. "I am completely unharmed."

She was completely under his thrall, as well. He could have her wedded and bedded inside a week.

The knowledge didn't come with any kind of glee. Indeed, it was a simple fact that brought with it the knowledge of his entire future as if on parchment. Lady Rebecca was too naïve to see that she worshiped a dream. Meanwhile, her much cannier parent would know of his deep pockets, ones that could help their coffers considerably if handled quietly. She would throw her own weight—and that of the Countess of Byrn—behind the idea that he was a hero, a prince among the peasants, who deserved to be admitted—provisionally—into their ranks.

If he kept free of scandal, helped various members of the *ton* now and then when they were in a tight spot, then his place among them was assured. They wouldn't welcome him completely. Far from it. But his children would have a place, and by the time his grandchildren arrived, his past would be all but forgotten by anyone but him.

All he need do was play to the crowd of onlookers.

So easy, and yet he was strangely reluctant to play the game.

Why had he kissed Iseabail? He was sure Lady Rebecca was the future he wanted, and yet he couldn't dismiss the feel of Iseabail's mouth, the scent of her skin, and the way her stiff body had softened beneath his lips. He remembered the desperation in her kiss, but also the well of passion she possessed, just waiting for the right man to uncover it.

What did Lady Rebecca have to offer against that?

Everything, and yet he couldn't forget Iseabail.

"That's one way of looking at it," Otto declared, "but they claim she's already married. Have a paper that says it."

"Have you seen this paper?"

"The witnesses did."

"As did I," Reuben said. "A blank piece of paper with random black marks on it. It was a lie."

The younger watchman spoke up. "They all swore it. And Sammy saw it. He said so. It was legal."

Fortunately, the countess knew her part in this display. She drew herself upright and spoke in the most imperious manner possible. "I demand to see this paper. If it's real, then we shall have something to discuss. But I *highly doubt it.*"

There would be no paper because they had already torn it to shreds.

He turned to the young watchman and pitched his voice low. "I regret what I had to do to Sammy," he said softly. "But the man lied to me, and this innocent girl was going to pay for that error."

Whether or not Charlie understood marriage law, the man knew who Reuben was. He knew that lying to Mr. Bates demanded punishment, and so his expression shifted from anger to grumpy silence. It was enough to end the problem.

"We'll look into this paper," Otto said, his expression troubled. "If it's real—"

Reuben held up his hands. "Then she'll go with them because that's the law." He shrugged. "But they don't have a real paper, Otto. I'd swear that to anyone."

That was enough to satisfy the law, even grumpy Charlie. So after a moment, the two men bowed to the countess and took their leave. One problem solved. Without that paper declaring a marriage, the Scotsmen had no legal way to take Iseabail home.

They would still come at her illegally, of course, and not in the open. Iseabail was right. She was in danger every moment that her uncle was alive.

But that was not his problem. He'd turn all that over to Jonathan and focus on securing his marriage to Lady Rebecca. Meanwhile, the countess touched his arms and spoke sotto voice in his ear.

"Neatly done, Mr. Bates. But I assure you, I can still turn this around to make you the villain."

He gave the lady his most winning smile. "I am much more helpful to you as the hero."

"No doubt," she said dryly. Meanwhile, she looked back at the girls, especially Iseabail. "Good idea to change into appropriate clothing. Can you both endure hours of simpering and claiming Mr. Bates as your hero? Or should you head upstairs with a headache?"

Typically, Miss Allen sniffed. "Like he did everything!"

"He did," the countess hissed. "No proper young lady fights."

"Then she's not a proper Scotswoman," the lady groused, but she lifted her hand to her heart and batted her eyes at Reuben. "My hero!"

Reuben wanted to laugh. He would have at any normal time, but all he could manage was a vague kind of smile since his attention was centered on Iseabail. She looked pale and her body was tight, as if she held herself together by will alone. That was probably true. She more than any of them knew exactly how much danger she was in.

Meanwhile, the countess had also seen her charge's distress. "Iseabail?" she pressed. "Perhaps you should go upstairs and rest."

"I'm safer among people," she said.

She was safest with him, but he didn't say that. Instead, he took her arm gently to steer her into the parlor. He remembered at the very last moment to bring Lady Rebecca along as well, and only because she all but tackled him to gain his attention.

That was a mistake on his part. If he intended to reel her into marriage, he needed to play the devoted suitor. And yet, he couldn't stop himself from glancing anxiously at Iseabail. She was the center of all the attention, now, with everyone asking about her wretched uncle and her very intriguing dowry. She handled it like the queen she was. She remained outwardly serene, though he could see signs of distress in the way she kept touching her necklace.

It must be a kind of talisman for her. A way to remember her mother, perhaps, but also a habit developed young as a subtle threat to any superstitious Scots. Bother her and she might put a spell upon you. And if it worked to keep her safe—at least throughout her childhood—then who was he to decry it?

And yet he longed to sit closer to her. He wanted his body heat to warm hers or to perhaps to entwine his fingers with hers. It would still her anxious fiddling with her necklace. And it would remind him that she was very alive.

Despite everything happening around them, he had only to look away from her face to remember that six very well armed Scotsmen had tried to grab Iseabail in the middle of Hyde Park. His mind's eye replayed the way those men had looked—brutal and determined—against one woman. What if he hadn't been there to help? What if Sammy had given her over to them? Any of a thousand of different things might have happened and she would not be here now. This regal, amazing woman would be in their hands and suffering things that would haunt his nightmares.

"You know," Lady Rebecca said, interrupting his thoughts. "I was so scared against all those horrible men. But you thought of me first, didn't you?"

He forced his attention back to the girl. "I needed to get you out of the way—" He winced. "Out of danger. You've never fought anyone, have you? Not even in pretend."

She gasped. "Oh, I couldn't. That not how a lady behaves."

"No, I suppose not." At least not well-bred English ladies. His niece, however, was a firebrand with her fists. His brother was right. It was a good idea to teach girls how to defend themselves. And the two Scotswomen had impressed him with their ferocity. "Do you know how to kick or bite?" he pressed. "Where to punch a man?"

Lady Rebecca blinked at him. "I am a babe in the woods," she said as if that were a good thing. "Utterly at your mercy."

He looked at her then, really looked. He saw her beauty and her youth, but also her innocence and all the doll-like qualities the aristocrats prized. She was an ornament to society, a beautiful attachment to any man who claimed her. She would echo the opinions of her parents in all things. And assuming she didn't turn sour, she would remain as absolutely useless as she was today. Which meant she would raise another generation of useless, beautiful girls.

Good God, she was boring. Marriage to her would be an endless tedium of sameness wrapped in a beautiful package.

He would go mad.

He stared at Lady Rebecca, his mind roiling from shock. He saw everything he wanted right there in front of him. A wife, an entry into the peerage, everything he had ever aspired to achieve—his for the taking. The gamble had paid off. He had won. All it took now would be to allow events to play out in their prescribed course.

Exactly as he'd planned.

What a shock it was to have it all and realize that two seconds after saying, "I do," he would be bored to tears. The game would be over. He'd have won. And then what would he do? It wasn't as if Lady Rebecca would be any kind of challenge. Indeed, nothing would be a challenge because he was the acknowledged King of London. The only thing left to him was to enter the peerage, and now here was Lady Rebecca giving him exactly that.

He'd won. He took a moment to savor the victory, to really feel it down into his bones.

And then he threw it all away.

CHAPTER SIXTEEN

ISEABAIL SAW WHAT was happening as if it were in a play before her eyes. Lady Rebecca with stars in her eyes as she worshiped Mr. Bates. He, of course, lapped it up, played to his audience, and would soon be accepted among their ranks. Her only hope of getting his help was the belief that the *ton* would revile him.

How wrong she'd been. They worshipped him. A man who could fight, was wealthy beyond belief, and had protected one of their own. Not her, of course. She was a Scotswoman with a dubious heritage and attackers coming for her in Hyde Park. No, it was Lady Rebecca who was their darling, and Mr. Bates was her hero.

She'd lost him.

Which left her empty except for the memory of two very delicious kisses. She almost wished she'd never experienced them because she doubted she would feel the like again. Sweet hunger and desperation, wrapped together in the meeting of lips. She never thought kissing could be like that. What she'd heard from the women of her clan had been about what happened afterwards. About the harshness of the taking. No one had said that kissing could be so wonderful.

Or maybe she was just thinking about the kiss because the rest of her life didn't bear attention.

"Were you not frightened, Mr. Bates? I would be quaking in my boots!"

"Does it hurt to punch a man like that? I would think your fingers might break!"

"Have you ever fought Gentleman Jack, Mr. Bates? I feel sure you would best him."

"How fortunate that you were there to protect everyone, Mr. Bates. I vow I shall never be safe at another ball if you're not in attendance."

That last statement came from one of the leading hostesses outside of Almack's. She didn't quite have Lady Jersey's status, but then her parties were a great deal more fun than an evening at Almack's. And if she was that anxious to have Mr. Bates around, then he was set inside the *ton*.

"But what are you going to do?"

It took a moment for Iseabail to realize that the question was directed at her and not Mr. Bates. Indeed, Sadie had to jostle her knee to gain her attention.

"What?"

"Oh, poor dear. You must be terrified. What will you do if they come for you again?"

What could she do? "Fight." Then she looked down at her hands, the weight of the truth making even her gaze too heavy to maintain. "I cannot win against them. They are too many, and I am alone."

An uncomfortable silence greeted her words. A few women murmured, "Surely not." Sadie squeezed her hand, silently offering her support. But everyone here knew the truth. A girl alone had no power against a brutal guardian.

She didn't mean to lose her composure. Indeed, she didn't even realize she was crying until tears spoiled the silk of her gown. Dark splotches expanded on her bodice and belly. She couldn't hide them. She couldn't stop them. And with every new blot, she crumpled inside. She still sat straight, she still breathed, though her body shook with the effort. But inside, she thought she was disappearing with every tear.

There went her face, lost in the wet. There went her head

because she could no longer think. Her shoulders had long since given way. And as for the rest of her—when had she last thought she could stand tall? Not since before her mother disappeared.

She felt him there before she could see. Her eyes were half-closed in misery when she felt his thumb on her cheeks, wiping away the wet. His fingers cupped her chin, raising her face up to his. He was on one knee before her, and his brows were knit with worry.

"Miss Spalding," he murmured. Then he smiled. "Iseabail, would you do me the greatest honor in the world and become my wife?"

She heard the gasps all around her and somewhere Lady Rebecca whispered, "But I thought he loved me."

It made no sense, this thing that was happening, and she blinked back her tears. "What?"

His expression softened. "You are not alone, Iseabail."

She nodded slowly. "You said you would recommend me to a friend of yours."

He nodded. "You shall meet him soon. I think we will need him when we go north to confront your uncle."

Her eyes widened. Was he saying…? Did he mean…? "You will go with me? You will fight with me?"

He shrugged. "It is what a good husband would do."

She blinked. "But…what?"

His thumb rolled over her lips. A tender stroke that nonetheless had her mouth tingling with awareness. Around her, every woman seemed to gasp with the gesture.

"Iseabail, marry me."

His words finally sunk in. His posture on his knee before her. Even the way he gazed into her eyes with such delight. Damn it, the man was grinning at her.

"Are you making fun of me?" she asked.

"I assure you, I have never proposed to a woman in jest." He lifted her hand to his mouth, flipped it over, and pressed his lips to her palm. "I want to be your husband, Iseabail Spalding. And I want to go to Scotland to save you from your horrible uncle."

"Why?" she gasped. "You said, no. You said—"

"Because to be a hero, one must have an equally fierce heroine."

"That doesn't make any sense."

He shrugged. "I don't want a child who is dependent upon me for her safety. I want a woman who can fight. And you, my dear—"

She didn't let him finish speaking. Finally his words penetrated her fog, and she answered as fast as she could, afraid he would change his mind.

"Yes! Yes, yes, yes." She had sworn to marry any man who would stand up to her uncle. That it was Reuben—

Her thoughts cut off as he pressed his mouth to hers. His hand cradled her face as his tongue swept inside. He thrust in with power, and he stroked her with a clever kind of frenzy. She could not explain it except that whatever he did left her weak. Not just the feel of their tongues intertwined, but the promise that he would help her. That she was not alone. That—

"There will be no more of that!" the countess exclaimed, and from the speed at which he withdrew from Iseabail, he'd probably been thumped on the head by the woman. He came away grinning, though, his body seemingly alive with energy while all Iseabail could do was sit in flustered confusion.

"A kiss between engaged persons is completely proper!" he said with a grin.

But the countess was not drawn in by his charm. Instead, she focused on Iseabail. "Think, girl, is this really what you want? It's been a difficult day. Perhaps you should—"

"Wait until Hamish comes back?" Iseabail asked. "Go to another party and wonder when they will try for me again? I'm surprised he hasn't stormed the house already."

All around her, people turned to the windows as if expecting a mad Scotsman to burst through. And truthfully, Iseabail couldn't discount the possibility.

"Perhaps you could hire someone to help you," pressed the countess. "You don't have to marry him for it." There was a wealth of disdain in her tone. One that was so often used to keep cocky footmen or cheeky maids in their place.

Iseabail would have none of it. She stood slowly, and when she found Mr. Bates remained on one knee, she tugged him upright to stand beside her. He moved fluidly, like a predator uncoiling beside her, and she smiled for what felt like the first time in years.

She had a hero now. He'd asked her to be his bride. She would not throw away this gift on the countess's preference for a title.

"He is the one," she said clearly. She turned toward Mr. Bates. "I accept. Please, how soon can we marry?"

He grinned as he wrapped an arm around her shoulders. "As soon as possible, I should think."

The countess sniffed. "Three weeks to read the banns—"

"No, my lady," he interrupted. "We haven't time for that. The danger is too imminent."

"But—"

"A special license. I can probably get one on my own, but it would be so much better if we went together." He looked down at Iseabail. "All of us now. They won't dare attack in a church."

She wasn't entirely sure about that, but she nodded anyway. Such was the force of his belief.

"My lady, please," he continued. "You have been the greatest of friends to Miss Spalding. She and I couldn't be more grateful to you. And though I don't have a title, I have enough money to keep her in a wealthy, happy life. This I swear to you and to her." That last part was added as he looked at Iseabail. "I will see you safe."

"I will honor my vows to you," she whispered. "To my last breath."

He grinned, then looked back at the countess. "Please, my lady, will you help us?"

The countess wasn't swayed. Not yet. But she clearly wavered. "This is happening too fast," she murmured as she peered at Iseabail. "Are you—"

"I am sure."

There was a moment when the lady studied them. A narrow-eyed scrutiny that would make lesser souls shrink into themselves. For the first time in forever, Iseabail had no wish to cower. She would marry Reuben. Hopefully within the next few days.

Seeing that her charge was resolved, the countess exhaled in a truly dramatic fashion. "So be it," she declared loudly. Then she looked at her butler. "Get my carriage ready immediately. We must go now."

Sadie jumped to her feet. "How soon will you leave for Scotland?"

"Immediately afterwards," Mr. Bates answered. "We must take the fight to her uncle."

"Immediately!" gasped Sadie. And it was echoed by everyone in the room.

Iseabail didn't know if it was true. Honestly, everything was moving too fast for her to follow everything. Five moments ago she had been certain that she would live out the rest of her life wedded to Hamish or someone much worse. And now…

She felt Reuben's thumb under her chin, tilting her face up to his. "Do you trust me?" he asked. "Will you obey me? We are treading in dangerous waters—"

"Yes." Indeed, her marriage vows would include that very promise.

"Then let us go," he said. He winked at her. "It will be a grand adventure!"

It could be the death of them both, but his glee was infectious. She felt it stir the embers of hope inside her body. As if the fire he lit slowly rebuilt her core, fragment by burning fragment. It was hard to believe soot and ash could become anything substantial, but then she had never had Mr. Reuben Bates beside her promising her everything she could possibly want.

And somehow, she believed. Despite everything she knew, every disastrous encounter with her uncle, and the furious hate of Hamish and his men. Despite it all, she believed that Mr. Reuben Bates would make it all right.

"To freedom," she said. Then she looked at the countess. "Where are we going?"

"To see the Archbishop of Canterbury," the lady responded, while everyone in the room gasped in surprise. Was the lady truly so powerful as to be able to call on so august a personage?

Apparently so.

"Be sure, Iseabail," the countess said. "Once done, this cannot be undone."

She looked at Reuben. In some ways, he was a complete stranger, and yet she was about to chain herself to him for the rest of her life.

Was she crazy? Yes.

Was she desperate? Absolutely.

Was this the biggest gamble of her life? Of course.

And yet, with him, she believed.

"I'm positive."

CHAPTER SEVENTEEN

ONCE COMMITTED TO an action, there was no stopping the countess. Iseabail admired such bold determination as the lady demanded an audience with the archbishop. Privately, Iseabail didn't think it would work, but to her shock, they were admitted immediately. Apparently, even godly men indulged their curiosity, and the attack in Hyde Park was the first topic of conversation. The countess took that opening and spun it into a tale that ended in marriage.

Immediately.

She and Mr. Bates were wed that very moment. She carried no flowers, her parents were not there, and no one sang songs for their union. But the countess was there to help adjust her dress and hair. Sadie stood by her side and gifted her with her favorite fan. And at the last moment, Mr. Bates's aunt arrived with rings.

Iseabail spoke the words of the ceremony as she was directed. She watched in stunned awe as he slipped an exquisite emerald onto her finger. Then she lifted her face to his for his kiss. She expected a quick buss on the lips. They were standing before an archbishop, after all. But Mr. Bates—Reuben—was not one to be restrained by the presence of a cleric.

He took her mouth slowly, teasing her until she softened into him. Then he plunged inside once, twice, in a scorching penetration, before he pulled back just enough to look into her dazed eyes. "Soon, love," he whispered.

She blinked, abruptly coming back to herself. Good Lord, they were in the archbishop's private chapel. Had Reuben just bent her over his arm and... and... Good lord, her face was flaming. As was the archbishop's! And the damned man—her husband—gave her a wink as if they were in a tavern and she a serving maid.

She looked to the countess, who merely shrugged. The message was clear. Iseabail had made her choice, and now she had to live by it.

Iseabail had no problem with that. She thanked the archbishop, pressed a kiss to Sadie's cheek, and turned to where her husband was speaking to his aunt in a low, urgent tone.

"He's to bring his best fighters and come quiet. No need to make a fuss."

"He knows what he's about," his aunt answered. "But what about—"

He shook his head. "You were right. I've held on too tight."

She frowned at him. "I know I'm right, but what has that to do—"

"You're on your own now. All of you. All the businesses, all the family. I've been holding on too tight, and it's choking the life out of you."

She gaped at him. "Is that why you're going to Scotland? Because you couldn't let us be for a while? You could have gone to Cornwall and dipped your toes in the water instead."

He chuckled. "I could have." He reached out and grabbed Iseabail's hand, reeling her to his side. "I chose Scotland instead."

"Are you coming back?"

"'Course I am. A month, probably. Maybe a bit longer. And I'll have an accounting from all of you. Those that have mucked things up will be out. And then I'll give someone else a chance."

The woman shook her head. "You're right crazy, you are, but then, that's always been true. No grass grows beneath your feet, does it?"

"It'll grow in Scotland."

The lady snorted. "I'd love to see that, but that ain't yer way." She looked to Iseabail and pressed a kiss to her cheek. "Best wishes to you. You nabbed yourself a live one, you have, but I doubt you'll keep him. Best set your expectations low."

"Aunt Judy!" Outrage hardened his tone, but his aunt didn't seem to hear it.

"I give it three weeks," she said to Iseabail. "He'll get restless, and you'll make yourself miserable trying to hold on." She lifted up Iseabail's hand to flash the emerald in the late afternoon sunlight. "Still, you got a good bargain, I'd say. And there are worse things than an absent husband." She grunted as she turned back to her nephew. "Best get going before the sun sets. I hear there are highwaymen on the road north."

It was clearly a joke between nephew and aunt. He chuckled loudly and she bussed his cheek, and then he turned to her. "Best say your goodbyes. We're heading north immediately. I don't want Hamish and his men to beat us to your home."

She stared at him, her mind completely blanked. They were heading to Scotland? *Now?*

The countess joined them, her voice overloud in Iseabail's ear. "Smart decision," she said. "Get away from all this gossip here, manage things back home, then come back next Season and I'll throw you a ball. Show everyone what a hero and heroine look like, yes? That's the story I'll tell. The two of you off to right a horrible wrong. Come back here for your victory party."

Reuben grinned. "An excellent notion."

Was it? It sounded like they would just wander up to Scotland and clean up a dirty room. They were going to confront her murderous uncle, and the idea that she was headed north *today* made her choke.

Good God, was she going to be sick?

"Easy—" Reuben began, but it was Sadie who came to her rescue.

"There, there," her friend said as she drew her aside. Then she held Iseabail's frozen hands until the nausea passed.

"I don't know what's wrong with me," she murmured.

"Attacked, married, and now off to Scotland? What could possibly be wrong?"

"But I have wanted this. I proposed to him for just this reason!"

Sadie touched her cheek. "It still takes time to adjust. I was ready for my mother to pass. We all were, but I still cried when it happened."

Sadie's relationship with her mother had not been easy. Indeed, her mother had been a vicious shrew whom everyone despised, Sadie included. But the girl had stayed by her parent's side until the cruel word was finally spoken. And still it had taken a long time for the end to come.

She hugged her friend. "I don't know if I will ever see you again," she whispered.

"Ach, no," Sadie said, letting her Scottish brogue become thick. "I'll see ye fer the victory ball, and do' ye forget it."

But that was so far away, and in the meantime... she shuddered. "What have I done?" she whispered.

"What you had to," Sadie returned. "And you're strong enough to see it through."

Was she? She felt like the harshest word would make her shatter right now. But before she could confess such a thing, her new husband interrupted. He came to them carefully, but his words were clear enough.

"It's time, Iseabail. Say your goodbyes."

She nodded. "This is what I wanted," she whispered to herself. Sadie heard it and nodded, her expression bracing. So, too, did her husband, and his expression tightened. It wasn't an angry expression, but neither was it kind.

"Come along," he said, his voice brusque.

She obeyed because she knew he was right. One last hug for Sadie and the countess, and then she joined her husband at a rented carriage. He handed her in, then followed, his expression serious and distracted. A moment later, the carriage started moving and she realized that she was alone with her husband.

Alone was scary. He was her husband now, and by rights could do anything he wanted to her. She sat in her seat, her hands folded in her lap while fears compounded inside her. What would she say to him? What was his plan? What would he do to her?

It was with a rude kind of shock that she realized he intended nothing whatsoever. He sat across from her with his brows furrowed as he ticked off things on his fingers as if committing them to memory. He never said his words out loud. Indeed, she wouldn't have known he was thinking so hard if she hadn't seen his lips moving. There was no sound, but his concentration was fierce.

She let him be. God knew she hated it when someone interrupted her thoughts. But a few minutes later her gaze went to the window, and she saw just how quickly they were traveling out of the city.

"I don't have any bags," she murmured. She looked down at her lovely green gown. As a wedding dress, she could have done much worse. "Am I to wear this all the way to Scotland?"

His head jerked up with a frown. "What? No, of course not. My men will bring your things to the inn tonight."

Oh. Did she dare ask him where they would sleep tonight? Normally, she would boldly demand answers. Indeed, the urge to do so was strong inside her, but every time she started to open her mouth, she heard her mother's voice in her head urging caution.

A man is different in private. Be careful how you upset him.

She knew it was true, and so she stuffed down the urge to ask questions. She suppressed her need to manage her own future, and she prayed that she had not made a bad choice today.

And the miles rolled by.

London slipped away though it took nearly two hours to leave it fully behind. The sun dropped in the sky, and she regretted having nothing to pass the time. Sleep would not come, even though boredom stalked her. All she could do was sit and fret while she watched her new husband frown as he apparently worked through a torturous knot of thoughts.

It was several hours before there was a sound inside the carriage. And when it came, it wasn't by her choice at all.

Her stomach growled.

His head shot up and she flinched backwards in alarm. It was too big a reaction. He'd only looked up, but such was the state of her nerves that she nearly bolted from the carriage.

"Are you hungry?" he asked. His tone was cordial, but he was frowning at her.

She pressed a hand to her belly. "Only if you are, my lord."

His frown turned into a scowl. "Why are you, 'my lording' me? If you're hungry, just say so."

Lord, she was an idiot. She had no idea why the "my lord" had slipped out. Her uncle liked it when people referred to him as such even though he had no right to the honorific. She was just nervous.

"Well?" he pressed, his tone even more foul.

"Sir?"

He bit his lip and looked unexpectedly awkward. "My mind is hither and yon. I have so many thoughts and no focus. And I can't seem to remember the most basic things. So please, my wife, if you are hungry, you must say so. Then I will see to your refreshment."

She swallowed. "I would enjoy some food." In truth, she wasn't sure she could eat it. Her nerves were in such a state. And yet that seemed to be the answer he was waiting for. He nodded as he looked about them.

"Where are we?" he asked.

She had no idea.

When she didn't answer, he rubbed a hand over his face. "How long have we been traveling?"

"Three hours?" She didn't really know. Time had no true meaning when one was sitting in a carriage with nothing to do but fret.

"Don't ask me. Do you know the time or not?"

She winced. "I do not." She had no watch.

He patted his pockets. "I gave my watch to Jonathan. He has no sense of time." He looked out the window. "You know we must consummate this marriage tonight."

She jolted. To speak so boldly of this made her breath freeze in her chest.

"If you are terrified of me now, how will we ever make this work?"

She had no answer. She didn't know what to do. What did he want?

His gaze returned to her face, and he made an effort to soften his expression. His lips even curved into a semblance of a smile. "I am usually more adept at things, but I have thrown myself into this endeavor with so much speed that I can scarce believe it."

He felt as if they had moved quickly? "I feel the same," she said. Her words were deliberate. A testing of whether he wanted conversation or just an ear.

He nodded. "I would think so. Did you have a plan for after the vows? For how we would gain your dowry?"

She shook her head. "I thought you were the man of war."

His grin was lopsided but still charming. "Not war," he said. "That is for commanders with hundreds of men fighting in lines against an enemy of similar size. I was raised in the London battleground with fisticuffs in the streets and knives in the dark." When she stared at him without comment, he shrugged. "It is fighting, I suppose, but of a different kind."

"It is the kind that is needed, I think." Indeed, it was a primary reason why she chose him.

"Perhaps we should discuss what I have already worked out."

She nodded. That sounded like an excellent idea.

He looked out the window again, pressing his nose to the pane as he turned left and right. "I think I know where we are. There is an inn an hour or so north of here. I thought we would rest there and wait for my men to join us." He looked to her.

"Can your stomach wait until then?"

"Of course, I can. It is only anxiety that makes it rumble so."

"I do not want you to be anxious around me." He opened both his hands. "You are safe with me. I cannot promise what will happen in Scotland, but you have nothing to fear from me."

Except the consummation of their marriage tonight.

"You do not seem convinced."

She swallowed. "I married you of my own free will. Whatever is to come, it was my choice."

"Damned by faint praise. I chose you as well. Surely you know that I protect what is mine."

She looked at her hands. "I know that people are different in private than they are in public." She squeezed her fingers tightly together as she met his gaze. "We need to learn about one another in private." She bit her lip. "You said your thoughts are hither and yon. Would it help to share them with me?"

"They are things I must remember about people you haven't even met, except for my aunt. You know her."

"I have a good memory," she said. "Perhaps if you told me?"

He looked doubtful, but then gave in with a shrug.

"You could hardly be worse than I am right now." He took a breath. "Very well, wife, let us test each other's memory, shall we?"

A game, then. It was how her mother had taught her with rhymes and quizzes, letters scratched in the dirt, and water stroked onto rock that faded in the sun. She could read and write as well, but paper and ink were dear, and so she learned to memorize lists as if they were written out before her in black and white.

She squared her shoulders and faced him. "I will surprise you," she vowed.

"That would not be the first time," he answered. "First, I must tell my brother to measure the bread loaves. I believe the baker is shorting him. Next, my aunt mentioned something strange about one of her new girls…"

The list trailed on, one after the other in no discernable order, while Iseabail set her memory to the task. And that worked very well indeed…for a time.

CHAPTER EIGHTEEN

REUBEN KNEW HE had a good memory. What a joy to discover that Iseabail's was excellent. No matter what he said to her, she remembered it. And when he tried to trick her, she challenged him. Carefully at first, because she was a cautious woman, but then with increasing strength. Especially once he demonstrated that he was pleased when she disagreed with him.

And what a revelation that was for them both. The first time she said, "No, that is wrong," he experienced such a surge of joy that he giggled. It was not a manly sound, but it was an honest one and she read it as such.

"You *want* me to catch you," she stated as she leaned forward. "You like it when I am as clever as you."

He shook his head. "I like it when you are cleverer than I." He blew out a breath. "I cannot do everything, and so few people can match me."

She did not comment except to lower her gaze as if she were a demure miss. But he had long since deduced that her quiet demeanor was to encourage people to underestimate her. He was not that foolish.

"When we arrive at the inn, I shall call for ink and paper. I would like you to write all of that down in a letter to my solicitor. He will see that everyone is told what I want."

"So I am to become your secretary?" It was not spoken in insult, but as simple question. She was trying to understand what her role in their marriage was.

"If you would like that, I should be grateful. I find my penmanship is not enough to garner respect."

"Only a fool judges a man solely on his penmanship."

And yet, so many solicitors believed him to be a fool merely because his letters appeared as so much chicken scratch. "And now," he said, "I should like to hear all about your home. What does your uncle do every day? How many men does he have and what do they do? I need to understand everything I can about your home, and then you can test my memory."

Information was the first task in any endeavor, and so he pressed her for the tiniest details of life at her castle. It worked his memory hard, especially since he had little knowledge of how a castle functioned. He viewed it as a tiny upright city with the bakery in one corner, the livery in another. A tower for the classroom, another for the armory, and two large rooms as taverns. It boggled his mind as he imagined all these workers crammed together like a rookery and yet she talked about fresh air, moments when there was not a soul around for miles, and how everything had to be created by themselves, as there was little that could be bought without great expense and time.

It was as though she talked of a fantasy place, and yet he hung on her every word. Indeed, he pressed her always for more. More stories, more memories, more snippets of life in Scotland. And the more she spoke, the more she relaxed. No longer did she flinch every time he moved abruptly. Indeed, she smiled a few times, especially when she spoke of her parents.

And so he kept her talking even when they stopped at the inn. He plied her with wine and hearty fare while she spilled tales of pigs birthing piglets into her hands and men bringing home stags for the women to clean and cook. Soon they settled in chairs by a good fire, and he sat with rapt attention while she curled her feet up beneath her skirts and shared yet another tale.

She was a fine storyteller, and he could listen to her tales throughout the night. He noted that she avoided all stories about witchcraft, and he would need to press her on that soon. But in the meantime, he listened to her voice as her words thickened with her accent, and he tried to imagine himself living among her people.

All he could see in his mind's eye was her as a child, running free in the sun. Her as a young woman working as midwife and healer. Her as a grown woman watching everything while planning her escape.

She dazzled him, and he could not wait to take her to bed.

Unfortunately, that would not come until after he spoke with his men. They had arrived a few moments before. He had seen and heard them through the window onto the courtyard. So he took his lady's hand and squeezed it.

"I must speak to my men. I have asked the innkeeper to bring you paper and ink, and his daughter will act as maid for you tonight. Are you still able to remember the things I asked you to write this afternoon?"

Her cheeks were flushed with pink, and her lips teased him with their darker color, but her eyes were no less bright as she laughed. "I remember everything," she said with an expansive flick of her hand. It was not a large movement for most people, but for her it was as loud as a shout.

The wine had done its work, and she would welcome him this night. Or so he hoped. He lifted her hand to his lips, pressing a kiss first on the back of her hand, and then more slowly into her palm. She smiled when he did that, her eyes sparking with interest, and so he let his tongue carve a small circle there before he slid up to her wrist.

Her brows rose, the skin above her bodice flushed, and—

Thunk, thunk.

That could only be Jonathan. He used his fist for everything, including a simple door. He sighed.

"I must go, but I'll meet you in our chamber soon."

She bit her lip and nodded, and he could not resist. He stretched forward and caught her mouth with his. He tasted the wine on her lips and the sharp onion from dinner. He smelled the citrus perfume she used and felt the ease with which she fell into his kiss. And just as he was thrusting inside her mouth—

Thunk, thunk, thunk!

He growled low in his throat. Especially as the sound was followed by Jonathan's heavy tones.

"Reuben! We're nigh to fainting with hunger. Are you deaf or dead?"

He broke the kiss, stomped to the door, and hauled it open. "An' what need do you have to lay your fist down to interrupt me and my lady wife?"

"What lady wife—" Jonathan cut off his words as he sighted her sitting there all flushed and pretty. Then he looked back at Reuben who made sure to glower as dark as any husband interrupted on his wedding night would. "Is that Lady Rebecca?"

Oh, damnation. As far as his men knew, nothing had changed since this morning when his determination to wed Lady Rebecca was well-known. He cursed under his breath, then quickly amended his tone.

"My darling," he said in as courtly a manner as he could manage. "May I make known to you Jonathan Armstrong?"

"I remember him," Iseabail said as she stood with graceful ease. "He was with you when you rescued me from the highwaymen."

"Blimey," Jonathan breathed. "You married the maid?"

"I married Miss Iseabail Spalding, ward and niece to Baron Bain."

"Oh! The one with the dowry."

Trust Jonathan to think of the money first. Though in the man's defense, that's what Reuben himself had taught.

Iseabail laughed, a cascade of notes that likely would not be so pretty without the wine she'd consumed. "I am the one with the dowry, assuming you and your men can wrest it from my uncle's cold, dead hands."

Jonathan sobered, his gaze hopping between Iseabail's

amused expression and Reuben's colder one. "Truth? Cold, *dead* hands?"

Reuben did not have a ready answer. He knew his wife believed that the only way to gain her coins was to kill her uncle. But that was a dark business, and he was unsure that killing a woman's kin was the best way to begin a marriage no matter what the bastard had done.

"I'll speak to you in a minute," he said. "Get some food in the main room. We're resting here for the night."

Jonathan's expression lightening into a grin. "Your wedding night, yes?"

Oh, damn. The boys would want to celebrate that. That was the custom after all. "It was a special situation," he began, but the man's grin had widened.

"Then it's up to us to see you get a proper party."

"There isn't any need."

"Aw, no trouble. No trouble at all."

He looked to Iseabail, but she clearly didn't understand what was going on. And it would only help his case if there were a rowdy bunch of men to testify that she was well and truly bedded. This was all part and parcel of getting married.

"She's not even got a maid with her," he said in an undertone. "Have your fun downstairs. I'll pay for the drink." He winced at the cost to his purse, not to mention the delay in leaving tomorrow. "But don't—"

"I'll see that it stays proper," Jonathan said. Then with a formal bow to Iseabail, he took his leave.

He should go after the man. He should make things clear about what was and was not acceptable, but as soon as he turned to Iseabail, the innkeeper scratched at the door.

"Begging yer pardon, sir, but I've got ink and quill fer you. There's a desk there with paper. And when it's done, I'll be able to set it in the mail for you."

"Very good," Iseabail said as she waved for the writing desk to be set in the corner of the room. "Put it all there. It won't take me more than a few minutes."

Reuben hesitated, torn between staying by her side and speaking with his men. Normally, he would never worry about a woman when there was men's work to be done. But he had never been married before, and this was his wife.

"Iseabail—"

She waved him away. "Don't worry. I remember everything."

He had no doubt. Well, not a lot of doubt. "I'll read it over before we send it."

"Of course." She smiled sweetly at him. "See to your men."

She was right. She had her task, and he had his. He could not live the rest of his life forever hovering over her. "Are you sure?" The question wasn't for her but for himself. He did not want to leave her.

"I'm sure." She smiled. "I will await you in the bedroom."

His body tightened at the mere mention of it. And perhaps hers did, too? It was so hard to tell. Were her cheeks rosy from drink or desire? Did she ache for him until she was flushed and bothered? Or was it merely hot near the fire?

He couldn't tell and he didn't have the time to figure it out. The faster he saw to his men, the quicker he could return to her. And so he gave her a formal bow and left.

Two hours later, he at last climbed the steps to their bedroom. The innkeeper's daughter had told him a half hour before milady awaited him. His men had roared their approval and toasted him—several more times—before he could leave them to their revelry. And now he was rosy with drink and desperate to see his woman.

If nothing else, tonight would see his wife well and truly bedded.

Or so he thought until he pushed open the door and found the chamber warm, scented with perfume, and completely empty.

CHAPTER NINETEEN

I SEABAIL SET HER bare feet in the stream and shivered at the chill bite to her toes. The water splashed up around her ankles, burbled against the rocks, and did nothing to soothe away the anxiety knotting her stomach.

She tried to do as her mother had taught her. She listened for the hoot of an owl or the scurry of mice in the underbrush. She focused on the wind against her cheeks and the squish of mud between her toes. All these things were of nature, and they were the basis of witchcraft. At least it was the basis of her mother's witchcraft. A woman connected to these things—air, water, soil, and fire. She had no flint to make a flame, but she tried to touch the spark of life in all the living creatures around her. And if not them, then she felt her own lifeforce. The beat of her heart, the heat of her breath, and the memory of a bonfire at Hogmanay.

From these things, her mother would cast spells that bless the land or aid in an easy birth. She would try to heal the sick or ease the passing of those who could not be saved. And if she failed in all of that, at least her whispers brought hope and peace to many who had nothing else to believe.

Or so she had told Iseabail, and so her daughter had believed. Until tonight.

Tonight, when the connection to earth and all the life within meant absolutely nothing to her. When no matter how she tried, she could not quiet her heart or still her thoughts. The wine had helped dull the panic inside her for a bit, but as the alcohol wore off, her fears returned a thousand-fold. So she had escaped out into the night to find peace. And though she had felt gifted to find this corner of babbling brook, she found no solace here.

So she soaked her feet and waited, pretending that an answer would eventually come to her. Unfortunately, her heart did not believe it.

She heard him coming long before he found her. No one else had that light step that was both heavy enough to be a man and yet quick enough to be a clever woman. No doubt he had seen the window open and the sturdy tree knocking on the panes, just as she had. And so he had followed her before she was ready for him to find her.

She dropped her head onto her knees and prayed for wisdom, for comfort, for anything that would calm the fears that were so familiar they had become a part of her blood.

"Iseabail? Is that you? Are you hurt?"

There was panic in his voice that shot her with guilt. She should have left a note.

"I'm fine," she said. "I needed to get outside for a bit."

"In the middle of the night?" He quickly crossed to her side, but hesitated before touching her. "You cannot run off like that. Not until things are settled with your uncle."

Part of her wanted to scream at him that she was not his to command, but of course she was. She was his wife now and had sworn to obey him. So she ducked her head and answered as demurely as she could manage.

"Of course, m—sir. I shall return immediately." She pulled her feet from the stream and began to stand.

He cursed under his breath, the words so graphic that she was momentarily shocked. And in her moment of stillness, he grabbed her elbow and pulled her all the way upright.

"What have I done to make you so afraid of me?" he snapped.

Her brows rose. How could she answer such an aggressive question?

He seemed to recognize the comedy in his question. He released her arm and stepped back, but his frustration didn't ease. He dropped his hands on his hips and stared at her. "I should like to play a game with you."

She frowned, not trusting his seeming change of topic. "A game?"

"I will ask you some questions and have you answer everything with total honesty. If you are angry, you should say so. If you want to curse, please blister the air. If you want to—"

"Have a simple conversation, then perhaps we could start with that?" Only a man would think that he could get better answers from a game than a discussion.

He frowned, his lips pursing as he no doubt reworked her words in his head. "You want to converse?"

"That is the usual way of things, is it not?"

"But I have been trying to get you to do just that, and you have trembled and flinched in my presence as if I am a terrible monster. And I am not!"

It would seem she'd married a man who valued plain speaking. He certainly did in public, but now she knew he wanted that in private as well. Very well. She began by imitating his pose. She stood with her feet apart and her hands on her hips. "Shall we say that what is sauce for the goose is sauce for the gander as well?"

He canted his head as he looked at her stance. "What are you saying?"

"That if you want plain speaking, then so do I. You asked me what you have done to turn me timid. You have taken control of everything without a word of explanation and a great deal of angry looks. What am I to think?"

"Exactly what I told you! My thoughts are all akimbo and I am having difficulty sorting through everything. I did not expect to get married this morning. Nor was it my plan to harry off to Scotland to confront your nefarious uncle!"

"You are in a foul mood because of that?"

"Of course!"

"I did not expect to get attacked this morning or to get married this afternoon. Neither did I think I would ever return to Scotland, much less today."

He took a breath. One clearly meant to calm himself, but it seemed to make him more frustrated. "Well, of course you're upset! And it's no wonder you ran out our window. From what I gather, you ran across Scotland, too. You're a runner, and I should have realized that!"

She stared at him. He appeared angry. In fact, his hand waved before her face as if he were batting away thoughts. But she couldn't reconcile his kind words with his furious movements. So she waited, doing her best to appear calm while he either settled down or became more agitated. Given that she felt no real threat from him, she was beginning to enjoy watching him sort through his thoughts. Especially when he glowered at the tree over her shoulder.

"You are a lady," he said, "and I am a coarse ruffian. I have no idea how to make you comfortable." He shrugged. "I thought the wine would be enough."

She shrugged. "I have always been able to handle my drink."

He nodded. "That is a useful talent, but it does not help me at all."

No, it would not. She waited for him to come to the obvious conclusion. Indeed, she had stated it out loud to him. She needed to have a conversation with him, but he just stood there with his arms on his hips. Was he truly this dense?

"Why not ask me what I want?"

"Why not tell me what you want?"

"A conversation."

"So converse!"

She stared at him a moment before she realized the truth of her own hypocrisy. She had waited for him to initiate the discussions, to give her the answers to her questions, but when had she taken the initiative and demanded what she wanted? Or even asked politely for it?

She felt her cheeks heat as her hands dropped from her hips. "I have never been allowed to ask men directly for what I want."

"You asked me to marry you."

Her cheeks heated to flame. "I was desperate."

"So be desperate now." He touched her arms. "Iseabail, what do you need from me?"

"What are you plans for when we reach Scotland? How will you…" She swallowed, but forced herself to say the word. "How will you kill my uncle?"

"I don't know them yet. And I don't know that I will."

"But you must!"

"I must defeat him. It is a grave thing to kill a man, even an evil one."

She nodded. "Will you tell me your plans when you make them?"

"You will help me make them. I cannot do it without you."

Oh. Good. "Then plan for me to kill my uncle. You need not do it." She said the words—and she meant them—but they also felt like a lie. She had never killed before, not even by accident. Unless Albie had died from the wound she gave him in Hyde Park.

"That is a discussion for tomorrow. For tonight, tell me what else you are thinking."

She wasn't thinking about anything else. It was more that she was feeling anxiety about how they must consummate their marriage tonight. But she couldn't talk about that yet. Instead, she reached for the stupidest question.

"I finished your letter. Did you read it? Shall we send it?"

"I did not see it. I was too concerned with where you had gone. But I will look at it in the morning."

"Oh. Good. That makes sense."

Now he was the one rocking back on a heel, his mouth curving at the corners. Was he laughing at her? It very much looked like it, but not in a mean way. Indeed, he seemed to be as amused as she had been a few moments before.

"Are you, perhaps, wondering about our wedding night?"

She swallowed and looked at her hands. "I am, of course, at your disposal—"

"If you say *my lord,* I shall be very cross with you."

"Sir?"

"Worse."

He was teasing her, his tone growing lighter with every word.

"I could call you Mr. Bates."

"That's my father."

She grinned. "My most devoted husband?"

He snorted. "Reuben. We are married now. I began using Iseabail the moment those bastards attacked."

Did he? She didn't remember. But the thought warmed her. It established an intimacy between them that was appropriate to engaged couples. Engaged couples who were now married.

"Reuben," she said, trying out his name.

He smiled. Apparently, he liked the sound of his name on her tongue. "Yes?"

"Must we…um…consummate things tonight?"

"I think it would be best. Do you wish to wait?"

What a question! If only she had an answer. She had always been one to get something over with. If it was inevitable or necessary, she took a deep breath and did what had to be done. But that was hardly the way to approach intimacy. Even she knew that. And yet, the idea of finally experiencing something that so many others spoke of, whispered about, or even praised…well, that was something she very much wanted right now.

After all, who knew what was to come in Scotland? For one night, she would like to know what it meant to be a full woman.

"Iseabail, we don't have—"

"I think my uncle will kill you," she blurted. Then she gasped and covered her mouth. Whatever had possessed her to say that?

His eyes widened, then he gently pulled her hands down. "I

am very good at staying alive," he said.

She nodded. She was sure of it. And yet…

"You think he will win anyway?"

"And he will marry me to someone awful, and I will try to kill him and fail. Because what other choice do I have? And then…" She closed her eyes as she tried to blot out the one fear she had lived with nearly her entire life. "I know so many ways to kill myself. I have thought of them all. A small knife, a sharp nail, a rope. So many ways."

"Good God," he murmured as he drew her into his arms. "What you have endured."

She shook in his arms. These were not the fears that were uppermost in her mind, and yet these were the ones that came out at the oddest of times. In the middle of tea with Sadie, out on a walk on a pleasant afternoon, or now when faced with her new husband on their wedding night. She tried to choke them down, but they always resurfaced at the most unexpected times.

He held her until she stopped shaking, until she could catch her breath and shove down the panic that choked her. And then he pressed a kiss to her forehead.

"If you put your shoes back on, we can take a walk. We'll see where this stream goes, and I shall tell you a story about myself. We will get to know one another as husband and wife."

That wasn't what people usually thought of when discussing husbands and wives, but she was grateful for the offer. She nodded and turned to get her shoes. Her feet had gotten muddy, so she sat on a rock as she rinsed the dirt away. And then, when she was about to put her shoes on, he knelt beside her.

"Allow me," he said.

He shook out his handkerchief and used it to wipe the wet away. His hands were large where they cradled her feet, his fingers strong as he massaged as much as he dried. And when the water was gone, his touch grew gentle. He caressed her foot, stroking gently around her ankle and along her instep. He touched her toes playfully and teased the callouses along her heel.

"Even your feet are ladylike."

She peered down at her knobby ankle and painfully high arch. So many nights her feet had ached from a night spent with a laboring mother or an ill child. She had never thought of them as anything but unequal to the task of her days. "How much ale did you drink?"

He laughed, the sound filling the night with warmth. "Your feet are clean, and the shape pleasing. Your bones are straight, the arch high, and I can feel the strength in them." He looked up at her. "You told me how the castle functions, who does what and on what schedule."

She nodded.

"I'll wager you have performed every task, attempted every skill, and have even taught others."

"Of course, I have. My mother always kept me busy. When I was a child, I thought it was because she hated me. Why did I have to gather eggs or wash laundry? There were others more suited to the task."

"And now that you are grown?"

"She wanted our people to know me as one of them. I worked alongside them. I grew up with their children. I could not have escaped if I didn't have their help."

He smiled. "So your people love you?"

She nodded. "The women do, I think. The men are afraid. My uncle can be cruel to those who don't obey."

He pressed a kiss to the top of her feet. It was a reverent gesture and she blushed to see it. He was treating her like a princess, and she had never seen herself as such. But she couldn't deny the appeal, especially as he slipped her shoe onto her foot.

"My childhood was different than yours, and yet similar in that. My mother set my hand to everything at home, and then my father put me to work with everyone he knew. He said it was because I was too expensive to feed." He grinned up at her. "I did eat everything I could find."

"Most boys do."

"But now I see the wisdom in what I learned."

"Which was what?"

"Every business, every task. I learned how shoes are made by living for a season with my father's cousin, the shoemaker. I protected my uncle's fruit cart from thieves during the summer. I spun yarn in the winter with my mother, and even made soap with the nuns."

"The nuns had a hand with you?"

He nodded. "When my mother was sick one winter, we all stayed with the nuns. That is where I learned to read."

"From one winter with the nuns?"

He nodded. "I had already figured out the letters, some words, and the numbers." He winked at her. "Numbers are important for money."

"Certainly."

"But putting the words together into stories fired my imagination. And the Bible has plenty of stories."

She gaped at him. She had known he was clever, but this was something beyond. She had spent many winters teaching children to read with mixed results. Most had little interest, some had no ability, but there were a few whose minds caught fire with learning. Those were the special ones, the smart ones, the ones she sent away to find better schooling. At night when she despaired of her future, she thought of the little ones she had saved merely by sending them to relations in other clans. Ones who had educated people among them. Those children had a future even when she did not.

"If you had been born in my clan, I would have sent you to Edinburgh to study. And I would dream about your future."

He touched her chin. "When we are in charge of your clan, we will bring the tutors to us, and they will teach all our little ones."

That was the first she thought of anything beyond the end to her uncle. Never before had she imagined that she could be a true mistress of their clan with a say in how the castle was run, who could come, and who might teach their children. Certainly, she had pretended things as a child, but her mother had silenced her the moment she spoke of when she might be in charge. "Your uncle will never allow it." And so, she had given up dreaming the day she understood her uncle was a monster.

He must have seen the shock on her face. He must have realized how her mind was spinning at the possibility of a real future. Because while she was reeling from the thoughts he put in her head, he cupped her face and whispered words that she never thought a man would say, much less believe.

"I can make it happen. You only have to tell me what you want."

CHAPTER TWENTY

WHAT A BOLD thing to tell any woman. *I can give you whatever you want.* It was a ridiculous statement, but Reuben didn't care. Iseabail needed reassurance, and he was the man who would do it. Especially since he didn't think his promise was unreasonable.

With her uncle brought to heel, the two of them could re-make her clan into whatever fit best. Education for the young was the least of the possibilities.

So he pulled her up to a stand, tucked her elbow into the crook of his arm, and began to meander as if this were a sunny afternoon in Hyde Park. Perhaps the continuation of the one this afternoon that had been so horribly interrupted.

"Take a breath of that air," he said. He took a loud inhale relishing the sweetness of it all. "Not a speck of coal in it."

"In Scotland, the air is so clear, I swear we can see halfway around the world."

He wanted to see that. Indeed, he was itching to stand at the top of his castle and spread his arms wide as if he embraced the whole world. Especially if he had her and his son standing right next to him.

"Remember how I said I watched a fruit cart? To protect it from thieves?"

"You must have been very young."

"So were the thieves."

She tilted her head to listen more closely. Better yet, the stiffness in her body eased as they walked.

"Every day, young children would come to the cart with dirty faces and empty bellies. Pitiful, sad creatures or quick-fingered little ones who ran faster than I ever could. I kept them away as best as I could, but there were always more. I would catch the littlest ones, but it broke my heart to take their only food away. Sometimes, I would let them have an old apple or a mushed one that would never sell. But as hungry as they were, they never ate it."

"What? Whyever not?"

"Because they had to give their prize to an older boy, and he in turn gave it to an older one, all the way up the line until a very large man named Gill had it." He paused to watch her. Were there thieving rings in Scotland? He was certain they existed in every major city, but apparently not in her corner of the world.

"I don't understand."

"He was the man who ran the children. He taught them to thieve and bring him the goods. He prostituted the girls, taught the boys to pickpocket or worse, depending on their inclination. And the youngest ones begged. In return, he gave them a miserable place to sleep in the worst of the rookeries, fed them from his leftovers, and gave them a sad bit of protection from other predators."

"That's horrible."

"I thought so, too."

He had her attention now. Her steps had slowed, and she turned her face to him. They were strolling beneath trees now, so there was a great deal of shadow despite the three-quarter moon.

"I guess you found a solution," she said.

"I did." He spoke with pride. "It was my first good win, and it set the course of my life." He stayed silent after that, just to be sure he had her caught. A good storyteller knew when to pause for his audience to prod him forward.

"You must tell me the rest," she cried. "How could you—still a boy—stop a whole ring of thieves?"

"I became one of them."

"What?"

"I pretended to be lost and alone. I waited, shivering, in a place I knew he traveled."

"You let yourself be caught by Gill?"

"I did. He was very kind at first, giving me food and a warm coat."

"That's how he gets them to trust him."

"Yes."

"And then once he brought me to his place, I figured out who was in charge, who was mean, and who was just scared."

"But you were a boy yourself."

"I was twelve, but I knew how to look even younger. Plus, I was scrawny."

She shook her head. "I cannot imagine it."

"I didn't fill out until I began working at the docks."

She shook her head. "Such a life you've led."

"No more fantastic than what you've done. I couldn't deliver a baby if you dropped one in my hands. You've managed it since you were the same age."

She smiled. "I suppose everyone's life seems normal until they talk with someone else." She squeezed his arm. "Don't keep me in suspense. What did you do once you were trapped inside with this terrible Gill?"

"That's the thing. I wasn't trapped inside. We were sent to thieve, remember? But he had a system. Bigger boys disciplined the smaller ones, but there's always one who will break. I worked with the weakest of the supervisors." He winked at her. "That's what Gill called them. His supervisors. As if they were more than brutes beating up on weaker children."

"What did you convince him to do?"

"His name was George. The older boys teased him about being Mad George because of the king and some other nonsense I can't remember. It doesn't really matter what they said, only that it made him furious. Then once he became angry, they pointed him at some drunken sot and told him to take out his fury on them."

"My mother taught me to keep my emotions hidden because feelings are the easiest way to manipulate a person."

"Your mother was right." And he was learning more about why she kept herself so quiet, so cut apart from the others, even her friends.

"So what did you do to this not-mad George?"

"I didn't do anything!" He pretended to be insulted. "I merely explained what they were doing to him. And I convinced him he could be his own boss."

"What? You mean set up his own thieving ring?"

"Good God, no. He wasn't smart enough for that."

"Then what?"

"With his help, I gathered all the little ones and the others that I could trust. There were so many of us and only a few of them." He grinned. "We attacked the ones who were mean, and I took them all to the nuns." He grinned. "They took us all in, and with George as their leader, they grew up safely."

"All of them? Truly?"

He shrugged. There were always a few who refused to learn. "Most of them. The nuns praised me all over the place. Said I was the cleverest boy ever and that surely, I had a spot in heaven reserved for me." He laughed when he said it. If God weighed everything he had done in his life—the good and the bad—he wasn't sure where his soul would come out. "It helped that I checked in on them. Georgie and I knew how to keep them in line and away from Gill."

"But surely the man was furious with what you'd done. Didn't he try to get revenge?"

"The little ones were out of reach. The nuns kept them close with Georgie's help."

"And what about you?"

He grinned. "They knew where I was. Figured out I was the

boy who protected my uncle's fruit cart." He grinned. "But when they came, we were ready for them."

"We?"

"Me and some older boys, plus my uncle's cousin and his friends."

She swallowed. "How bad was it?"

He chuckled. "What do you mean? It was—"

"Glorious? Bloody good fun?"

Well, yes, that's how he usually described it. But that was the braggadocio of a boy. Thinking back, he'd also been terrified. He'd seen blood gushing from a skull for the first time. He hadn't been seriously hurt, but some of the others had. Certainly, Gill's boys had, and the old bastard himself had been killed. It was the only possible fate for a man like that, or so his aunt had said.

"It was necessary," he finally said. "And we saved over a dozen children who have gone on to live happy lives." Most of them at least.

She nodded. "What happened to Gill's boys? Did they live good lives?"

"No. I don't know exactly, but…" He remembered all that blood. "No." And he realized now as he had not then, that the people who fought for Gill had been children. Little boys and a few girls who never had a chance. At least one had died that night. Meanwhile, he turned her to face him. "So you understand battle?"

"I have seen the results. Everything from a taproom brawl to a clan skirmish. And I have heard all my life about those who died in Culloden. Good men who should not have been butchered like that."

He nodded. "And yet you want me to kill your uncle."

She looked past his shoulder into the shadows. "I am a woman who has stitched wounds, set bones, and comforted widows and orphans. I have held a man's hand as he died because he punched the wrong man." Her gaze turned to him. "And yes, I want you to kill my uncle. Or allow me to do it myself."

He felt strength in her statement. He had assumed she was an angry child or a beautiful debutante who had no idea what she was asking. That image was undercut by the way she fought in Hyde Park, but he had still clung to it. He liked thinking of her as pure or at least innocent.

But he couldn't cling to that mirage any longer. "You've thought about this for a long time?"

"Every day and every night since my mother disappeared."

"How long ago was that?"

"Nearly a decade. I had just turned sixteen."

There was more to the story. Pain echoed through her words. Perhaps he was being cowardly, but he didn't want to darken his wedding night with those memories. Instead, he cupped her cheek. "What terrible things you have survived. I am in awe."

She shrugged. "I endured. You saved a dozen street boys and girls from a monster."

He caressed down her jawline to stroke her neck. "I wanted you to know me better. Instead, I see you more clearly." He let his fingertips trail across her collarbone. "But this is not a night for ugly thoughts. Do you think you could stand to rest beside me and not be afraid?"

"I wanted a fearsome husband. It would be silly if I despised you for it."

"I wanted an aristocrat for a wife, and I chose a queen in all her fierce beauty." He angled her face to match his. "I want to make her mine as surely as I want my next breath."

Her expression turned wistful, as if she couldn't possibly believe what he said. But her nostrils flared as well, and there was a hitch to her breath that told him she was not sleepy.

He drew her face closer, he let their breath mingle, and she knew he intended to kiss her. Still, he waited long enough for her to deny him. He would not force her, even on their wedding night. Instead, she surprised him by leaning in, by lifting onto her toes, and by pressing her mouth to his.

Hunger burned in his blood. The spark had been lit long ago, but now it roared in his ears and beat in his cock. As she stroked across his mouth with her tongue, he let his hands slide from her neck to her bodice. He shaped her breast with his hand and felt her nipple pebble beneath his palm.

His other hand cradled the back of her head, supporting her while she explored his mouth with her tongue. It was torture to feel her tentative probes and not take over. It was exquisite delight to feel her twist her tongue around his.

He could not hold out much longer. Not with her breath catching and his blood thrumming with hunger. He pinched her nipple through the thin fabric of her gown and felt her entire body tighten against his. But it was the way her head fell back from his that was his undoing. Her head rested in his palm, her chest lifted in invitation, all while the moonlight bathed her skin in an ethereal glow.

Her eyes fluttered open. Her gaze caught and held his as surely as any goddess entrapped a mortal man. Then she set her hands on his chest. He wore nothing over his torso but a fine lawn shirt, and to his shock, she rubbed her nail across the nub of his nipple.

Lust burst through him. Need ripped away his restraint.

They were in shadow, alone in the middle of the night. No one was about, he was sure of it. And so while she rubbed her hands across his chest, he unbuttoned her dress from neck to hip. His fingers were clumsy, but what he couldn't manage with dexterity, he pulled apart with strength. Her gown slipped off her shoulders and down her arms.

He already knew she wore no undergarment. He'd felt the lack of stays when he began to caress her. But now he saw the truth of her in the moonlight.

High breasts, pointed nipples, and skin flushed from desire. And when the gown dropped to her ankles, he knew exactly where he would feast.

CHAPTER TWENTY-ONE

ISEABAIL WAS NO stranger to sexuality. She had birthed hundreds of babies from both animal and human mothers. She had seen the results of it, heard detailed accounts of it, and knew with clear understanding everything that was involved.

But she had never experienced anything herself. Her mother had seen to that when she was sixteen. No soul touched her for fear that her mother's witchcraft would strike them dead. That had suited her just fine in Scotland—for the most part—but the heart shriveled without touch. Her body longed and her mind imagined.

She had no idea why she had run from her marriage bed. She'd felt claustrophobic at the idea of being locked inside when all his men came banging at her door. It was the custom, she knew, to harass the newlywed couple, but she could not bear it.

And so she'd rushed outside where the air was clean, the water burbled, and he could find her. Out where the moon bathed everything in its purity. And here, she could let him touch her, caress her skin, and kiss her breasts.

But she didn't expect the power of his caress or that a single kiss would set her body on fire. The way he touched her was so different from anyone else. There was a reverence in his stroke, as if she were the most precious thing in the world to him. That couldn't possibly be true. Thanks to their discussions in the carriage, she had an idea now of the extent of his wealth. He had a hand in businesses throughout London. He had men and resources that dwarfed what her uncle commanded in Scotland. And yet when he touched her, she felt like she was the center of his whole world.

"Do you like this?" he whispered against her skin.

He had been kissing across her shoulder, licking her skin with tiny nips as he moved lower. The feel of it was so exquisite that she had to clutch his shoulders to keep upright.

"Yes," she gasped. He already knew she did, but she liked the way he smiled against her skin. And then he caught her nipple between his lips.

Lightning shot through her blood, followed by a thunderstorm of feeling when he began to suckle. She felt dizzy with the pleasure of it all.

So this was sex when it was good. And in case her mother's magic still lingered about her, she whispered the words. "I allow this. I *want* this."

He pulled back, his expression quizzical. She touched his face, marveling at the man she would spend the rest of her life with. "In case the magic needed me to say it."

His brows rose. "You were cursed?"

She shook her head. "Only those who would touch me against my will."

He grinned. "Then I am pleased."

His hands had not been idle as they spoke. He touched her breasts and her torso, spanning her waist with his two hands and using his thumbs to press in the crease between hip and thigh. The pressure felt good there. Hot and tingly. She wanted to feel him grip her there. She wanted…she wasn't sure what.

"I can take you back to our room. Your first time shouldn't be—"

"Here," she interrupted. "Outside with the moon and the water."

He nodded then shrugged out of his jacket. "As you wish."

He lay his jacket down to use as a bed, but she shook her

head. Kicking off her shoes, she walked naked to the stream. The water wasn't deep, but it was swift enough to cool her heated feet and to add to her heightened sensations. Though he stood on the bank in shadow, her body still felt his hands on her breasts, his mouth on her nipples, and his thumbs edging toward the juncture of her thighs. He had imprinted himself there, and she needed a moment to remember these feelings he engendered.

Then she turned back to him. "Will you join me in the water?" she asked.

"I'll join you anywhere you want," he returned as he shrugged out of his shirt. Then he quirked an eyebrow at her. "I'm going to Scotland, aren't I?"

She nodded, lightheaded with the joy of the moment. She watched in delight as he stripped out of his clothing. Soon he was as bare as her, but it wasn't until he stepped out of the shadows that she saw his true beauty.

Moonlight limned his body in silver, showing her the hard cut to his muscles. There was little fat on him, and so she marked the strength in his sinews as they bunched and released with his movements. She saw, too, the crisscross of old scars, some reflective in the light. She would ask about every one, but not at this moment.

Not when his cock stood up proudly between his corded thighs. When it looked too large to fit and yet so tempting to touch. She looked at it bob before him as he strode forward. And when he stepped into the brook to face her, she reached out her hand.

"May I?" she asked.

"Milady, I am yours to command."

He sounded so serious when he spoke, but when she looked into his eyes, she saw the merriment that danced there. His lips were curved as he smiled at her. And then he spread his arms wide.

"It has always been my dream to be worshiped by a queen," he said.

"You are teasing me," she said as she touched him. "But I don't care."

He was hot and hard. Flesh stretched taut enough that she could stroke it with her fingers, hold it in her fist, and even squeeze tight enough to make him groan.

And while she played, he cupped her chin, lifting her gaze to his. His eyes were hooded, and his head was tilted back as he breathed deeply. But when he spoke, she understood every word.

"You amaze me, Iseabail. You surprise me at every turn, and that is something very hard to do." He stroked his thumb over her bottom lip, tugging until he could slip inside. She teased his callouses with her tongue. "Never has a woman enthralled me so." He brought his lips to hers but didn't quite connect. "I begin to believe witchcraft is real."

She gasped and pulled back. "Never say such a thing!"

His eyes widened at her reaction and then he nodded, his gaze canted down. "I did not mean it the way—"

"I know," she said. "I know." She brought her hands to his face, cradling his jaw as she kissed him. She pressed her tongue to his lips, then widened as he swept inside.

And when he was done, he trailed kisses across her cheek until he could whisper into her ear. "I am a lummox with words. Let me show you what I mean."

"Yes. Please."

And so he did. He lay her down at the edge of the brook on soft grasses still bathed in moonlight. He teased her nipples until her back arched and her hand clutched at him. With steady hands, he slipped between her knees, gently lifting one leg until she lay open to him. He set his knees between hers, spreading her further open as his hands teased through her curls.

She had never been in such a position with anyone looking downward at her, and yet he gave her no time to think how she must appear to him. His fingers did such things to her. He stroked between her folds; he thumbed the point that she had heard about but never experienced. And when she dug her heels into the soft dirt, lifting herself up to him, he set his mouth to kiss her in ways she had never imagined.

The stroke of his tongue made her cry out. Then he pushed his fingers inside. First one, then more. In and out, she barely understood what he did, except that she would not stop it. She wanted more. She wanted him. She wanted—

Her body tensed. Her breath caught.

And then he abruptly pulled back.

"No!" she gasped. *Don't stop!*

She felt the press of his organ, thick and blunt. He rubbed it across her most sensitive place. Once. Twice. And then he tilted his angle and thrust inside.

The penetration ripped through her consciousness. Not pain, exactly. She was stretched. She was full. And she was ecstatic.

Pierced. Deflowered.

Amazed.

"Iseabail," he gasped as he dropped down upon her. His weight made it better somehow, and she lifted her legs to cradle him deeper.

He moved inside her. In and out while she held on.

With every thrust he ground down against her.

With every breath, she thrust up toward him.

And soon the tempo increased. Faster and faster.

Frenzy.

Light!

A burst of light exploded through her entire body. It spread pleasure everywhere. Joy suffused her. Delight consumed her.

He was there with her, shuddering with his release. He whispered her name as he gave her his seed. And she smiled.

This was what it meant to be a woman. Not everything that was womankind, just the part that was denied to virgins. And now, she knew.

Now, she…loved?

The thought didn't frighten her, which was a surprise. In her experience, love was something that could be exploited and few women ever got the good end of that. Perhaps it was a remnant of the bliss that still suffused her body, but for now, she allowed the idea of love. She could let it live in her mind for a time and see what came of it.

For now.

CHAPTER TWENTY-TWO

THEY CLEANED EACH other up in the stream, washing away the dirt. Iseabail regretted allowing the water to take away his seed, but she knew it was only some of what he had given her. She could still bear his child, and that thought pleased her.

He used his shirt to dry her off, then helped her with her gown. She brushed away the dirt on his backside, and he caught her hand with a laugh, drawing her to him to share a kiss.

The moment was playful, but she felt a simmering desire beneath the delight. She wanted to do everything again, and so, apparently, did he. The more she looked at him, the more the bulge in his pants grew. And he laughed.

"I had not thought to be so fortunate in my marriage bed," he confessed as they headed back toward the inn.

She did not tell him what she'd expected in her marriage bed. He could probably guess, and she was too sparkly happy to even think of such things.

They strolled calmly back to the inn only to hear the raucous sounds of drunken men singing bawdy songs. She didn't have to ask to know where they were. The men were outside her bedroom, and they clearly thought she and Reuben had been inside this whole time.

"I blocked the door with the furniture to be sure they couldn't get in," he said.

"Thank you," she said. It would not be good for anyone to

know she had run out the window on her wedding night.

"Can you climb up?" he asked, as they got to the base of the tree.

She laughed, pressed a kiss to his lips, then scampered up. It wasn't the easiest thing to do in a skirt, but she had managed worse. He followed behind her, ready to catch her if she fell. She didn't, and soon they were both inside the room and he was shutting the window before crossing to the bed.

"Quickly, now," he said. "Undress."

She did, oddly embarrassed now to be naked inside. She pulled on a wrap and grabbed a brush for her hair, but he stopped her.

"Leave it," he said. "It's better wild."

Better for what? She didn't have time to ask as he pulled out a penknife and flicked the fleshy side of his hand. Bright blood welled up and he smeared it into the bedsheet. He looked at her in apology with a shrug.

"It's custom," he said.

She knew it.

Then he stripped out of his shirt and boots, doing everything he could to appear as if he had just roused from bed and pulled on his breeches. But before he went to the door, he paused to look back at her.

"Do you feel up to a show?" he whispered.

Her eyes widened.

"Just noise, my dear. Just some very fun noise."

He kissed her then, drawing her close as he plundered her mouth. Then he pulled back. "Do you know the sounds of lovemaking?"

She nodded. She had heard it many nights of her childhood. Her uncle liked it when everyone in the castle knew he had a woman in his bed. But she didn't know if she could do it herself.

"Can you moan? Loudly?"

He caressed her breast and her whole body shivered. She had no idea how she could still be so sensitive after their walk back, but every part of her seemed to rise at his touch. Her chin lifted, her legs tightened, and even her breath pulled in and up in a quick inhale.

But she didn't moan. Not even when he released a loud moan of his own. He waited until there was a pause in the song and that made sure he was heard. As was her giggle. She hadn't meant to make such noise, but he was so funny as he pulled fists to his belly like a man before lifting a great weight. He looked like he was about to toss a caper in a Highland game. Instead, he was creating a show for his men.

There was a great roar of approval outside her door, and she felt her face heat a fiery red, but he just wiggled his eyebrows at her. Then he went to the bed and grabbed the wood at the base of the bed.

"Cry out?" he whispered to her.

"What?"

Then he slammed the bed against the wall, making a loud thump.

"Oh!" she exclaimed, but probably not loud enough.

He grinned at her. Then he banged the bed again. She understood this time, and her exclamation was loud enough to gain a roar of approval from the hallway.

He winked, then he growled loudly as he slammed the bed again. But it wasn't loud enough. She knew that from her uncle's copulations, so she joined him at the base of the bed. Fortunately, she knew just what to say, assuming her blushes didn't rob her of breath.

"Oh my…my lord!" she cried as she helped him push the bed again.

"Har, har, har!" he returned with a ridiculous expression, and she burst out laughing.

His eyes widened and he shook his head. "This isn't supposed to be funny," he whispered.

Oh, right. But she was laughing, and he was making her do it as he began to slam the bed faster, his grunts becoming louder and louder as he worked.

Truthfully, it was exciting as she saw his muscles bunch with the work. He was an attractive man, and she had no trouble building her own gasps with the movements.

"Oh! Oh!" she cried.

The tempo was really fast now. Too fast for her to keep up, but he was banging the bedframe with such power that she was sure the entire inn would lose sleep over it. And then, with a sudden roar, he left off the bed and leaped straight at her.

She cried out in surprise as he tumbled them both onto the bed. He rolled them as they flew such that she landed on top of him. And then she burst out into a laughter that she tried to muffle against his chest. He held her close, his own humor shaking them. And outside, there was an enormous roar of approval.

He looked at her then, his eyes alight with merriment and whispered into her ear. "Well done."

She shook her head. "That was all your doing. I merely—"

"Played along," he said. Then he pressed a quick kiss to her lips. "That makes it all the better, you know. To have someone—"

"Who plays along," she said, suddenly understanding her husband on a new level.

He was a brilliant man, one with money and connections throughout London. But who in his life could match him for intelligence? Very few. And who in that world would dare play with him without fear? Powerful men like her uncle intimidated others with brutality. Powerful men like Reuben intimidated not from their actions but because others felt inferior just from standing in their presence.

She straightened up on her elbow. "You want a playmate."

"Aye," he rumbled, as he pressed his thick cock against her.

She chuckled. "Aye, indeed."

Yes, he wanted that kind of playmate, but what they'd done was something better. They'd joined together in fun, and that was something few people valued as they should. As a woman who had spent her childhood with very few friends, this was something precious indeed.

So she teased him with her nose, rubbing back and forth against his cheek until they both grinned. And then he drew her close for a kiss, one that stretched and deepened. That made her heart speed up and—

"Let us see! Let us see!"

Reuben groaned, and she sighed. She was still cradled in his arms, supported by his body, which meant she felt how desperately he did not want the interruption. And she felt the power in his lungs when he turned his face to the door and shouted.

"Shut up, ye buggers!"

That didn't work. If anything, it pushed them to greater excess. And so with a sigh, she rolled off him.

"You meant for them to come in," she whispered as she motioned to the blood smear on the sheet.

He groaned as he sat up. "All right, all right," he growled.

Another roar from the hallway, and Iseabail mentally apologized to the innkeeper and any other soul who might be trying to sleep this night. Fortunately, it would end soon, and then they could get back to what they were doing before.

She stood up and wrapped a blanket over her nightdress. He stomped over to the door but didn't open it. Instead, he waited for her nod before he hauled open the door. His men tumbled inside, laughing with good cheer. Two scooped Reuben up on their shoulders in an unsteady display that had her gasping in fear and him slamming his hands out toward the beams in the ceiling.

"Easy, easy! Set me down!" he cried.

They ignored him, of course, especially since the other men shone a lantern on the blood smear. Another great roar of approval shot through the men and two came toward her to scoop her up as well. They meant nothing by it. She was merely to be held aloft as was her husband, but Iseabail had been trained from birth to fear large men. She feared them putting their hands on her body. She feared what they might do "all in fun."

She shied backwards, scrambling for a place to hide as she sought any weapon—

"Leave her alone!"

Reuben's bellow filled the room with a fury that stopped every soul cold including her. And lest anyone miss his words, he followed them up with ones that were designed to chill even a drunk down to his bones.

"If any man touches her without her leave, I will cut off his hands. See if I won't."

The two men who were closest to her jumped backwards, their heads averted. "We were just—" one of them began, but he never got to finish his words.

"She is my lady wife," he bellowed. "And you will protect her *before* you protect me."

Now their heads shot up, their eyes wide with confusion.

"Wot?"

Reuben grimaced and then jumped out of the arms that had been holding him aloft. He landed as sure footed as any cat, and then he went through his men, shoving or kicking them one by one onto a knee.

"Down, you damned fools," he cursed.

Those he hadn't reached dropped quickly to the floor.

"Do you not understand who she is?" he demanded. "Do you not know what the fairies would do if you frightened one of their own?"

What?

"Wot?"

"Huh?"

Her husband growled, low and deep in his throat. "Think, ye blockheads. Why would I so easily give up Lady Rebecca? I could have married her in a week's time, had I the mind."

Two of the men nodded at that.

"What is better than a lady?" he pressed. And when they didn't answer, he rolled his eyes. "A queen, ye daft clods."

The men looked at her confusion. Even in their inebriated

states, they knew she wasn't the Queen of Scotland.

"Do ye not know who her mother is?" His accent was changing as he spoke. It wasn't exactly Scottish, but he had the beginnings of credible brogue. "Ach, she's the most famous witch in all Scotland."

Infamous, actually, and it was her grandmother, but she didn't correct him.

"A witch and a fairy king sired my lady wife, and all of Scotland knows it. Why do you think her uncle is so fired up to keep her around? He's got her dowry, hasn't he? What does he need her for?"

A good question, and one that she had spent many nights wrestling with.

"Because of her blood, you fools. He knows the fairies bless her and protect her. And they'll bless all who keep her safe." He stopped long enough to study the men's faces. They were confused, still trying to sort his words through their inebriation. But mostly, they were uncertain as to why they were on their knees before a woman in a dressing gown covered by a blanket.

"Look at her, you fools! Have you not seen a more regal woman? She's dressed for bed, she is, and yet do you not see the fairy queen inside her?"

Now that was ridiculous, but she couldn't argue with him. He'd declared it, so she lifted her chin and stared coolly down at them. She had to pretend to a nobility she didn't deserve. And thank God for all the lessons her mother had given her in how to stand, how to walk, how to do nothing but exude enough confidence and power to make a man tremble.

It was about confidence. And it was about feeding into their superstitions.

So she stepped out from where she'd been cowering between the bed and a chair. She spoke clearly, modulating her voice as she had been taught. And she made the story simple because they were still very drunk.

"I knew nothing of my past," she said, "until the night I

turned sixteen. I was born at midnight, you see, as it was the moment when fairy and woman do their best work."

Several heads nodded at that. It made no logical sense, of course, but what fairy tale did? There were only custom and guesses, but her mother had showed her how to use it.

"Many know the tale of my sixteenth birthday. Mother brought me to a field under a full moon—" Actually, it hadn't been exactly full. Neither had it been her sixteenth birthday, but close enough. "She put symbols on my body in blood and copper and gold." Dirt and paint, but even at home the tale had grown with the telling. "I was a child. What did I know of magic and fairies? But as the clock struck midnight, standing there in the moonlight with symbols of power on my body—" She took a deep breath. "I knew. I saw." She lowered her voice. "I *felt*."

"What was it?" Reuben asked, his voice rich in the quiet room.

"My mother's curse or blessing. I'm not sure what to call it. But she said that from then on, any man who touched me against my will would suffer terribly. Any soul who crossed me would fare ill. Any—"

"Ach," one of the men scoffed, along with a loud belch.

"Scottish nonsense," one man—a big one barely in the room—said from the doorway.

"Is it?" Reuben asked as he turned on the man. He pointed to the sheet. "You see what all of us see tonight. Her virgin's blood. Now look upon her. She ran on foot across all of Scotland. A woman alone. A girl of such beauty. What would happen, do you think, to any English girl who tried that? Would she end here, tonight, as a virgin?"

That, apparently, made sense to them. Any girl who managed to keep her virginity as long as she had was obviously cursed or protected. In her case, apparently, it was both.

Reuben squatted down before them. "Shriveled cocks is the least of what has happened to those who would touch her. Pox comes next and the waters." He shuddered. "Men wasted away in days. It was powerful magic formed at midnight from blood and blessed by the fairies."

"My mother put all her power into the spell," Iseabail said. "Two weeks later, she was gone."

"Taken back by the fairies?"

Killed by her uncle. "I don't know."

Reuben gasped. "She doesn't know," he said, his voice hushed. "But no man has touched her before or since."

The closest man to her twisted to look at Reuben. "You did," he said, his voice filled with awe.

"I did," Reuben returned, a very masculine grin on his face. "I certainly did, but she had to say it aloud. Before the first kiss, she had to say she willed it. She allowed it. I heard it clearly and I felt—" He paused on a dramatic gasp. It was done so well that she hung on his breath, waiting for the rest of the sentence. "Magic," he whispered. "Such beautiful fairy magic as unravels a man."

"And a woman," she said. It was the truth.

"Aye," he echoed.

Good lord, what a story he was weaving, and she was as caught up in it as everyone else. And then he continued. He thunked the shoulder of the man nearest to her.

"I've saved you, I have. A shriveled cock, had you touched her. The waters if it had gone further. A fairy curse is an evil thing."

Every man seemed to gulp at that.

"But I've married her, I have," he said, "with all their blessing and the church as well. Did I not say my vows before the Archbishop of Canterbury? Did I not wed her in the most proper way? Do I not worship her as befits a fairy queen among men? Kneel, kneel before her, I say!"

They were already on one knee before her, but every man straightened his pose and dropped his head.

"Swear, men, swear to protect her with your very lives. She is the queen among us, and I am but her servant king."

Never could she have imagined what happened next. The

days when knights swore fealty to a queen were long gone, and yet every man swore themselves to her. At first it was a stuttered, "I s-swear." But before long, every man there took up the chant. "I swear! I swear!"

Then she heard a female voice among the men. She looked to the door where the innkeeper crouched on one knee and his wife bowed to her, her cap askew as she curtsied. It was incredible and wholly inappropriate.

She was no fairy queen, neither was it clever to have men swearing fealty to her as if they meant to take up arms against England.

"I mean no harm to anyone," she quickly said. "All I ask is…"

Oh hell. What exactly did she ask? It was more than safe passage back to Scotland. It was freedom from her uncle's tyranny. A home in which to abide with her husband and raise her children. Safety to live her life was what she wanted. But how to phrase that?

"She asks that you keep her safe," Reuben said, taking up the tale. "We travel to Scotland to claim her dowry. We travel to magic and beauty the likes of which you cannot imagine."

"Yes," murmured one of the men.

"Yes!" cried the next one.

"Yes! Yes! Yes!" they chanted together, as if any of them knew what they were agreeing to.

It was bizarre, and yet it filled her heart with such happiness. How had her husband turned a frightening moment into a cheering mob intent upon her safety? Insane! And yet it was completely within his ability.

It boggled her mind, and yet she could not deny his power.

Her breath caught as he accepted the cheers as entirely appropriate adulation. And then, to her enormous relief, she watched him gently guide them back out of the room. Not a soul came close to her. No man dared approach her, though they murmured their devotion as they continued to bow in her direction.

Somehow, he had completely turned the situation to his advantage. And she…

Fell in love.

CHAPTER TWENTY-THREE

REUBEN SLEPT IN the next morning. He hadn't meant to. Normally, he was awake with the first light of day, but everything was different with this woman snuggled tight to his side. Something about her scent settled him inside. It tempted him to linger in bed, to taste her skin, and to stroke—

"Hmmmmm," she purred against his side. Then she jolted and he felt every part of her stiffen away from him.

"Iseabail?"

She blinked and looked around the inn room, her mind clearly taking a moment to absorb her situation. He let her move as she willed, though he sat up slowly to look at her. In time, she focused on him, and he got to watch the delightful creep of her blush.

"All you all right?" he asked.

She nodded as she rubbed a hand over her face. "I slept so deeply," she said, her voice filled with awe.

"That's a good thing, yes?"

She turned to him. "I felt safe enough to really sleep." She looked down at the coverlet. "I cannot remember the last time that happened. Not since my mother disappeared."

He touched her face, drawing her gaze up to him. "I am pleased by that."

She swallowed, and there was a message in her eyes. Hope, fear, or some mixture of emotions he couldn't name. All he knew was that it touched his soul. Never had a woman looked at him that way. It wasn't worship. She knew better than to think any man was a god. And yet there was an openness to her, a warmth that she hid from the rest of the world. That she would let him see that part of her stirred his heart.

And his loins.

"We have time," he whispered as he stroked her neck. "If you want to linger in bed. If you're not too sore."

Her eyes fluttered closed as she let her head rest against his hand, but he could already tell this interlude wouldn't last. Not because she was unwilling. Indeed, it appeared that he could seduce them both into a delightful morning.

But both their thoughts had engaged. He was already thinking about when his men would wake. They needed to make plans, and she needed to give him more information about what they faced in Scotland.

She caught his hand and pressed a kiss to it. "It appears that I am not the only one distracted this morning."

He smiled at her. "You are the best distraction, but you are right. I think we should get going. We can take a slow pace to Scotland, but I do not want to linger here too long." He dropped his forehead to hers. "I want to spread the tale of my fairy queen further north."

"You know none of that is true."

"Whatever do you mean?" He laced his tone with humor because it covered his anxiety. He'd chosen a risky gambit. Fairies and witchcraft were closely aligned in people's minds, and not usually with kindness. He needed to instill fear, not terror. And he had no wish to bring back the witch hunts from a hundred years ago.

She cast him a wry look. "I'm not the child of a fairy king."

"And how would you know that for sure?"

Her expression sobered as she pulled away from him. "It is a dangerous business to be called a witch—"

"You're a fairy child. A queen!"

"That's treason!" she exclaimed. "And by now, every soul for miles around will have heard the tale."

"That's my plan," he said with a grin.

"And will the English king accuse me of raising an army?"

He snorted as he rolled out of bed. "Don't be daft."

She matched him, standing tall and proud despite her nakedness, and by God, she looked glorious. "They dropped to one knee before me. They swore fealty!"

He shrugged. "They were drunk. Besides, we're not heading to London. We're going north to Scotland. And the king cares bugger all for a bunch of drunken revelers heading out of England."

"But—"

He came around the bed to face her. Damn, his cock was getting hard just looking at her. But he could see she was genuinely worried, and besides, she deserved to know his plan. She was the primary component in it.

"Do you know, I heard the tale of your sixteenth birthday while I was searching for your necklace."

"What?"

"Without ever going to Scotland, I had heard of you, granddaughter to Scotland's most famous witch."

"Infamous. She was killed—"

"But she wasn't killed, you see."

Iseabail stiffened in outrage. "She was hounded! She was chased! She died sick and alone—"

"Exactly." He touched her arm. "They made her life miserable, but they didn't actually touch her."

She glared at him. "She was killed."

"The same way your mother was killed," he said gently. "She disappeared in the middle of the night with no one knowing what happened."

She blanched, and he felt horrible for bringing up her past like this. He tried to pull her into his arms, his tug insistent despite her stiffness. Eventually she relented and he was able to feel her heat against his skin, know when her breath hitched and finally released, and then press a kiss to the top of her head.

"In public, they still believe in magic and the power of your blood."

"I have no magic!"

"Yes, you do! It's just not the kind where you wave your hands and mumble things." He drew her back to the bed. She'd already grabbed a robe, so he waited while she pulled it on. It helped his focus when she was covered, but he mourned the loss of the sight. "Why do you think your uncle kept such a tight hand on you?"

She shrugged. "Because I took care of the castle and saw to the health of the clan. I made sure there was food on his table and—"

He waved his hand in dismissal of that. "That's useful, to be sure, but there are others who could do the same."

She sniffed. "Not as well as I."

He grinned. "Of course, not as well as you, but do you think he saw that value in you?"

Her lips pursed as she puzzled out his meaning. "He saw no good in women beyond the most basic things." She snorted. "He liked to say that all women looked the same upside down."

What an idiot her uncle was. "To him, your value was in the tales he spun around you. Of how you blessed the clan. I would bet the other clans did not attack for fear of you."

"That's ridiculous. I have no real magic."

"You have whatever magic people believe you have. And if that is fierceness in battle, then so it is."

"It's a lie."

"Only to those who don't believe it."

They were talking in circles, but he had made his point. Tales of magic—both good and ill—had swirled about her for her entire life. He meant to use it to regain her proper place in the Spaulding clan. With him alongside her.

"I mean to use your fame to advantage," he said.

"How?"

He grinned. "By making you into a fairy queen and me your king."

She snorted. "I believe you said, 'servant king.'"

"That I am," he said.

Then he began to caress her, unable to resist the lure of her body and the trust in her eyes. She believed in him, and that was a potent aphrodisiac. So while he searched her face for doubt, he stroked the robe from her shoulder until her breast was bared to him. And then he pressed her back into the bed.

"Allow me to show you," he murmured as he feasted upon her breast.

She clutched his shoulders, she lifted herself into his mouth, and she gave herself to him with an openness he treasured. And when he thrust into her, she smiled at him as if he were the answer to all her prayers. How could any man resist that?

TWO HOURS LATER they were fed, dressed, and ready to head north. Reuben's still-inebriated men were sleeping it off in rooms, thanks to his very generous payment to the innkeeper. They'd follow soon. Meanwhile, the inn was overflowing with curious locals, all wanting to get a look at the fairy queen. He was about to remind her to be extra kind to everyone, but then realized she was already generous with her praise. She expressed gratitude for the efforts of the innkeeper's daughter as her maid, she praised the groomsmen for how nicely they'd managed the horses, and she especially thanked the innkeeper's wife for the excellent meals.

It was part of her regal charm, and he adored it.

Unfortunately, the delight was going to end very soon. Once they began their journey, he would have to press her for details she wouldn't want to answer. But he would go slowly.

Soon.

After a kiss or three.

And a little more…

But even such a wonderful interlude had to end. When she was relaxed against him, her body barely clothed, he asked her who were the people—exactly—who helped her escape her uncle's control. He wanted every name and everything they did on her behalf.

Entwined in his arms, these stories came easily to her.

Her clan ran the largest highland market. Every clan brought their goods here to sell and fair days were a sight to behold. As such, so were pregnant women, children with illnesses, and injuries to man and beast. Iseabail usually worked night and day, helping wherever there was need. So when she had cause to hide in a potato cart leaving a day early from market, she was just another lump in one of several wagons that came and went that day. From there, she found other carts, other rides, all to get her to Sadie's clan and the final trip to London.

"You didn't trust any of your own clan?"

She shook her head. "There are some who would help, but they are always intertwined with someone who will tell. Everyone knows what everyone else is about."

He grunted. That did not bode well for their success.

Now for the harder part. "Tell me about your mother's disappearance. How did you realize she was gone? Who helped look for her?"

She moved restlessly against him. He let her shift how she willed, but he could not let her escape the questions. "She went to help a sick family and never arrived. Never returned. I knew she was gone the very next morning when no one, not even the women, could tell me where she was."

"And your uncle?"

"Feigned great distress. Sent out Hamish and a few others to search. They found nothing."

"Hmmm."

He pressed for more details, discussed who she thought tried to help her and who maligned her. By her reckoning, the numbers were equal. He hoped she was wrong and that the Scots were not blind to her skills.

Which led him to the last and most difficult questions. "Why do they despise your grandmother? And what has she to do with you?" The answer was simple, if somewhat confusing to his English mind.

"My grandmother blessed the men at Culloden. She praised them, cast spells to protect them, and swore that they would win the Jacobite cause."

Obviously, that hadn't happened. The Scots had been decimated at Culloden. "They blamed her for the loss?"

She shrugged. "They blame everyone, the Sassenach most of all. But they can't vent their hatred onto you. You're all the way down south and you have cannons."

"But she was in Scotland. She blessed them and predicted a glorious win."

Iseabail nodded. "I wasn't even born yet. My mother was a child. But they turned their anger on her, said she was a witch who trucked with the devil." She shuddered. "They said awful things—"

"But they didn't kill her."

"She ran. She hid. She changed her name and pretended to be yet another clanless widow with a child."

"Did someone recognize her?"

"Someone recognized her skills." She lifted her chin to look hard at him. "They are the same as mine. The knowledge of herbs to fight infection, unguents to soothe old joints, midwifery, and more. Could you sit by and watch a woman in labor die merely because no one else knows how to turn the babe in the belly?"

"No." And neither could she.

"She had a habit of humming songs as she worked. Hymns or lullabies, folk songs or just notes." She looked back at him. "You understand I never met her. This happened long before I was born. I heard it from my mother."

"I know. But the Scots have long memories. I need to know why they damn you because of her."

She threw up her hands in disgust. "They said she was invoking the devil to curse Scotland." The scorn was heavy in her tone. "Many people hum when they work, but it was enough to identify her. I learned young to keep silent."

"So she ran?"

"To a cave somewhere. She was sick with a fever. It was winter and they had no food. She died while my mother shivered beside her."

"How did your mother survive?"

"Kindness from a Spalding shepherd with a pregnant wife. She was half frozen and starving, but she knew her trade. She repaid him by helping with his sheep and his wife. In time, she worked at market day and met my father before he was laird."

Reuben nodded. "And he figured it out?"

"She told him." There was insult in her tone. "She would not begin their marriage with a lie."

"Of course not," he said, knowing full well that many would. Indeed, it probably would have been better for everyone if she had kept her identity secret. But she had been honest, and that was a credit to her mother, and something that Iseabail clearly valued.

"He kept it quiet as long as possible. Many knew, but while he was alive, he would brook no talk about magic. But after his death…" She shook her head. "My uncle started telling everyone. He stoked the fear about us even as he bragged about it."

"He was stirring everyone up about it—both good and bad. It probably made it easier to control you and gave him someone to blame if things went wrong."

"Yes," she agreed. "Every stillbirth was Mama's fault. Every bad storm came because she had prayed for it or not prayed enough. She would be delivering a child and the father would threaten her if it wasn't a boy." She looked at him, her eyes filled with pain. "It was awful. Every day, every night. Awful."

He wrapped her in his arms and set her head on her chest. He tucked her close as she lay on him, not crying but still taking comfort. Or so he hoped. "Those days are over," he promised. "You will never live like that again."

She nodded against him, but he could tell she didn't fully believe it. Neither did he.

He didn't yet see a way through. At the moment, every direction ended with him dead. Someone, somehow would gut him in the night if he didn't finish this fast. It had to be public, and it had to leave Iseabail vindicated. Otherwise, she would likely be gutted along with him.

Or married to Hamish, which was even worse.

CHAPTER TWENTY-FOUR

"WHY DID YOU go to outsiders for help?"

"Hmmm?" Iseabail stretched against her husband, feeling her body slide against his. There wasn't a soft spot of fat anywhere, and yet when she snuggled next to him, she felt as if he softened to accommodate her. Never had she thought such physical sweetness could exist between man and woman. She'd always heard about the passion, never the sweet aftermath.

She liked it. But she didn't like his question.

"I have been speaking of this all day with you," she murmured. "Must we do so now in the middle of the night?" They had stopped south of Scotland to give the horses a night's rest and wait for his men to catch up. For all that their departure from London had been abrupt and desperate, they were now taking their sweet time as if he had no fear of being caught.

"And why are we going so slowly to Scotland?" she added.

"Because I am not prepared to face your uncle yet."

"They why did we have to leave London so quickly?"

"Because his men knew where you lived. He does not know where we are now." He rolled her so that she lay on her back while he set his chin on his elbow above her. He was studying her, his expression grave, and she took the opening to move against him again. Would there be more bed sport tonight? She had already enjoyed—

"You are ducking my question. Why did you go to outsiders

instead of your own people?"

She looked at him for a long moment. It wasn't that she was ducking the question, exactly. It was that she had no answer for him.

"Iseabail—"

"I couldn't be sure they would help me. I didn't think it through. I just did it." She sighed. She had already told him the details, just not the why. Because she didn't fully understand it herself. "I was cleaning and stitching the hand of a farmer who sold potatoes and other vegetables at the fair. He'd cut his hand open on the market stall and if it was not tended well, he would lose the use of his fingers. And if it got infected—"

"That's a serious wound. He was lucky you were there."

She shrugged. "Someone was always hurting themselves on the market stalls. My uncle did not construct them carefully and they are hard used."

He pressed a kiss to her hand. "Tell me what happened next."

"There wasn't anything. Talia's daughter came to see me. She was bursting with excitement. She said I was to be married to Hamish on the last day of the fair." Her chest tightened as she remembered the moment. She'd been dumbfounded at first, but the fear had built with every beat of her frantic heart. She would not marry that horrible man. Death would be preferable. "I ran."

"How?"

"I asked the farmer to take me away." She flushed. "I begged him, and his wife agreed. So we packed up and left with me hidden in the back of the cart under empty potato sacks."

He nodded. "And you never thought to ask your clansmen? Not even the women?"

"I ran, Reuben. The first way that I could."

He sighed as he pulled her close. She snuggled into his comfort thinking that the conversation was at an end. But he kept pushing while she grew increasingly angry.

"You have tended the sick and injured in your clan since you were a child."

"Yes, along with my mother."

"You managed the castle, too, serving as chatelain?"

"My mother did at first, and then my uncle's woman. But she was so terrible at it, I took over."

"No one complained?"

"They asked me to do it."

"And you did not barter for it. You simply stepped in to see that there was food for everyone, safety and comfort as needed."

"Why would I let the clan suffer when I was able?"

"What did your uncle say?"

"He thanked me. He proclaimed I would make an excellent wife to one who paid enough coin to him to have me."

He shifted, clearly annoyed by that. "He spoke loudly of selling you in marriage?"

"Often."

"But that is a guardian's right in Scotland, isn't it? A bride price."

"In England, too. Or it used to be."

"So why, do you think, did he give you to Hamish?"

"I don't know, and I don't care! I won't do it!"

"Of course not," he soothed, pressing a kiss to her forehead. "But you should know. Is Hamish rich? Did he buy you?"

"He has some sheep and a badly tilled garden. His mother tended it until she died last winter. I doubt he has any coin."

"But he has a powerful need for a wife, it would seem. Else who will tend his sheep?"

She snorted. "Not him. He's the laziest of my uncle's men."

"And yet he got you. Why?"

An interesting question. "He and my uncle grew up together. They each other's secrets. Always have."

He soothed her with a long caress along her arm. She could have turned away from him, but she liked the way he held her. He had a way of teasing circles along her body, then sometimes tapping her between long strokes. He wasn't conscious of his actions. She knew his mind was churning about something and when that happened, his fingers were rarely idle. But as someone who had so rarely been touched at all, this was a treat she would not refuse. Not even if he annoyed her with his questions.

"Who in your clan do you trust?"

She shook her head. "No one."

"Surely there is someone—"

"There are women who are kind, men who are generous, but they are busy with their own work. They care nothing for me except in the services I can provide when someone is ill."

He was silent, his hand continuing the stroke along her shoulder. She thought for a moment that he had accepted her words, but very soon he was at it again with questions she thought had obvious answers.

"How do you know they care nothing for you?"

"They just don't."

"Do they beat you? Say mean things to you?"

"They wouldn't dare. Otherwise, I might be busy next time someone scrapes up a leg or catches a fever."

"So you threaten them."

She shoved back. "Never! I have never said such a thing to them. My uncle has threatened it if they don't follow his orders, but I have never refused anyone who asked for aid. Even at times when my uncle forbade it."

His brows rose. "Did that happen often?"

She shook her head. "Only twice after my mother disappeared."

"So they have cause to be grateful to you."

She huffed out an irritated breath. "Grateful, yes. Bold enough to defy my uncle? No."

"Did you ever ask?"

"No!"

"Then how do you know they wouldn't help you?"

She stared at him, struggling for the words that would make him understand. "My uncle is in charge, and no one fights him."

"Has anyone ever tried?"

"My mother did after my father died. She was sure Papa had been poisoned, but there was no proof. And my uncle acted so grieved and outraged by the suggestion, no one listened." Iseabail took a deep breath. "They did not stand up when my father died. They did nothing when my mother disappeared. Why would I think they would do anything for me?"

"Did you ask them after your mother disappeared?"

She sighed. "To do what? My mother was gone. None had seen her. What could I ask them to do?"

"So you kept quiet. You feared your uncle and did not trust that anyone would fight for you."

"Because no one would!"

"Did you ask them?"

She glared at him. Why wouldn't he understand? "They didn't stand up for my father, they didn't find my mother. Who would care about me?"

"A great many, I think. Did anyone look for your mother? Or was it just you?"

She swallowed down the painful memories of that time. She didn't even want to look at something buried so deeply. But his words forced her, and honesty made her confess the truth. "I already told you. There was a search party led by Hamish." She rolled her eyes. "They stomped around for a day and declared her gone. My uncle made a great show of grief."

He touched her hand. "I do not mean to upset you—"

"This is very upsetting!"

"But do you not see? You believe you are hated; you believe your uncle has complete control of the clan, but no one has challenged him." He squeezed her hand. "Is he openly vile? Or does he smile and make reasonable choices—generally?"

She wanted to declare her uncle a monster, and so he was. But on the surface, she understood why people followed him. "He makes reasonable choices. Except when it comes to me."

He nodded. "So that gives others less reasons to overthrow him."

"But he *is* vile. He murdered my parents!"

"I believe you," he said. His tone was gentle, it was also uncompromising. "But does anyone else?"

She shook her head, misery welling up in her. Reuben was going to go soft on her uncle. Just like everyone else. He wasn't going to kill her uncle. He wasn't even going to fight him. He would just try and take her dowry and then what? Abandon her?

She pushed up from the bed, setting her feet down on the cold floor. But when she stood up, it was just like every other night after her mother died. She stood there with nowhere to go, no choices at hand beyond accepting and enduring.

"Iseabail—"

"You are just like everyone else. You offer me hope and then do nothing."

He growled as he pushed up in the bed. "What *everyone else?* Who? Iseabail, you said you didn't ask anyone."

She rounded on him. "And what am I to say? I will not set your broken leg unless you kill my uncle? I will not tend your fever-ridden child unless you throw my guardian from our clan?" She stomped her foot, so frustrated that she now acted like a petulant child. But she couldn't stop herself. "He smiles and acts reasonable, then threatens me when we were alone. He struck my mother repeatedly in places that didn't show. She complained about him often, but no one would listen. And he never hit me after my sixteenth birthday. I'd taken beatings when I was younger, but not after her spell."

"Is he cruel to the other members of the clan?"

"He has a mean temper, but…" She shook her head. "As long as he is kept in whisky and women, he is happy and even generous." She stared at him, her heart breaking. "You don't believe me."

"I do believe you," he said coming to his feet. "But I am not the one who needs to be convinced. It's your clan—"

"They won't fight him! They're too afraid!"

"Or are they too busy trying to survive to bother? At least

until someone makes them care."

She folded her arms. She wasn't stupid. She understood what he wanted. "You think I should make my case to them. You think they'll turn on him just because I say so." She shook her head. "They won't. They have no love for me. I am granddaughter to the witch who trafficked with Satan. I am child of a doomed father and a mother who so despised me, she ran away."

Reuben drew back. "You don't believe that, do you?"

"Of course not. But it's what my uncle has been saying."

"And you think they believe that nonsense?"

She nodded, miserable to her core.

"Why?"

"What?"

"Why do you think they believe that? Have they said it to your face?"

She frowned. "No. But they have said nothing against my uncle."

He touched her face. "Did you ask what they believe?"

She threw up her hands. "What does it matter? They believe it!"

He lifted her chin, his caress exquisitely gentle. "I think you are the one who has believed."

"I told you, I don't—"

"Not about your parents. It has been your uncle, I think, who has convinced you that you are worthless except in your dowry. That no one cares for you except in that you nurse their sick and manage the castle." He wrapped her in his arms, and though she allowed it reluctantly, she still let him tuck her against his body. "What if they are merely waiting for you to demand your due?"

"And what if they aren't? What if they care nothing for me? What if—"

"You'll never know unless you ask."

Was it possible? Did her clan have feelings for her? It was hard to believe. Certainly, here had been kind looks and whispered thanks, but nothing that suggested they knew her uncle was an evil man Nothing that told her they would take up arms against him if she only asked.

"They know you who you are," he whispered into her ear. "How could they live with you, see you, and not love you?"

She pulled back. "That is a ridiculously romantic notion. I thought you were a sensible man."

"And I thought you were a woman with magic."

"I'm not."

"I'm not either. But I'll wager we can make everyone believe it."

"But—"

He cut off her questions with a kiss. And when they separated, he looked her straight in the eye. "First, you must believe you are worth defending."

She snorted. "Of course, I am. Why do you think I traveled all the way to London if not to find a man who would fight for me?"

"And I will. But first you must fight for yourself. You must believe that your people will see you for who you are."

That was a step too far for her. Ever since her father's death, her people had been distant with her. Or perhaps it was her mother who had clung too tightly to her. The woman had been overprotective and let no one near. Eventually, everyone stopped trying. And then when her mother disappeared...what? They were out of the habit of talking to her? Of sharing anything beyond the most general of topics?

"I can see how lonely you have been," he whispered.

She hadn't thought it. Her life had been a constant series of tasks mingled with fears. Take care of this task. Don't let her uncle near there. Don't laugh too loud or appear too friendly with anyone. Day after day until she collapsed into bed and slept. Alone. Untouched. Unloved.

So much so that the only person she thought to find when she ran was Sadie, a girl from a different clan who she'd been friends with years before. It wasn't until London that she had begun to realize how good it was to laugh with a friend. In

London, she had passed entire days without worrying what might make her uncle angry.

Her breath caught on a sob. "You have to kill him," she said. "Otherwise, he'll find a way to make you disappear, too!"

"Ach, lass," he said in an awful Scottish accent. "I'm terribly difficult to make disappear. Better men than him have tried."

"You sound like a sick cow," she muttered. Then she sobered. "I mean it," she said. "He will find a way."

"I know," he returned, as he stroked her face. "And now you must trust me. Your people know you better than you think. They will come around with the right encouragement."

"What kind?"

He stroked his lips across hers. "Tomorrow," he whispered.

"But—"

His kiss was deep and clever. By the time he was done, she had lost all memory of their discussion beyond her usual fears and his vague reassurance. It was enough, she decided. For tonight, it was enough.

Together, they returned to bed and the pleasure to be had there.

CHAPTER TWENTY-FIVE

REUBEN HAD TAKEN a great many risks in his life. They ranged from the childishly stupid (a leap from a moving horse over a fence made of spears) to the brilliantly lucky (several businesses managed by people of questionable competence). Never had he felt the stakes more than when arriving without his men at one of the tiny crofts well inside her uncle's land.

He and Iseabail were alone and on horseback. After much discussion, they had agreed upon a plan. She didn't think it would work. Indeed, she had repeated that they would fail, and so he would need to hold off her clansmen long enough for her to gut her uncle. She didn't seem to care if she lived or died afterwards so long as her uncle's reign ended.

He was trying an approach that would not make his new wife a murderess.

He didn't give them good odds, and that made everything more frightening. The cost of being wrong was unthinkable. His own death would be bad enough, but if he died and she survived…well, that would be a fate worse than death.

No choice now as they slipped through the dark to knock on a door of a crude hovel. Reuben took stock of the area, noting that it was roomier and more pleasant than many homes in the London rookeries. It was the air, he thought, and the space. Livestock usually smelled bad, but there was enough separation to let the stink blow past. And that made this home better than a good portion of London.

"Talia?" Iseabail called at the door. "Talia, are you awake?"

For a long moment, there seemed to be no response. Then there came a grumble from inside the hut before a thunk and a curse. Suddenly, the door was hauled open by a darkly bearded face backlit by lantern light. That left the man's face in shadow with still enough light to fall on an upraised sword clenched in a heavy fist.

Holy shit! Reuben was used to lots of different types of weapons, but this was the first claymore he'd ever seen held by a man with strength enough to wield it. No one in London carried so large a thing. Damn it, the man shouldn't be able to raise it in one hand, much less maneuver it through a doorway, but this one seemed to be doing it easily.

Nevertheless, Reuben jumped in front of Iseabail, shoving her back as he tried to figure out how to defend them from that sword and the giant beast wielding it. But before he could do more than make himself a target, the woman holding the lantern peered around her beast of a husband.

"Iseabail? Is that really you?"

"Fergus, put tha' away! We mean ye no harm!"

Iseabail's brogue had grown more pronounced as they'd traveled through Scotland. It was in full force now. Even better, Fergus seemed to understand the sharp tone.

"Miss Iseabail? That canna be you."

Iseabail pushed forward. "It is," she said, her voice becoming less certain as she stepped around Reuben. "May we come in? I've need to speak with ye both."

Fergus frowned, his massive brow making calculations that Reuben couldn't guess at. His wife, however, had no such hesitation. She pushed her man aside and gestured with her lantern. "Get inside. Quick. It's no decent hour fer anyone."

Iseabail nodded and quickly entered. Reuben tried to stay close, but these were her people. He would not endear himself by being overprotective. Neither would he leave her completely exposed, though his back prickled as he ducked beneath Fergus's claymore.

"Fergus," Talia ordered. "Get some drink for us all. I mean to have a talk with Miss Iseabail."

She meant to have an accounting. The woman was older than Iseabail by about fifteen years, and she had the attitude of a difficult aunt as she placed her hands on her full hips and rounding belly. She was with child for sure, but not so far advanced that she couldn't whip an errant child—or husband—if she had a mind.

Apparently Fergus understood that, so with a hard look at Reuben—who immediately raised his hands in surrender—the large man stomped outside to wherever the drink was stored. Likely a cellar of some kind. Meanwhile, Iseabail was looking hard at Talia's belly.

"Oh my," she murmured. "The herbs didn't work, then."

"They worked fine until you left, and I couldn't get them anymore. Orlaith threw out all your jars of medicine. Said we didn't need yer witchcraft no more."

Iseabail gasped. "All of them? But there was no witchcraft in—"

"All gone." Talia snorted. "Then she was gone a month later once she turned up barren."

She would have been better to learn something about what she destroyed, but Reuben knew too many souls who would rather throw away something than learn why it was important.

Meanwhile, Talia put her hands on her belly, clear worry in her face. When she spoke, her voice wavered with fear.

"I don't know what to do, Iseabail. Little Blake nearly killed me. You remember that, don't ye? You said the next child would be the death of me—"

"I said it would be difficult, but not impossible," Iseabail soothed. "I said—"

"To use a sheath. I know. But we didn't have any and I finished the herbs, an..." She shook her head. "We got seven kids already, and I'm too old—"

"Not that old." Iseabail took her friend's hands. "I'm here now. I'll see you through."

Talia's swallowed, her body straightening as she gained enough strength to face her future. "And you'll make more of that mixture, yes? After this one's born—"

"And get more sheathes." She nodded. "I'll do whatever I can."

Reuben saw hope enter the woman's eyes. Hope and suspicion as she looked over at him. "And who is this?" she asked, her voice low.

"He's my husband, Reuben Bates."

Reuben had already pulled off his hat. Now he performed his most courtly bow. "Pleased to meet you, madam."

"A Sassenach!" Talia accused.

There was no hiding that truth, but he did his best to make himself seem friendly. "I'm here to protect Iseabail. I'm her husband, and she's my responsibility. I have no wish to stir up trouble."

"And yet it's trouble ye've brought," she said with a harsh spit at his feet. Then she looked back at Iseabail. "Oh lass, if ye've found yerself a fine Sassenach husband, whyever did ye come back?"

"Because this is my home. You are my family. Why wouldn't I want to be here?"

"Because Hamish will claim ye, that's why. And who here will stop it? We were all there when he married yer necklace."

"This necklace?" Iseabail asked as she held up her pendant. "I don't know what he married, but it wasn't my token."

"And what difference does that make? The baron said it was, and he's got the men to make it so."

That was Reuben's cue. "Does he though?" he pressed. "Hamish and five others went down to London to get her. They attacked her in broad daylight as if she were a common thief without a word first. Have they come back?"

Talia opened her mouth to answer, but it was Fergus who spoke from the doorway. "The baron's been grumbling that the Sassenach killed them. Cut them down—"

Iseabail snorted. "The English did nothing but stand there and gape. Except Reuben here, who was caught without a weapon. He kept them from rushing me while Sadie Allen and I fought. I put a dagger in Albie's leg, I did. And then my husband and I headed back here to find out what nonsense my uncle's been spouting." She lifted her chin. "I'm not married to anyone but Mr. Reuben Bates, and by the Archbishop of Canterbury, no less."

Both the Scots gaped at her. "Never say so," Talia breathed.

"I do say so. And with the Countess of Byrn at my side." She touched Talia's hand. "You know I would never agree to Hamish. You sent Lizzy to me, didn't you, to warn me?"

That had been Reuben's guess, and it seemed he'd been right. Talia looked at her hands. "Hamish was bragging about it, and I sent Lizzy to find you."

"And warn me." She lifted both Talia's hands and squeezed them. "Thank you for that. Thank you. I couldn't be standing here now if you hadn't—"

Fergus clunked down his drink and glared at his wife. "It wasn't her place. We don't interfere in the baron's ideas. We don't do it."

Talia's gaze dropped to her hands, but Reuben had seen this dynamic before. Here was a wife who bowed to her husband's decrees to his face, and yet still found ways to do what she thought was right. In this case, she'd sent her daughter to save Iseabail from a surprise wedding.

"I'm right glad you did," he said, his voice as earnest as he could make it. "Iseabail deserves better than that bastard."

Fergus glared at him. "And is that you, Sassenach?" His tone was derisive, clearly meant to be an insult. But rather than bristle, Reuben held up his hands.

"Me? No. She deserves far better than me, and that's the truth." Then he smiled at Iseabail. "But I'm the lucky one who caught her fancy."

She smiled back with equal warmth. "That he did, and I accepted his touch." She looked down at her belly. "And maybe more."

Silence descended on the four of them, each one staring at Iseabail's belly. She looked positively beatific at the idea. Fergus and Talia looked alarmed. But Reuben was absorbed in a wave of love that had his jaw flapping open in shock. He certainly knew that bed sport could result in children, but that hadn't been in the forefront of his mind until this moment. Until the possibility of their child growing beneath Iseabail's hands *right now* thrust into his brain like a knife blade of clarity. His child could be beneath her hands right then. Her child in her belly.

Their child. Reuben swore right then that the child would have a future unlike anything he'd had growing up in London or she'd had beneath her uncle's thumb. Their child would have every advantage, every possible future. He could not have felt it more strongly if God Himself had set a babe in his arms.

"The baron will kill it," Fergus said, his voice dull. "No Sassenach in his kin."

"His grandda was a bluidy Sassenach collaborator!" Iseabail snapped.

Fergus shook his head. "Don't matter. He's denied that. Won't hear a word—"

Reuben spoke, the words as final as the death in his tone.

"I'll kill him."

Fergus eyed him darkly, but Iseabail turned to him with hope in her eyes.

"Will you? Truly?"

"No one will harm you," he stated firmly. "I swore that to you on the day we wed." Then he reached out a shaking hand. She gently set it on her belly. There was no movement there yet, no bulge to indicate a babe. It was too soon. And yet, he felt a child there all the same. "No one hurts our child."

And so his fate was sealed.

CHAPTER TWENTY-SIX

T HEY SLEPT THAT night in the hayloft. Iseabail was embarrassed by the accommodations, but Reuben kissed her cheek and whispered that he had lived in worse. That sparked a conversation about exactly when and where he had lived so crudely, and she heard the tale of his first home as a young boy where he daily faced down vermin the size of dogs. He was so funny as he spoke that she laughed, even though the tale was excruciatingly sad. Her childhood had often been harsh, but she'd always had food and a warm bed. And normal-sized rats, at least by Scotland's standards.

He roused her early, and she wondered if he had slept at all. She had rested deeply thanks to his presence. She always felt safe around him, and that made all the difference.

"Is there something wrong?" she whispered.

"No," he said as his thumb stroked down her cheek. "But there are people you should talk to before you confront your uncle."

"Who?"

"I've no idea, but Fergus arranged it—"

"And Talia would have helped." She stretched as she worked out a kink in her back. "There's a stream nearby. I'll—"

"I've brought water and a towel," he said as he pointed down from the loft. "Don't go about without me."

She knew better than to argue. She'd married him for his

ability to protect her, and so she did as he instructed. Instead, she asked him what he and Fergus had talked about last night. She and Talia had whispered about all the clan's children as they peeked in on her sleeping seven. Without a trained midwife, the women were nervous about their babes. And without a trained healer, even the men felt the anxiety.

"I asked him who wanted to marry you," Reuben said as he tidied the loft. Apparently, he wanted no evidence of their presence. He glanced at her. "You had your pick of men here."

She shook her head. "My mother did not allow it—"

"Before your sixteenth birthday? I wouldn't either."

"And my uncle kept everyone away afterwards. He said my witchcraft would kill them."

"And you believed him?"

"Of course not. My craft is with medicines and blessings."

"But they believed it."

She nodded.

"Were you hurt by that? That your friends, the people who had known you all your life, could believe such a thing?"

She looked down at her hands. Yes, she supposed it did hurt a bit. How could they think she would ever harm them? "My mother made sure they believed it."

He wrapped her in his arms, and she settled into his comfort. "There will be an end to this today," he said. "You will finish it."

She jolted. Today? But—

"This is your fight, Iseabail. These are your people. If I say anything, it will only damage your cause." He chuckled. "I'm just the Godless Sassenach."

She lifted her face to his. At one time in her life, she had believed the tales she'd heard about the English, but she had long since discarded those stories as foolish. "You have never been such to me."

He smiled as he stroked the line of her jaw. "How did you manage to leave them?"

She frowned. "I have told you how I traveled."

He shook his head. "You left everything you know, every soul you'd ever met, to find your fortune in England. Even now, I can hardly believe you were so brave."

She'd been desperate or she'd never have tried it. And now she saw how fortunate that gamble had turned out. He was here with her, and they would soon face her uncle together. It didn't matter if he was a silent presence nearby. He was with her, and she felt safe.

"When will we confront him?"

"When he finds us. Which will be sometime today."

"Why not take the fight to him? Why not go now—"

"Because he will be on the defensive then. I want him to feel confident."

She snorted. "He is always that."

"No, my dear," he said as his lips neared hers. "I think he's always been afraid of you, and rightly so." He paused as he looked at her. "You said he had many women. Did any give him a child? If so, I need to know—"

"No." She shrugged. "He is unable to father children."

"That's a lucky break," he said. "How do you know that's true?"

Did she dare confess her mother's crimes? Most men would surely consider it such. She shrugged. "Some secrets are passed down among healers. Such as where to cut a man such that he canna father children."

He jolted. "What?"

She smiled. "A man—if he were very drunk—might not even feel it. And if the right woman were to help him to bed, undress him because of his stink, then she might accidentally slip with a knife. Indeed, he might never even know, especially if he were already unconscious."

"The devil you say!"

She shrugged. "It is something witches know. At least so my mother told me."

He pursed his lips and nodded slowly. "I begin to admire her more and more."

"I think she would have liked you."

"Because I will not fault her for being ruthless?"

"Because you are a canny one and you fight for me."

He grinned. "Always," he said. And then she lost herself in his kiss, his arms, and the sweet tangle that…

Was interrupted by Lizzy, who wasn't at all as quiet as she thought.

Reuben pulled back and winked at the girl. "You're up early," he said.

She shrugged, her attention fixed on Iseabail. "I thought Hamish married you. Or he married yer necklace. It seemed verra strange."

"That it is," Iseabail agreed. "And not done right."

The girl nodded, her gaze going to Reuben. She didn't ask, but her gaze was very direct. So Iseabail did the introductions and was pleased to see the girl take it in stride. She curtsied, as was appropriate, then turned back to Iseabail.

"Mama says to come now."

"Aye. Thank ye."

The girl nodded, then with one last look at the pair of them, she dashed away. "That girl is always running everywhere," she murmured. And she set her hand on her belly, wondering if her own child would be like that.

He must have seen her gesture. He must have been thinking along the same lines as her because he caught her hand and kissed it. And then he bent down and pressed another to her belly.

She set her hand on his head and let her fingers slide through his curls. Whatever the day brought, this moment now was good. Pure and full of love, and so she gathered that feeling inside herself and used it to strengthen her determination to find a solution. Even if it meant murder.

There was time for one last kiss, one final caress, and then she turned to face the day. She thought she would be lost in a mass of anxiety. She had feared her uncle for so long that the idea of confronting him today seemed immense. Instead, she had no time to think. Talia's kitchen was filled with the old and the sick, and she spent a great deal of time tending to them. Reuben, on the other hand, stayed with Fergus near the sheep, speaking in low voices to all who came by.

And by the looks of things, every soul in the clan stopped by to speak. Some came out of curiosity and with nothing good to say about a Sassenach. But more came to seek her skills and for the first time in her life, she drew a line.

Any who spoke ill of her husband could find another place for their healing balms and possets. To her shock, she heard no more ill talk about the English. She was sure they whispered it, but in front of her, they remained respectful. And when they still needed to curse at something, they cursed her uncle's woman Orlaith for destroying her stillroom and all the medicines contained there.

Before long, talk turned to how things had gone poorly for the clan since she left. It was nothing more than the usual complaints. Most would have happened with her here, but with Orlaith gone as well, there was no one to even pretend to take care of the clan.

She listened with growing surprise. Her people did see her worth, or they saw her skill with medicines. And one by one, they were letting her know they valued her. And she never would have realized that if it hadn't been for Reuben telling her exactly that.

By mid-afternoon, she began to feel happy and appreciated, feelings that were so rare in her earlier life.

Which was why it was no surprise when her uncle rode up, resplendent on his white stallion, to destroy her every good feeling.

CHAPTER TWENTY-SEVEN

HER UNCLE WAS cleanshaven, and his white teeth gleamed in the sun as he dismounted with all appearance of good will. He practically oozed charm and he made Iseabail's skin crawl.

"Iseabail, I've been worried sick. Where have ye been? Never mind that, come here. Let me give ye a kiss. How grown up ye look."

His voice was warm, his expression everything a doting uncle's should be. But Iseabail knew the truth behind that smile, and she refused to be pulled in by it. She stood her ground and gave him the barest inclination of her head.

"Uncle."

"Ach, it's like that, is it?" His brogue was thick, and she prayed that Reuben could understand the man's words. More, she prayed he wasn't fooled by her uncle's pretend concern. But then, of course he would be. Everyone was. Everyone, that was, except her mother who was long gone.

Rather than greet him, she turned and gestured Reuben forward. "Uncle, I have great news. I've come back with my husband, Reuben Bates. We were married by the Archbishop of Canterbury himself."

"Ach lass, but that's a terrible thing to lie like that. Yer neither titled nor wealthy, and we all know the archbishop won't be marrying any mister to his missus. He's fer the titled folk."

Reuben smiled and put a reassuring arm around her. It was all she could do to not sink deep into his embrace.

"He's a priest for all souls," Reuben said. "Isn't that what the church says? And I've a great many friends. Enough, it seems, to get his help to wed my true love."

Reuben lifted her hand and pressed a kiss into her palm. It was a sweet gesture, but overdone. She doubted anyone would believe he was overcome by love for her. And yet, she could feel the heat of her blush at the way he looked at her. As if she were the woman he'd been looking for his entire life. And she couldn't stop her blood from rising at the thought.

If only it were true.

"Ach, but she's lied to you, sir. Lied to you and to the arch-bishop, then. She's already wed and no true lass."

"Not a lass anymore," Reuben countered smoothly. "But I swear she was pure on our wedding night. And a good woman she is." He looked at her uncle with a demeanor that seemed amused. As if this whole thing were a huge joke, and yet, she knew from experience that her uncle could turn ugly fast.

"She was wed to Hamish, likely before you ever met. He's got her dowry and the right of her, no matter what slut-filled tales she's told you." Her uncle shook her head. "It's her witchy blood come through, that's fer sure."

Anger burned hot through her. "I have not married Hamish! Nor would I ever!"

"Yer wishes are not my concern, girl. Hamish is the man for you. He wed yer token before the priest and the whole clan. He'll tame yer dark ways."

"What token?" she scoffed as she pulled her necklace out of her bodice. "This one? The one I've been wearing since I left two months ago?"

Her uncle groaned as he looked on her with clear pity. "An' how much did you pay to make a new bauble in London? 'Tis the witch in you, I'm sure, that drives you to such lies."

Damn it, she'd forgotten what it was like to have her every word questioned, her every thought painted in the worst possible light. Two months surrounded by people who believed what she said had changed her. It had reminded her that she wasn't crazy, and it was her uncle who was wrong.

"Lies?" she taunted. "Shall we talk about lies, Uncle?"

She drew in a full breath, unable to prevent the hesitation. This was a mad plan, but Reuben swore it would work. Of all the accusations she could lay at her uncle's feet, this seemed the silliest, but Reuben had been adamant, and she put her faith in him.

"Do you know," she said the clan at large, "I would have married Fergus had he asked, but you told me he was too old for me, and then he fell in love with Talia." To the side, Fergus dipped his chin in acknowledgement. So she went on. "I would have given my hand to Ciaran, as well, but you said he had unnatural appetites—"

Ciaran jolted in shock. "That's a lie!"

"I don't even know what you meant by that, but it kept me away from him. And then there was Ashton. Sweet Ashton who brought me oat cakes and asked me to dance. You told me he had a man's disease, and I should not breathe the same air as he."

Ashton stood up from where he was leaning against the barn. His face was tight with fury. "I've no illness," he declared.

She gestured to all the men around her, most of whom had found other wives, other women. "Shall I tell them what you said about all of them? The lies you told me—"

"You were too young, Iseabail. I had to tell you something. You were not ready for marriage." She could see he was aware of the fury building in the men around him. "Come, come," he said with his arms spread wide. "We will talk about this over dinner, yes? The two of us in the castle."

As if she would go anywhere with him. "I should like an answer now, Uncle. Where did these men fail that Hamish succeeded? Why did you try to give me to him, of all people? He beat his wife to death. I cleaned her body. I saw what he did. He drinks and does no work. Why did he deserve me when all these good men did not?"

She had never spoken to him this way before. Her mother had, but she had always told Iseabail to keep quiet and to be busy far away from her uncle or his men. Now she stood in the late afternoon sun and faced him as her mother once had.

"I am your only heir," she said.

"You are a witch—"

"I am a blessing to this clan and to Scotland. Ask any here if this is not true. I have set bones, stitched wounds, and delivered babies. Why was I denied all these good men?"

He was done with her defiance. She could see it in his face. His cheeks had gone ruddy, and his crossed arms dropped such that his big fists planted hard on his hips.

"Verra well, Iseabail, ye forced me to tell the truth. Do ye think Hamish so ill fer you? Well, he's the only one what wanted ye. A black witch with a black heart. But he's a good man, he'll keep ye in line fer sure. And as fer yer Sassenach here, I'll show ye all what he's about and why Hamish is the man fer ye." He clapped his hands loudly as he looked up the road. "Bring em out," he bellowed.

Everyone turned. Her uncle knew how to create a show, that was for sure, as Hamish appeared with three of his men...and four of Reuben's men. Every Scot had a Sassenach before him. The English, for all their size and strength, looked beaten and ashamed. Their heads were bowed, and their hands were bound tight before them.

"Hamish caught them," her uncle called out. "They were coming here to kill the clan. To steal our cattle, rape the women, and destroy everything we have built. Hamish is the one who caught them. Hamish is the one who is fierce enough to defend our land."

Several of the men openly doubted such a statement, but the evidence was on her uncle's side. After all, the Sassenach did appear defeated. And then Reuben made it worse. He turned and addressed the crowd.

"It's true."

Everyone gasped in shock, even Iseabail.

"Oh, not the raping and pillaging part. We've got women and money aplenty in London. We don't need yours. But I did come with four of my good men. Not my best, mind you, but those that wanted to see Scotland and the fair lasses they had heard about here." For emphasis, he winked at young Lizzy, who blushed prettily. "I had them sneak around. I needed to see what your defenses were like. Jonathan, what did you find?"

Jonathan looked up. Hamish held a dagger to his throat, but that didn't seem to bother him as he answered.

"A couple of them chased us right well. It's their dogs, Reuben. You can hide from a man, but their dogs smell ye clear enough. We couldn't get anywhere at the first two farms. The ones that belong to them." He jutted his chin at Murray and Elliott. "But it was right hard getting these clots to see us. We had to start singing like we were drunk and sit our arses down by the main road. They'd missed us twice when we were beside the road."

"Lies!" cried Hamish as he pressed the dagger against Jonathan's throat. "We caught ye sneaking about with evil on yer minds."

There must have been some signal. Or perhaps Jonathan got tired of acting submissive. Iseabail couldn't tell, but she certainly saw when all four of Reuben's men—with their hands bound— managed to disarm and free themselves from the Scots. Jonathan appeared to take special pleasure in putting an elbow to Hamish's face. And when the bastard cursed and tried to attack, Reuban's man twisted the knife away, banged the hilt into Hamish's eye, then stood back while the idiot dropped to his knees and whimpered.

Given the great many black eyes he'd given his wife, Iseabail had no sympathy for his pain.

Meanwhile, Jonathan passed the dagger to Reuben, who neatly cut the binds.

"They're piss-poor fighters," Jonathan said. "Strong enough, I'll give you that, but little discipline." He wrinkled his nose. "I don't know how they have any whisky left to sell. They drink more than the gin sots."

Reuben turned to Fergus. "Do you have enemies? Clans who want the land and the market for their own?" He jerked his head at the four men on the ground. "This lot won't be able to protect you."

"Aye," Fergus said grimly. "There's a few clans that'll stir up trouble. Especially when word of this gets out."

Her uncle curled his lip. "Well, it won't get out, will it? Not a one of ye will talk. It's yer head and mine that will pay." He stomped over to Hamish and kicked him in the thigh. "Yer a damned disgrace, you are." He lifted his head to look at the clan. "Don't worry none about it. I'll see to their punishment and their training myself."

Iseabail laughed, the sound loud and mocking, just as her mother used to do. "But you have been seeing to them, Uncle. You've had control of the men ever since my father died." She pointed to where they sat on the ground. "This is the result."

Her uncle shook his head as if sorely betrayed. "I trusted Hamish. It was my love for him that had me believe him so long. It's brought me low, it has." A king devastated because he loved too dearly. It was a lie, but he was a fine actor. All around him, the men shuffled their feet awkwardly. The women mostly kept their heads down. In private, they would scoff at her uncle's antics, but the core of the clan—the men—would hesitate to go against one of their own.

Which meant she had to remind them. "And this is the man who is better than Fergus and Ciaran and Ashton? What about Rudi, who you said is not a man at all."

Rudi's head shot up. "What?"

"Lying bitch!" her uncle bellowed.

She didn't see his hand raise until too late. She couldn't have avoided it if she'd tried. Just as well because she wasn't sure her courage would keep her standing. Reuben had told her she had to take one blow. He'd never hit her after her sixteenth birthday, but he hadn't been so restrained when she was younger. She knew how he could set her ears to ringing.

It landed as they always did, with enough force to throw her to the side. She moved with it as much as she could, softening the impact as her mother had taught her. And when her entire body flew to the right, Reuben was there to catch her. His arms were solid where she fell into them, and he murmured into her ear.

"Well done," he whispered. "Finish it now, and he won't ever touch you again."

She didn't need to answer. Indeed, she couldn't, given that every soul had their eyes on her. Reuben helped her stand to her full height. His expression was murderous, but she spoke to him loud enough for all to hear.

"I'll handle this," she said.

He nodded, though she could see his jaw clenched with anger. Was it an act? She didn't think so. She knew his body now, and his was strung tight with violence.

Meanwhile, her uncle sneered. "Even your man won't defend you. He knows you're evil."

She arched a brow. "He knows I am strong enough to manage you without him." A lie if ever there was one. "You have touched me without my consent," she declared.

She turned slowly, showing everyone the thick swelling on her face, the blood welling on her cut lip, and the righteous indignation in her eyes. He hadn't even used his open palm but had struck her with his fist.

"That is my right," he bellowed. "You are an undisciplined child."

"I am a married woman," she declared. "And therefore the only man who has rights to my body is my husband."

Reuben growled out his response. "Only a coward takes out his embarrassment on a woman. I have never struck a girl in my life," he declared. "And certainly never with a fist." Reuban spat at her uncle's feet, showing all what he thought of the man. "Is this how Scots treat their women?"

Not a soul answered. They were ashamed to see what her uncle had done. And she could now use that shame to plunge a knife into her uncle's dark heart.

"By the magic in my blood, by the witchcraft gifted to me by my mother, I could now take your life. I could squeeze you in the palm of my hand until your eyes pop and your guts spill black blood on the ground." She'd never tried the kind of dramatic pronouncements her mother had used. By all accounts, Iseabail came from a long line of dramatic women, but she had always kept quiet, kept contained.

Not today. She invested her voice with power and raised her hand as if she could indeed squeeze him to death by magic. Her uncle was sweating. She saw fear in his eyes, but his pride would not allow him to run.

"Stay back, unnatural witch!" he hissed.

She lifted her hands to the sky, twisting her wrists as if to say, I surrender. Her pose was casual. "Very well, Uncle," she said, her tone conversational. "I have the right to kill you, but all I ask is that you answer the question."

He gaped at her. Then, he sneered. "What question?"

She sighed as if sorely put upon. "The one I have been asking for the last half hour, Uncle. What does Hamish have that Fergus does not? Where do Ciaran, Ashton, and Rudi fail?"

She had picked those names carefully. Each one carried weight in the clan, each man had kin who supported him and would have made a fine clan laird. And to a man, they stood and faced her uncle with their arms crossed and their brows drawn low.

"You were promised to Hamish!" her uncle snapped. "Long ago, I made that promise."

"Why?"

"That's none of your concern! Especially now that he's shown himself to be useless." He turned to glare at the man.

"Where is Albie?" he demanded. "You left with five men to London. Not only did you fail to get your wife, but you have left one of yours behind. Where is he?"

It was a deflection. A way to draw everyone's attention away from the primary question, but Iseabail allowed it for the moment.

"Did you abandon him in London?" her uncle demanded.

"He's dead!" Hamish bellowed.

"Not by my hand," Iseabail said. "I cut him for sure, but he would have survived." With proper treatment. "Six men attacked us in daylight, in the middle of Hyde Park, but still could not take me." She straightened. "Such is the power of my magic."

"Witch!" Hamish hissed.

"Idiot!" her uncle spat at Hamish. "How can ye be such a failure?"

Iseabail turned her attention to the man her uncle had chosen for her. He was just now standing up from where he had collapsed on the ground. His hands and his body were dirty, and he had an ugly pout twisting his lips. He looked as worthless as a Scot could be.

She *tisked* loudly. "He's turning on you, Hamish. That man who you thought was your best friend. He's betraying you."

"Enough!" her uncle bellowed. "You are back but a few hours and look at the chaos you bring!"

"Only to those who will not answer the question!" she returned. "What does Hamish have that makes him more deserving than any other in the clan?"

Her uncle stomped forward, his expression ugly. "Ye will be silent, witch!"

His fist was raised, his temper boiling between them, but Iseabail did not flinch. Reuben was close enough to stop any blow. She had absolute faith that he would protect her. But it was not his voice that surprised everyone. It was Fergus's.

"Nay."

Loud and heavy, the one word dropped into the air like a

stone. Her uncle's head shot up.

"I am laird here!"

"Aye," Fergus agreed. "But the witch's spell stands. Do ye answer her question? We have all seen that he struck her when he had not the right."

"I am her kin!"

"But she is wed, either to Hamish or to the Sassenach, we don't ken. But she be wed fer sure."

Her uncle drew himself up to his full height while his expression turned tragic. "Do you not see, Fergus, how she is destroying this clan?"

"I only see a question gone unanswered." His eyes narrowed. "How was I unfit? How is Rudi less than a man?"

Her uncle shifted his stance, no doubt looking to see if he could storm out and regroup later. But he was surrounded on all sides by the clan. Hedged in and much too close to flee through them. As for his horse, well, Lizzy was walking it to Fergus's barn.

So he fell back onto what he had claimed from the beginning. "I am laird here. I can strike any woman I want." Then he pointed a hard finger at Hamish. "It is his fault! I trusted where I should not have! I believed—"

"You fecking bastard!" Hamish said his fists bunching at his side. He did not lunge yet, but he was ready to attack. He didn't get the chance as Fergus stepped before him, slouching a bit as he stared at the man eye to eye.

"Answer the question, Hamish, and I swear to you that you'll not be harmed by me. Not me nor any man here." He looked back to cast his hard stare at the clansmen around him. When they all seemed to agree, he turned Hamish. "Tell the truth now, or we let him lay all of it at yer feet."

"My feet!" Hamish growled. "My feet, when it was he who put the poison in his brother's drink?" He glared at her uncle. "I got it fer ye, but it was yer hand what put it in."

Iseabail felt the blood rush from her head. It was true. Her uncle had killed her father. Her mother had always said so, but there'd been no proof.

"And what of my mother?" she asked.

Hamish rounded on her. "She gave all her magic to you, so there was nothing to stop us, then, was there? Nothing to stop him."

"Lies! Lies!" the baron screeched, but this time, Reuben was fastest. He pressed a dagger to her uncle's throat as he hissed.

"Be silent. Let the clan hear everything."

Her uncle tried to attack then, but it was Ashton who grabbed him on one side and Rudi on the other. And though the man struggled, they gave no quarter. Indeed, they stretched his arms back enough to make him whimper with pain.

"What did he do to Iseabail's mother?" Fergus demanded.

Hamish spit into the dirt at Iseabail's feet. "What she deserved. Then we filled her dress with rocks and cast her in the fen."

Iseabail closed her eyes. She'd always felt it was true, but to hear it stated so clearly hurt. Indeed, the pain of it coursed through her like a thunderstorm, and yet she said nothing. She did nothing.

Once begun, Hamish would not keep the secrets inside.

"And for what reason," pressed Fergus, "did you kill a good woman? One who tended our bairns as if they were her own?"

"He did it! I did it on his order!" He looked at Iseabail. "And for that service, he gave me her. Her magic would be mine, and her dowry too." This time he spat at her uncle's feet. "But there ain't no five hundred gold coins, are there? Ye already spent it, didn't ye?"

Her uncle couldn't speak. Reuben's knife was still pressed against his throat.

Meanwhile, Talia stepped forward. She didn't meet Hamish eye to eye as her husband did, but she leaned over him, her mouth twisted in disgust. "Ye were married to Annie when Iseabail's mother disappeared. How could ye be promised to

Iseabail?"

Hamish grinned. "But I wasn't married long, was I?"

Nausea roiled in Iseabail's belly. She held it back by force of will. She would not disgrace herself or her parents by being ill. She would stand and face their murderers, and she would use every ounce of whatever magic she had to see that they paid.

When she could finally speak, her words came out dripping with acid. "This is the good man for me, Uncle?" she taunted, her tone heavy with sarcasm. "The one who is better than any other clansman here?"

She stepped backwards, her eyes burning with unshed tears. "I have the answer to my question," she rasped. "I shall leave it up to the clan to decide what to do."

She nodded at Reuben, who stepped away as well. He and his men closed in around Iseabail, ready in case they were needed, but she knew they wouldn't be. It didn't matter if her uncle had done good things for the clan. Thanks to him, the market had flourished. Indeed, he appeared as a generally benevolent laird except for when he lost his temper.

But the murder of their laird was too much for the clan to stomach. Two dead women was bad enough, but her father's death tipped the balance.

Fergus took the clan's vote. Man after man nodded his consent, and none cared that her uncle kept screaming, "Lies! Lies!" Indeed, when it was time, Ciaran slit her uncle's throat as much to gain silence from the screeching as anything else.

A single slice done in full view of the clan, and her troubles were ended. She could scarce believe it, though the stench of blood nearly undid her.

Next came Hamish's turn. The clan regarded him with heavy eyes, but no man moved to harm him. Indeed, Hamish straightened his filthy clothes and glared them all back.

"You swore!" he said. "You swore no one would touch me. I told you everything. I confessed it all."

"Aye," Fergus agreed. "And no man will harm ye."

So it was that Annie's mother did the deed. She stabbed him from behind as he looked at the men. And as she cut him, she muttered, "I wish to God I had done this years ago."

Hamish died with a gasp and a sputter.

Last to be judged were Fergus's other men. There was no proof of a crime other than incompetence, and so they were banished, their names stricken from the Spalding clan. In an act of mercy, they were allowed to keep their horses, but their weapons were forfeit to Reuben's men who had so easily defeated them.

Jonathan held up the heavy sword with a grin and said, "'Tis a fine weapon to start my own collection."

So it was done. All in a single day, just as Reuben had promised. Her head was swimming from the suddenness of it all. After a lifetime lived in fear, it was over. Her parents were avenged, and she was safe from retribution. Only one question left to answer.

Who now would lead the clan?

CHAPTER TWENTY-EIGHT

"MAGNIFICENT!" REUBEN MURMURED as he mounted one of Fergus's horses. He wasn't referring to that creature, but to Iseabail who rode ahead of him to the castle.

She couldn't hear him, of course. She was too far in front, sitting on her uncle's white stallion with her head held high and her body held seemingly still despite the movement of the horse. "Seemingly still" because he knew just how difficult it was to sit so regally on a horse. She was, in fact, so attuned to the animal that she appeared statuesque even when the creature labored up and around the terrain.

Other adjectives came to mind. She was regal, intuitive, smart, and brave. So damned brave to face down an uncle who had murdered her parents and abused her trust. And yet as he watched her move steadily toward a truly impressive castle, his thoughts were on her heart.

Was it broken? Her last blood kin was now dead. She'd learned the truth of her parents' deaths, and now she might or might not have the leadership of the clan. She was the blood heir, of course, but she was also a woman. He had no idea how the Scots picked their successors, and he didn't want to betray his ignorance by asking. He didn't care if everyone thought him an ignorant Sassenach, but he didn't want that to reflect badly upon Iseabail. So he kept his mouth shut and directed his men to stay as quiet as possible while the Spalding clan did whatever it was going to do.

But oh, it was hard to stay back from her. It was hard to admire her from a distance and know that she might now be wracked with heartbreak, and he could not give her the smallest support. He contemplated riding forward. In truth, he was directly behind her and could easily speed up enough to touch her. But she had declared that the clan would eat at the castle, then had started to walk toward the structure, leaving the disposal of the bodies to the men.

It was Talia who had brought her the stallion and Reuben who had urged her to claim it. That was the extent of their exchange, though he had hoped for more. He could see that she was barely keeping herself together, so he hadn't pushed. Then he'd rocked back on his heels and watched her sit her horse with more poise than the Queen of England.

It had taken him a few minutes to see that Fergus was directing his clansman with a competent hand, then he'd whispered his instructions to his men before taking one of their horses to follow Iseabail. By the time he caught up to her, though, she was suffused by such regal presence that he felt it would damage her consequence for him to speak to her.

So he hung back far enough to watch and admire, while inside he wondered if she needed him anymore.

As soon as they arrived at the castle, two stable boys ran out to manage the horses. They were wide-eyed at seeing her, but they didn't speak until she addressed them. They nodded, then scampered away while she slowly dismounted, then turned to look at the castle.

That's where he caught up to her. He stepped up beside her and took a moment to absorb the sheer size of her home. It was a fortress meant to defend against invaders. It came complete with an outer fence, a raised metal gate, and a huge courtyard, not to mention four towers and who knew what else inside. He'd never been in a castle before, and the sheer size of it stole his breath. All his relations could live comfortably inside that thing and still have room for their friends. Indeed, all it seemed to lack in his mind was a moat, but the cliff on which it sat was intimidating enough.

Then he admonished himself. It wasn't on a cliff, exactly. The castle sat on a raised jut of land that felt to his London eyes like the tallest mountain. He grinned at the thought of his children running around the place, defending it from imaginary pirates and rescuing damsels from dragons.

He reached from Iseabail's hand, wanting to share the moment with her. But when he caught her fingers, all he felt was her coolness. Her fingers were icy, her body absolutely still. And when he turned to look at her, her expression was remote.

"Iseabail?"

She turned to him. "I don't..." She swallowed. "What do I do now?"

"What do you want to do?"

"I've promised the clan food, but according to Talia, the kitchens are a mess and the rooms filthy. I've no idea who still works here. Orlaith upset a great many folk before my uncle—" She choked on that word and took a moment to reset. "Before she was run off. The men will want drink, but they need to be watched. I don't know who I can trust to carry away those who cannot hold their liquor. And what of lamp oil and bed linen? I'll not sleep in—"

She was panicking, her mind racing ahead to problems that weren't here yet. And so he silenced her in the way she responded to best. He turned to face her eye to eye, and he stroked his thumb across her lips.

"Reuben, I canna—"

"Those are tasks you must do. What do you want to do?"

"What?"

"You are mistress here now—"

"Mayhap. It's not settled, you know. They could still run me out—"

"Hush," he said as he pressed his mouth to hers. She accepted his kiss—for a moment—then she pulled back.

"It's everything I wanted," she said. "But I cannot run the clan myself. It needs my mother and father. It needs a man who knows how to manage the market and train the men. Fergus is respected, but he's a farmer. He's never wanted to count coins. Talia does it for them, and she's pregnant again. Ach, and that's a danger to—"

He kissed her again, this time more forcefully. She didn't fight him as he thrust his tongue into her. Better yet, her shoulders relaxed a bit, then a bit more before her body softened against him. And only then did he raise his head.

"They're not going to cast you aside. They just killed your uncle on your behalf."

"Not my behalf. He murdered—"

"Stop thinking in excuses. That's your uncle's style. He lied to you as he spoke in dazzling ways to confuse people all while making excuses for himself. Iseabail, your people chose you."

She looked him in the eye, her body tightening as she fought through her fears. "There is so much to feel, I canna think."

Her brogue was coming in thick with her distress, but he understood her. "Will you listen to my advice?"

She frowned at him as if he were daft. "All of this is because of you! Of course, I will listen."

He smiled. "All of this is because of you," he said. "Years of caring for them, years of being kind despite all the witchcraft nonsense. I merely saw the pattern." He grinned as he pressed a kiss to the tip of her nose. "It's what I'm best at."

She smiled, though the expression was strained. "What does the pattern say now?"

"Take command of the castle. You ran it for years, yes?"

"Yes."

"Then do that first. Start with the meal. Everyone is happy with a full stomach."

Her brows rose. "Not everyone. And not if the food is bad."

"Start there."

She nodded as she turned to face the castle again. "What will you do?" she asked, as if it were an afterthought.

He squeezed her hand. "I shall be looking for more patterns."

She cast him a sidelong look, her expression anxious. "Do you want to be laird?"

He did. The need burned in him as fiercely as when he'd wanted to marry into the aristocracy. This would be his own kingdom to shape as he willed. As it ought to be done for the benefit of all.

But he shook his head. "They will never accept a Sassenach, even one as brilliant as me."

"Do you think they will accept a woman?"

He shrugged. These were her people. "I think you can declare it so, if it's what you want."

She bit her lip. "I don't think they'll want me. I'm afraid to ask."

He touched her face. How did she not see how wonderful she was? How did she not understand that every soul in her clan depended upon her? She was the one with medicines and magic. She was the one who organized and maintained order. She was the one who inspired. He was merely another soul who stood in awe at her feet.

"They'll want you if you demand it. You cannot hesitate. You must act and declare. But most of all, you must believe."

She shook her head. "I'm not sure."

"Then be sure by the time the food is done."

"Another pattern?"

He nodded. "Make your decision by then."

She took a deep breath and started forward. He matched her steps, wondering what would happen next.

"I'll start with the bread," she declared.

"Good choice. Do you mind if I start with the books?"

"An excellent idea," she said as she handed over the keys that had been lifted from her uncle's body. "Whatever accounts he had will open with one of these."

A great many keys, but he was a man who loved to open new doors.

CHAPTER TWENTY-NINE

ISEABAIL DECIDED.

It began when she saw the dirt in the kitchen. A castle, indeed a clan, ran on its food. And the heart of that food was here, where the pots were dirty, the food burnt, and the bread hard. She was cleaning when Talia appeared with several women in tow. They more than anyone knew how much Iseabail had done for them.

They joined her in the work of cooking.

Seeing their faith in her bolstered her, but determination came when she stepped into her stillroom. Every bottle was smashed, every herb discarded. Orlaith had been very thorough in her spite. What idiocy to destroy healing ointments and calming herbs in a fit of temper.

"Why didn't anyone stop her?" she wondered.

Talia shrugged. "Why? None of us have the knowledge to use it."

And here she saw her mother's wrong. She had taught Iseabail, but no one else. To have only one healer in a clan was foolish.

"I will change that. Any who wish to learn may come to me."

The words came from a place of certainty and from fury. No clan could survive if they failed to take care of their own in so basic a manner. And as the women nodded their support, Iseabail gathered her will.

She would lead this clan as laird, and she would be certain that no woman under her protection was lost or abused. It was high time for a woman's perspective in clan matters.

She followed Reuben's suggestion to wait until the food was consumed but before the whisky began to flow. The fare was adequate and a far cry from what it would become, but for tonight, it served.

She sat at the high table between Reuben and Fergus. In clan matters, Fergus would need to appear preeminent because he was born and raised a Spalding. But as her husband, Reuben took an equal place beside her. And he was especially gallant as he drew out her chair for her.

"What did you learn about the coffers?" she whispered as she took her seat.

"They will recover," he said. Then he cast a look at Fergus. "I suggest someone search your uncle's rooms. I have not entered there, but I suspect—"

"I'll do it," said Fergus.

And so Fergus did not eat when everyone else did. Neither did the three men he took with him. Three who were the most disgruntled about the situation. They returned with riches squirreled away, fancy purchases for vanity, and—most damning of all—the golden chest of her dowry.

It was empty.

Given how much her uncle had touted her dowry, had held it out to tempt the men to vie for her hand, that discovery reinforced everything Hamish had said. And in the end, even the ones who had benefited by her uncle's occasional bouts of generosity, shook their heads in dismay.

And while Fergus and his men began eating, Reuben squeezed her hand beneath the table. "If you've decided," he murmured, "now is the time for a bold declaration. Do not hold back. Do not hesitate. Say what you want and be done."

He was right, and so she rose from the table and spoke clearly, calmly, and with a boldness that she could scarce believe came from her own mouth.

"My uncle deceived us all, and he has paid for his crimes. We must now look to the future." She paused for breath only. Nothing more before she said what needed to be said. "I claim the right of leadership. By blood, I am the laird. And by right of battle."

For a moment there was deafening silence. And then laughter, full and scathing from the men. Reuben didn't laugh, and neither did Fergus. And neither did a single woman in the room. They remained silent, and in time, their dark looks quieted the rest.

Iseabail continued.

"I fought Hamish and five strong men, and I did it in a dress in the middle of Hyde Park. Who among you can say the same? I fought disease when I stitched your wounds and set your bones. I fought death with every child I have delivered. And I fought for Scotland with the magic invested in my blood from generations of women."

"Your grandmother cursed us at Culloden!" exclaimed one. It was the perpetual curse of her witch blood.

Iseabail lifted her hands in a kind of shrug. "If she did, she has paid for it. If we set my uncle's sins to rest this day, then hers are long gone as well." She lifted her chin. "I will be your laird. Who stands with me?"

This was the boldest moment of all, and she held her breath when not one soul moved. Was this the moment when her uncle was proved right? When none would see past her grandmother's crimes, whatever they might be? When everyone believed the men and not a soul respected the women?

It appeared so.

Until Talia stepped forward. "She is my laird," she declared.

And one by one the women of the clan stood, echoing the statement.

"She is my laird."

"She is my laird."

She, she, she.

The men looked about themselves in confusion while the women stared defiantly at them. And one old sot shook his head, his voice loud in the silent hall.

"Ach, sit yerself down, woman. Laird is a name for a man."

At his words, more than one woman wavered. Shoulders lifted as if expecting a blow. Heads ducked down in fear.

"Be bold," Reuben whispered behind her. "Say what you want."

What did she want? She wanted her clan to be safe. She wanted them to stand strong together with good food and strong families. It seemed so simple, but life was never simple. And nothing was given to the timid.

"Verra well," she said, her accent coming out. "Then I will take those who stand with me, and we will cook and clean for ourselves. I will deliver their babies, heal their cuts, and tend our stock without ye."

"There won't be a babe to deliver without us!" scoffed a young man, barely shaven.

Talia grunted. "We've babes enough, thank ye Colin. And even if we didn't, ye'd still be alone until ye bathe yerself properly."

That produced guffaws a-plenty, but in a moment the hilarity died down. It was Fergus who broke the silence as he pushed to his feet.

"I won't follow a Sassenach," he declared.

Talia spread her hands. "Am I not Scottish through and through? I'll fight any man or woman who says otherwise."

No one scoffed at that, though many could best her in a fight. It was as if she was of no account, though she stood in the center of the hall and had declared herself laird. All eyes were on Reuben.

He stood slowly, then moved around the center table at an easy saunter. With a jerk of his chin, he ordered his four men to stand behind him, each one bringing a bag with him. They were large bags, clearly heavy, and Jonathan even grimaced as he dropped his on the floor before Reuben.

"I have lived most of my life in London," Reuben spoke, his tone casual. "I have no title, no claim to fame beyond the wealth brought to me from eighteen businesses started and flourishing there." He grinned. "Commerce is my lifeblood, and I make no apology for that." He stepped forward and looked about the room. "But in all my years, I have never seen such beauty and strength as what I have seen in Scotland." His gaze roved across the people to the castle itself. He admired the stones that surrounded them, but then his gaze turned to her. "Scotland is truly to be admired," he said as if she were the personification of her entire country. He took her hand, pressing his lips to the back of her hand. "Fierce," he said. "And astounding."

She blushed. How could she not? Then he dropped to one knee before her.

"I pledge all that I have and all that I am to you, Iseabail Spalding. And if you'll allow it, I'll take your name and foreswear Bates."

The gasp was audible, not from her clan but from the men behind him. None had ever heard of a man who took a wife's name. But to join a clan was no small thing, even if it was in a marriage such as theirs.

Behind them, that same old coot scoffed. "And wot have you that we would make ye one of us? Wot battles have ye fought? Wot strength do ye bring?"

Reuben probably didn't know it, but those were the standard challenges to any man who wished to add his strength to the Spalding clan. Or perhaps he did, because he smiled.

"Oh! I do have one other peccadillo, so to speak. An oddity that I started as a boy that I have maintained over the years because it amused me." He turned to the largest men in the clan. "I keep the weapons of every soul I have defeated in a fight. Most were simple fights in dark alleys, but in my time, I have defeated highwaymen and two gangs of a ferocity that would shock most souls." He grinned. "I kept their weapons, too. Perhaps they could be added to the Spalding armory."

Then with a nod to his men, they each opened the sacks they had brought. Opened the top, then tipped them over such that their contents spilled on the ground. Daggers, short swords, and not one but two heavy Claymores.

So he had killed Scotsmen, too. He must have seen the direction of her gaze because he turned to her.

"Two Scots and seven English attacked a set of three carriages I guarded on their way to London from Edinburgh. They wore no clan colors, and they fought like brute animals. I killed them both." He gestured back at his men. "There were nine total, and my men handled the rest. I received this scar in that battle."

To her shock, he stripped out of his shirt to show the scars he bore along his body. There were several, evidence of a lifetime of fights. He pointed to one particularly nasty cut that ran from shoulder blade to waist. One she had kissed a hundred times already.

"If you care about strength in battle," he said with a chuckle. "I have that, too."

She cared because her people cared. And not a one had a word against him. Not even old Harley.

Then Talia whistled. "Maybe we should form the Bates clan."

Fergus rounded on her. "Ye would never!"

No, Talia wouldn't, but her shrug was eloquent. "I'll not remain with fools who canna see a gift from the Almighty when it drops in yer lap. Iseabail has shown herself true. She has fed, cleaned, and healed all of us at one time or another." She set her hand on her rounding belly. "And we will all have need of her again. She is here now bringing with her a man who fights well, who has knowledge of commerce, and who will bow his head to follow her. We're lucky, we are, that she has returned to us and not left to make a life on her own. So, Spalding, do we take the gift that she has brought? Or do we nurse the ignorant pride that has been the death of so many?"

She spoke to the clan, but it was Fergus who answered. He wrapped his arm around his wife, touched her rounding belly, and turned to Iseabail. "I will follow you," he said firmly. "Wherever you lead." Then to emphasize his statement, he dropped to one knee before her.

And Reuben did the same.

Warmth flushed her body, shock and pleasure intermixed. Her heart swelled that these two men would bend to her. Iseabail the child had spent her life trying to be small. She had done her work as quietly as possible, then hidden herself away.

But here, she saw what happened when Iseabail the woman claimed her rights as an adult.

One by one, the others in the clan knelt to her. Men, women, boys, and girls. The last to kneel were Reuben's men. The four who were meant to return to London, but who looked around and threw their lot in with her.

And in such a way she became The Spalding.

"Thank you," she whispered. Then she tilted her face up to the sky. "Thank you," she said loudly, her words meant for her parents, for God, for any who had helped her along her very strange path. And then lastly, she went to Reuben. "Thank you," she whispered into his ear.

He grinned as he looked up at her. "To the Spalding Laird!" he cried.

"The Spalding Laird!" echoed through the chamber.

Then Iseabail held up the key to the storeroom. "Let us celebrate with whisky!"

CHAPTER THIRTY

WHILE THE MEN celebrated, the women worked. After all, someone had to serve (and control) the drinks. And someone had to put the children to bed. But they still found a way to celebrate in their own spaces. The kitchen was filled with laughter. The corners of the hall rang with it as well. And every woman found a way to speak with Iseabail, to tell her of what had transpired in the last few months, and of what they hoped for the future.

For the first time in her life, Iseabail felt drenched in the love from her clan. It had been there before, she realized, but her uncle and even her mother had kept her from experiencing it as she did now. Tonight, she felt soaked in the richness of it, and she could scare believe the magic of it all.

Eventually exhaustion caught up with her. Eventually, Talia pushed her toward her bed after confirming that Reuben's men had a place to sleep as well. Reuben, of course, would find her, she was sure. And before her eyes drifted shut, she saw him enter her chamber.

He was unsteady on his feet and grinning from ear to ear. He half fell into her bed, clumsily adjusting to be beside her. She snuggled close as he wrapped his arms around her. Then together, they slept.

She woke a little past dawn, her eyes heavy and her bed empty. And when she turned, she saw him standing by her window, his gaze surveying the land beyond. He'd pulled on his breeches, but nothing else. And he had the look of a king well satisfied with his kingdom.

Or a man after a job well done. One who was already setting his sights on a new challenge.

Iseabail sat up slowly. Her hair was a mess, there were a thousand things to do, but her thoughts would not leave Reuben. What was he thinking as he turned to look at her? Was he deciding when he would leave?

"Good morning," he said, his voice a low rumble that skated along her spine. "You look a fine sight."

She pushed her hair out of her eyes and tried to finger-comb out the tangles. "I am not at my best at first light," she confessed.

He caught her hand and pulled it to his lips. "I was not teasing you. You are beautiful."

She might not have believed him except for the way he caressed her cheeks and then rubbed his thumb along her lower lip. Admiration and hunger sparked in his eyes, and she found herself warming to his heat.

"When are you leaving?" she blurted out. If he were to depart in a week, she had to know. The pain would be easier to hide if she could prepare for it.

His eyes widened and his hand stilled. "Throwing me aside so soon?"

"You told your aunt you would return to London in a month." She bit her lip as she pulled away. "We've lost a week of that already. You are a Spalding now whatever you choose, and of course you may come back whenever you choose. But I would know…" She reached to the side and pulled on her plaid. She'd left it behind when she ran and now was grateful to feel it around her again.

"You would know what, Iseabail?"

She lifted her chin. She was The Spalding now, laird of the clan. She needed to act like one instead of cowering like a frightened child. So she stood and faced him, eye to eye. "If you lied when you swore yourself to me."

"Which time? As your husband or as your clansman?"

Both. Either. She didn't put the thought into words. The pain was already welling up inside her. It was because of him that she now stood as laird. It was thanks to him that her uncle was gone, and she no longer lived in fear. How would she bear it if he abandoned her now?

"Has no one ever stood by you?" he asked, his voice softening. When she didn't answer, he sighed. "Do you think I give my word so lightly? We were married before the Archbishop of Canterbury!"

"I think that you are a man who must always solve problems. That you grow restless otherwise. I think that you could find a way to forget the vows we spoke. I begged you to save me, and you have—"

"You saved yourself—"

"It was your plan."

"And you executed it flawlessly."

They were mincing words and she hated it. Why couldn't the man simply answer her question? When would he leave her?

He gathered her hands in his and studied her face. So many emotions flitted across his face, thoughts that she could not guess. He opened his mouth twice to speak, but then stopped himself. If he did it again, she would grow mad.

In the end, he pulled her hands up to his and pressed his mouth there. It warmed her, the way he sucked upon her knuckles. But it did not answer her question.

"Reuben—"

"I have searched all my life for a woman who is the match of me. One who is smart and brave, who will take a risk with me or check me when I am too bold. I want a partner in my schemes and a mother for my children. Iseabail, I have seen no better match for me than you. Indeed, I cannot believe there is another man for you either. We are a pair, and I would be a fool to leave you, ever."

But he would. She felt it. He would set things to rights here, get bored, and then abandon her. Such was the way of things. Tears sprang to her eyes, and she looked away. He let her go as she grabbed her comb and applied it to the knots in her hair. He watched her in silence, then sat down upon their bed to watch her.

"Do you want me to leave?" he asked.

"Of course not, but I cannot make you stay." She looked at him in her mirror. "You are a man who makes his way in this world. You wander. You conquer. And you—"

"I searched." He pulled her around to look at him. "I *found*."

She wanted to believe. Damn it, she wanted everything he said to be true, but…

"You're going to make me say it first, aren't you? Ach, lass—"

She winced. "You do not have a brogue! Stop trying to fake one!"

He chuckled. "Very well, Iseabail. For you, I shall break my manly pride and say it first." He dropped down on one knee before her. "I love you, Iseabail. I was attracted to you the first moment I saw you, but love came later. Love came when you fought like a warrior in Hyde Park. It came when you listened to reason and argued for logic. It bowled me over when you poked fun at my brogue, and it set my blood on fire when you faced down your uncle and claimed your birthright before God and your clan. Iseabail, I have not met a woman equal to you, and I cannot help but love you. You have my heart, my soul, and my body for as long as you will it. Iseabail Bates Spalding, will you allow me to stay by your side forever?"

It was true. He meant it, every word. She could see the truth of it in his face and body. He was devoted to her. He *loved* her!

"You won't get bored and leave me?" she asked.

"Do you not think there are challenges enough here? Good God, woman, I have such ideas for your market. I shall make your corner of Scotland the center of all commerce! And I have relatives in London who will let me market their wares here." He waggled his eyebrows. "London goods in Spalding. Scottish goods sent to London. It will take years to accomplish. But I will not do it without you by my side."

She snorted. "I am your laird. Of course, I will be here."

He laughed. "You are that, indeed."

He loved her, and the truth of that blossomed inside her as nothing else ever had. She felt it in her heart as well in as in his touch. And so she answered with her full truth.

"I love you, Reuben. Please stay with me forever."

"Forever."

He kissed her then, and she returned it fully. And though there were a million things to do, and a million more things to plan, the Spalding laird and her consort remained in their chamber for the entire day. One day for just them.

But on the morrow, they both got busy creating a future for themselves and everyone they loved.

About the Author

A *USA Today* Bestseller, JADE LEE has been scripting love stories since she first picked up a set of paper dolls. Ball gowns and rakish lords caught her attention early (thank you Georgette Heyer), and her fascination with historical romance began. Author of more than 30 regency romances, Jade has a gift for creating a lively world, witty dialogue, and hot, sexy humor. Jade also writes contemporary and paranormal romance as Kathy Lyons. Together, they've won several industry awards, including the *Prism—Best of the Best, Romantic Times Reviewer's Choice,* and *Fresh Fiction's* Steamiest Read. Even though Kathy (and Jade) have written over 60 romance novels, she's just getting started. Check out her latest news at www.KathyLyons.com, Facebook: JadeLeeAuthor, and Twitter: JadeLeeAuthor. Instagram: KathyLyonsAuthor.